Moonshell Beach

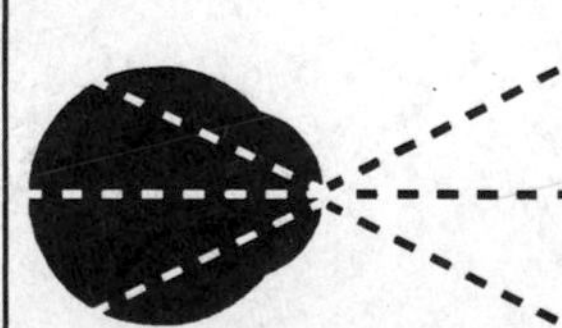

This Large Print Book carries the Seal of Approval of N.A.V.H.

A SHELTER BAY NOVEL

MOONSHELL BEACH

JOANN ROSS

THORNDIKE PRESS
A part of Gale, Cengage Learning

Detroit • New York • San Francisco • New Haven, Conn • Waterville, Maine • London

Thorndike Press, a part of Gale, Cengage Learning.

Thorndike Press® Large Print Romance.
The text of this Large Print edition is unabridged.
Other aspects of the book may vary from the original edition.
Set in 16 pt. Plantin.

LIBRARY OF CONGRESS CATALOGING-IN-PUBLICATION DATA

Ross, JoAnn.
Moonshell Beach : a Shelter Bay novel / by JoAnn Ross. — Large print ed.
p. cm. — (Shelter Bay novel) (Thorndike Press large print romance)
ISBN-13: 978-1-4104-4959-7 (hardcover)
ISBN-10: 1-4104-4959-9 (hardcover)
1. Large type books. I. Title.
PS3568.O843485M66 2012
813'.54—dc23 2012019137

Published in 2012 by arrangement with NAL Signet, a member of Penguin Group (USA) Inc.

Printed in the United States of America
1 2 3 4 5 6 7 16 15 14 13 12

Again, to all the men and women of the U.S. military — and their families — for their service and sacrifice.

To all those wonderful readers who've written to me over the years, asking for a story about Mary, from *A Woman's Heart,* the first of my Irish trilogy, this book is for you.

And, as always and forever, to Jay.

I have heard the mermaids singing,
each to each. I do not think that they
will sing to me.

T. S. Eliot,
"The Love Song of J. Alfred Prufrock"

1

Belying the song lyrics about it never raining in California, a dark gray sky was weeping onto the black Suburban's windshield as Marine captain J. T. Douchett drove through rain-slicked streets to carry out his mission. A mission he'd been catapulted into a year ago. A mission without weapons, which, given that every Marine was a rifleman, was not one he'd prepared for at Officer Candidates School, at the War College, or even during years of combat.

The rain was appropriate, he thought wearily as he pulled into the parking lot of a Denny's restaurant. As tough as this assignment was, it always seemed a lot worse when a benevolent sun was shining and birds were singing.

The drizzle reminded him of home. Back in Shelter Bay, his father and his brother Cole would've already gone out on their fishing boat. Maybe his grandfather, who often missed his days at sea, would have gone with them. The small coastal town would be coming to life — shopkeepers down on Harborview Drive would be opening their doors and lowering their bright awnings; beachcombers would be walking at the edge of the surf, gathering shells and agates; locals would be sitting around tables at the Grateful Bread, enjoying French toast and gossip while tourists lined up at the pier to go whale watching.

Memories of his hometown not only comforted; they reminded him of family, which, in turn, drove home the significance of this mission for which he definitely never, in a million years, would have volunteered.

But the first thing J.T. had learned at OCS was that every Marine was part of a larger picture. And the tradition of "Leave no Marine behind" was a sacred promise that went beyond the battlefield.

He and his passenger, a staff sergeant who, despite years of marching cadences, still had the slightly bowed legs of a man who'd grown up riding horses in Abilene, retrieved their garment bags from the backseat. They entered the restaurant, walking past the tables to the men's room, where they changed from their civilian clothes into high-necked, dark blue jackets, dark blue pants with a bloodred stripe down the outside of each leg, and shoes spit-polished to a mirror gloss.

Although he could feel that every eye in the place was on them, J.T. put on a focused but distant stare and glanced neither left nor right as he walked straight back to the Suburban. Neither man spoke. There was no need. They'd been through this before. And it never got any easier, so why talk about it?

After he was waved through Camp Pendleton's main gate, passing a golf course, a McDonald's, a Taco Bell, and a veterinary clinic on the way to his destination, it occurred to J.T. how appearances could be deceiving.

The treelined streets he drove through, set on hillsides behind a lake shadowed by fog, with their manicured lawns and children's play park, portrayed a sense of tranquillity. It could, he thought, as he turned onto Marine Drive, be any one of a million suburban neighborhoods scattered across the country.

What made his destination different from most was that these tile-roofed beige stucco houses were home to warriors. Another reason he was grateful for the rain. On a sunny day, more people would be outside and the sight of the black SUV with two Marines inside wearing dress blues would set off alarms that would spread like wildfire.

J.T. leaned forward, trying to read the house numbers through the slanting rain. He could have used the GPS, but found the computerized female voice a distraction in situations like these.

The house was located at the end of a cul-de-sac. A white Ford Escape with a child's car seat in back was parked in the driveway. A bumper sticker on the small SUV read *My Heart Belongs to a U.S. Marine.*

Exchanging a look with the sergeant, J.T. pulled on his white cotton gloves and climbed out of the Suburban. The heels of his shiny shoes clicked on the concrete sidewalk.

A pot of red geraniums on the small covered porch added a bright spot to the gray day. A blue star flag, signifying a deployed family member, hung in the side window.

J.T. took a deep breath. He knew the sergeant standing beside him would be saying a prayer. Wishing he still possessed such faith, J.T. found his own peace by envisioning himself back home. The remembered tang of Douglas fir trees and brisk salt-tinged sea air cleared his head.

Although he'd rather have been back in Afghanistan, facing a horde of Taliban, than standing at this front door on this rainy California day, J.T. squared his shoulders and braced himself as he reached out a gloved hand to ring the bell and shatter yet another woman's heart.

2

He came to Mary Joyce, as he had for each of the past five nights, in her dreams. His hair was as dark as a moonless night over the Burren, his eyes the color of rain. He was striding determinedly toward her on long legs that ate up the ground. Flames blazed across the battle-scarred landscape behind him.

His jaw was wide and square, his raw-boned face as chiseled as the stone cliffs of her native Ireland. He was every bit a warrior, in rough clothing, carrying a huge and dangerous sword in his large hands.

Having grown up in a country that had suffered centuries of hostilities from battling factions, Mary hated war. And, although she understood intellectually that occasionally such things were necessary for the greater good, she'd never experienced a moment's attraction to men who'd conduct them.

Which didn't explain why, as he stopped in front of her, his granite gray eyes intense as they glared down into hers, she felt her body melting like a candle left out too long in a warm summer sun.

There was no seduction.

No romance.

There never was.

The dangerously menacing stranger did not even bother to ask; he took, as if it were his perfect right. As if she were merely a battle prize granted without question to the victor. Dropping his weapon, his fist crumpled the front of the emerald green nightgown that had cost an obscene amount of money for such a scrap of silk and lace — and ripped it down the front.

When she gasped, as she always did, his head swooped down and his mouth — hard and demanding — devoured hers in a deep, forceful kiss, as broad, rough hands claimed her body.

Her head was swimming. As she felt her legs weaken, Mary struggled to keep from fainting. Such savage, primal passion made her tremble. Not from fear, nor outrage at being taken by this stranger without a single pretty word or bit of clever foreplay, but from a burning need for fulfillment.

Seeming oblivious to the death and destruction behind him, he dragged her to the ground beside a mountain lake, where, in direct contrast to the battle that was still waging, a pair of swans — one white, the other black — drifted on glassy blue water.

His body was all rock-hard muscle and sinew. They came together like thunder. Like lightning. Every coherent thought Mary possessed was swept away by the hot winds swirling around them.

When a soft, shimmering lavender dawn light began to filter into the bedroom, Mary woke, emerging from the storm shaken, as she had for the past five mornings.

And alone.

The house was quiet. Her guests must still be sleeping. Turning on the coffee, so it'd be brewed when they got up, Mary quickly braided her long black hair, pulled on a pair of shorts, a T-shirt, and running shoes, and went out her back door and down the wooden steps onto the beach.

It was early enough that the fog had yet to burn off, and as she ran down the packed sand at the edge of the surf, she could almost imagine that she was back running on the beach in Castlelough.

She'd always loved the ocean. Granted, this glistening strip of sand on Malibu beach was not the kelp-draped shores of home, and the houses crowded together like crows on a line were a poor substitute for the soaring, vertical west Irish cliffs, but the salt air still managed to clear her head, even as it failed to blow away those last lingering fragments of the erotic dream that had been bedeviling her.

Once upon a time, while growing up in a small county on the far west coast of Ireland, Mary had dreamed of moving to America, where she'd become a rich and famous movie star, live in a mansion in Beverly Hills, and have a worldwide audience of fans who'd follow her every move.

Despite having chosen an acting career that had thrust her into the public eye and onto the covers of tabloid magazines, Mary had always been an intensely private person. After surviving admittedly tempestuous teenage years, she'd emerged as what she liked to believe was a sensible, logical adult. A woman who was the polar opposite of the sexy Queen of the Selkies, a role she'd created by writing the screenplays that had garnered her wealth beyond her wildest dreams — along with a legion of fans who'd show up in droves at theaters for the opening of her movies and hold festivals where they'd enact favorite scenes and conduct workshops about selkie myths and culture.

At the urging of the studio's publicity department, Mary had attended several of these events, and as grateful as she was for these moviegoers who'd made her dream come true, she was bemused by the idea her stories, drawn from myths her late father loved to tell, could be taken by anyone as gospel truth.

"I'm simply telling stories," she'd insist to those who'd push her to admit otherwise. "They're make-believe. Like leprechauns or fairies."

Of course, one problem with that explanation was her own father had believed in leprechauns and fairies. Fictional or not, her stories had stimulated the imaginations of millions who preferred to believe in an alternate reality.

And lately she'd been feeling more and more trapped in a life of her own making.

The sun was rising in the sky, burning off the fog, as she returned to the house and found her houseguests seated out on the deck.

"Good morning!" Kate MacKenna waved as Mary approached.

"Good morning to you." Mary ran up the steps and gave the older woman a hug. "I'm sorry I wasn't here to be making you breakfast."

"Don't bother your head about it. We've only just gotten up." As Kate exchanged a look with her husband, a telltale flush rose in her cheeks.

The idea that her older sister's best friend had found such love with the American horse trainer after a miserable and abusive marriage brought Mary a rush of pleasure. Kate was one of the kindest, most nonjudgmental people Mary had ever met, which was why she'd been such a valuable sounding board during those young and foolish years when Mary's entire happiness seemed to have revolved around whether she'd be popular with the village boys.

Kate's smile faded, just a bit, as she swept a gaze over Mary's face. "You look a bit tired," she said. "I hope we haven't been a bother."

"Don't talk foolishness. I love having you visit. I just had a restless night."

"More than a few of them, I'd be thinking," Kate said, as her husband, Alec, went into the house, returning with a mug of coffee he handed to Mary. "Is something wrong?"

Damn. There was no hiding anything from this woman. According to Mary's sister

Nora, ever since childhood Kate had been able to "see" things. Like when she was five and saw the black wreath on Mrs. Callahan's door two months before the elderly woman dropped dead of a heart attack while weeding her cabbage patch.

Or the time, when Nora and Kate were teenagers, that Kate saw little Kevin Noonan floating facedown in the surf seconds before a white-crested wave swept the wandering toddler off his feet — but soon enough to warn his mother.

"Thank you," she said to Alec as she cradled the mug in her hands, breathing in the fragrant steam. When she was home in Ireland, she tended to drink tea. But she'd developed the coffee-drinking habit while living in America. "There's just a lot of stress involved with releasing a new film."

"I imagine it's a bit like an upcoming race," Alec said.

"I would imagine," Kate echoed. Then gave Mary an even longer, more pointed look. "Is that all it would be?"

"I've been having dreams," Mary admitted reluctantly.

"Would those dreams be about a man?" Kate asked. "And would they be a stranger?"

"Yes on both counts, but as for him being a stranger, that's undoubtedly because I don't personally know men worth dreaming about."

Before her warrior stranger had begun visiting her, Mary had experienced a particularly hot dream about Daniel Craig where she'd played a Bond Girl to his 007. Not that she was going to share that bit of information in front of Kate's husband, who was pretty hot himself.

It was time to change the subject. "You must be really excited, with Lady of the Lake's win yesterday."

The Thoroughbred, sired by Legends Lake out of Irish Dancer, was the reason for Kate and Alec's visit. They'd brought her from the couple's Kentucky farm for the American Oaks Invitational Stakes at Hollywood Park.

"I hoped she'd do well, but winning by so many lengths was definitely the icing on the cake," Kate said. She exchanged another look with Alec, who, on cue, stood up. "Well, if you ladies will excuse me, I have some calls to make," he said.

"What was that about?" Mary asked as he went back into the house.

"Oh, you know how it is." Kate brushed away the question with a graceful wave of her hand. "The stud business never rests."

"That may be. But why do I get the feeling you wanted to talk to me alone?"

"You've always been a clever girl, Mary, darling." Kate's lips curved. "And you can resist all you want, but I still believe you've inherited a bit of the sight, yourself. Undoubtedly from your father."

Kate had told her more than once over the years that her father had been known to experience a few visions. Having witnessed that such a gift could also be a curse, Mary had steadfastly closed her mind to the possibility.

"The only thing I inherited from Da was my storytelling. As for his visions, as much as I loved him, I can't overlook the fact that he was more than a little fond of his pints and Jameson's."

"Well, there was that," Kate agreed with a faint smile. Then got right down to brass tacks. "I had a dream of my own last week," she said. "About Eleanor."

"Mam?" Mary had been nine years old when she'd lost her mother. There were times she couldn't decide whether some of her memories were true or merely stories others had told that she'd grasped onto so tightly she'd come to believe she remembered them. "Does that happen often?"

"Not since your sister married. In truth, the last time I dreamed of her was right a lovely holiday there with her family after her sister had married.

"That's it. According to the letter — an actual letter, on town council stationery, not an e-mail — I received, they're throwing their first film festival."

There was a slight pause. "They asked if you'd make an appearance, since the festival is featuring your movies. Being a seaside town, it fits in with your selkie stories, and being that you're a former citizen of their sister city, of course they thought of you. Unfortunately, the letter got misdirected by the mail room, and after spending the past two months wending its way through the studio, it finally landed on my desk."

Another pause. "Of course I called and told the mayor I doubted you'd be able to make it on such short notice — it's next eek — but —"

"I'll do it."

You will?" The voice on the other end of phone sounded as surprised by Mary's er as Mary herself was. Not only was ealist; she was also not the least bit ve.

r say anything I don't mean." And tely hadn't meant to say that.

y. So . . ." She could practically eels spinning in the publicity

before Quinn Gallagher arrived in Castlelough."

Not only was Quinn now Mary's brother-in-law, the bestselling horror novelist was also the person who'd gotten Mary interested in both acting and writing. He'd also, on one memorable night, talked her out of giving away her virginity to a boy who would never have appreciated what such an act would have meant to her.

"It was much the same as last time," Kate revealed. "She told me to tell you she's sending you a man."

Although she'd never intentionally hurt the other woman's feelings, Mary couldn't help laughing. "Are you suggesting my mother's in heaven, pulling strings on my life? Because if she is, could you ask her to please cause a flood or tsunami that'll wash those tabloid cretins who call themselves reporters off the face of the earth without harming anyone else?"

"They'll get their comeuppance," Kate said mildly. "In this life or the next. And aren't you reacting with the same skepticism Nora had when I brought it up with her thirteen years ago? And look how wonderfully her life's turned out."

Her sister's life admittedly could have served as inspiration for a romantic movie.

But having been there to witness the beginning of her and Quinn's relationship, Mary knew that the road to their well-deserved happily-ever-after hadn't been all that smooth.

"I best be getting ready to go to the track." Kate stood up and kissed Mary's cheek. "Just keep an open mind," she advised. "And you never know when magical things might happen."

Perhaps to some people, Mary thought as she looked out over the deck railing to where the glistening sea foam was washing onto the sand. But despite making a living writing fantasy, Mary didn't believe in magic. Nor the banshees her father had once sworn he'd tangled with and escaped, nor glittering green sea creatures, nor even selkies.

Her feet were set firmly in the concrete of reality. Which was precisely where she intended to keep them.

3

Mary had just gotten out of the shower when her bedroom phone rang. Seeing it was one of the myriad publicity people the studio had assigned to her upcoming movie, she switched into work mode and picked up.

"Hi," she said. "What's up?"

"I have a proposition for you," the yo[illegible] woman said. "But you don't have to [illegible] it if you don't want to."

That got Mary's attention. Sh[illegible] remember a time when she [illegible] made to feel pressured [illegible] publicity. "What is it?"

"There's this small [illegible] supposedly a siste[illegible] grew up in."

"Shelter Bay[illegible] immediately. Ha[illegible] at both ends of [illegible] been in high school?

woman's head. "Let me get back with them and work on transportation and where you'll be staying. I didn't bother to look the place up online before I called, because I was so sure you'd say no, but I got the impression you won't be booked into a suite at the Shelter Bay Four Seasons or Ritz-Carlton."

"It'll be a challenge, but I believe I can handle that sacrifice," Mary said dryly.

"You're such a trouper! I'll call the mayor, get more details, and get right back to you."

Left listening to dead air, Mary hung up. Then cast a glance upward. "Good try, Mam. But if you did have anything to be doing with this, you've got your wires crossed. Because I'm definitely not in the market for a husband."

Ever since *Siren Song* had achieved block-buster success, she'd devoted so much time to her career, she had no time for men. Let alone a romantic relationship, which, from the few she'd attempted, had required her to do most of the heavy lifting and eventually ended, not with a bang, but with a whimper. Which had left Mary wondering if she even knew what it felt like to be deeply, madly, truly in love. Oh, she could write about love and passion, but she was beginning to suspect that she simply didn't possess a romantic gene.

Which wouldn't be the end of the world. She did, after all, have good friends like Kate and Alec, work she loved, and although living in Los Angeles would no longer be her first choice, she'd adapted.

Life might not be perfect. But whose was?

Unlike seemingly many of her fans, Mary fully understood that life really wasn't anything like the movies.

4

Shelter Bay, Oregon

It wasn't the same. J.T. wondered why he even thought it could be. Shelter Bay hadn't changed. But *he* had.

Giving up on sleep, he crawled out of the rack at dawn and ran out of town to the coast, boots pounding the empty streets, across the bridge, and along the hard-packed sand at the ocean's edge. He didn't run for physical fitness, or to achieve any elusive runner's high. The truth was, he was out in the morning fog, as he'd been every day since returning home six weeks ago, trying to wipe out the memories that ran like an unending video loop in his head. Even as he feared they'd always be with him, J.T. continued to run.

And run.

And run.

Arriving back in town, he passed the blue and white welcome sign announcing that the sleepy Oregon coastal town he once couldn't wait to escape was not only the Pacific Northwest's whale-watching capital, but home to Navy Cross recipient Sax Douchett.

Knowing how his former SEAL brother hated that hero tag, J.T. suspected that Sax cringed every time he was forced to drive past the sign.

Another sign was yet more proof that while *J.T.* may have changed during the dozen-plus years he'd been away, not much else had. The Rotary Club continued to meet on Tuesdays at the Sea Mist restaurant, the historical society on the first Thursday of every month at the museum, and summer concerts were still held on Sunday afternoons at Evergreen Park.

Although the calendar might say summer, a cool, misty rain blowing in from the Pacific had followed him, dampening his hair and brown T-shirt as he ran along Harborview Drive.

Again, everything looked nearly the same as it had when he'd left town in search of adventure. It was high tourist season, and although it was still early and wet, people were out in full force, crowding the sidewalks as they shopped in quaint little galleries and souvenir shops, stood shoulder to shoulder at the seawall taking photos of the sea lions lounging on the docks, and watching with binoculars for the resident whales that made Shelter Bay their home.

A fat orange cat lounged in the window of Tidal Wave Books next to a stack of Gabriel St. James's new photo book. The former jarhead (not that there was really any such thing as a *former* Marine) was J.T.'s brother Cole's best friend. While in Shelter Bay for Cole's wedding — which J.T., who'd been in Afghanistan at the time, had missed — St. James had fallen in love with a local veterinarian and stayed.

When he went inside to buy a copy, the friendly bookstore owner chattered away to him as she rang up the sale, but although he could see her lips moving, J.T. couldn't hear a word she said over the roaring, like surf, in his ears as another memory flashed through his mind.

When a pregnant wife had asked to spend the night before her husband's funeral next to the flag-draped casket, J.T. had sneaked her into the funeral home. Not wanting her to have to sleep on the hard tile floor, he'd gone to Target for an air mattress, a pillow, and sheets. Until he'd stood in the aisle, he'd never realized sheets came in so many damn colors. Since women liked flowers, he'd grabbed the ones with roses, which she'd seemed to appreciate.

Marine notification officers stayed with families for as long as they needed, which meant visiting her at the hospital after she'd given birth. While showing off the baby boy who'd never know his father, she'd confessed that her husband sometimes visited her at night and they'd make love.

The summer he'd turned ten, his family had taken a vacation road trip that had included a visit to Little Bighorn National Monument. Having felt the lingering warrior spirits, J.T. wasn't about to discount the young widow's story of ghostly visits. In fact, as he accepted the white bag with the blue wave and store name on it, he wondered if perhaps he was turning into a ghost himself. If the bookstore owner reached out to touch, would her hand go right through him?

Since that memory made him thirsty, on the way back to Bon Temps, his brother Sax's Cajun restaurant, where he'd been staying in the office, J.T. dropped into the VFW hall. The heads of various game animals still hung on knotty pine walls, while a snarling grizzly continued to stand over a jukebox that offered up mostly country.

While Trace Adkins's rumbling baritone sang about a solider who'd died and met up with his grandfather, who was also buried at Arlington National Cemetery, J.T. put the bag on the floor covered in peanut shells and took a stool. "I'll have a Bud."

The bartender, who'd shot the bear during R & R after participating in Operation Just Cause in Panama, lifted a brow. "Little early, isn't it?"

"Since when did Navy frogmen become the beer police?"

"Just saying." The former SEAL twisted off the cap and put the bottle on an ancient bar that had been carved with initials and symbols of various units going back to World War II.

"Well, don't."

The icy cold beer went down smooth and took the edge off the hangover that had continued to linger during his run. After polishing it off, he tossed some bills on the counter, picked up the book, and left. He did not say good-bye. Neither did the SEAL.

Maybe he'd turned as invisible as he felt.

Or maybe not.

"Where the hell have you been?" his brother Sax demanded when J.T. walked in the door at Bon Temps and found both his brothers waiting for him.

He tossed the bag onto a table. "And that's any of your business, why?"

"Because you're our baby brother," Cole, the eldest, said.

"I haven't been a *baby* for a helluva long time. And where I go and what I do isn't any of your damn business." He went behind the bar and pulled a bottle of Full Sail pale ale out of the cooler.

"That's what you think." Sax snatched the bottle away before he could open it. "Everyone's been walking on eggshells around you, waiting for you to settle back in. But it's been six weeks of you drinking up my profits, and you're still spooking everyone in town —"

"Not to mention worrying Mom and Dad sick," Cole broke in.

J.T. thrust out his jaw when he wanted to lower his head in shame at that unwelcome news. "Low blow, bro." He rubbed his stubbled face, trying to remember how long it had been since he'd shaved.

Sax heaved a long weary sigh. Raked his hands through his hair. "Look, we both know it's not easy."

"I had nightmares," Cole volunteered. "Once, I even grabbed Kelli by the throat while we were sleeping. Scared her nearly to death."

"And I had ghosts," Sax said. "Not just memories, but real ones who talked to me and followed me around for a while. Which, by the way, no one but Kara, Cole, and now you, knows about, and I'd like to keep it that way. But, like I said, we understand. So, if you've got PTSD issues, we're here to help you get help. Before things get worse."

"Thanks. But I don't have PTSD." He'd read all the symptoms and none of them had said anything about turning into a ghost. "And I don't need any stupid intervention."

He was just exhausted. And weighed down with a deep-to-the-bone sadness he couldn't shake off.

When he tried to snatch the bottle back, Sax pulled it out of reach.

Frustrated by this entire situation, J.T. lunged.

Sax dodged, threw down the beer, and connected with a strong left hook to the chin that caused bells to ring inside J.T.'s throbbing head. Which didn't stop him from jumping on Sax.

"Trust a damn SEAL frogman not to fight fair," he said as he took another blow that had him staggering. As his knees buckled, he dragged Sax down to the floor, where they rolled, fists flying, elbows swinging.

Cursing like the Marine he was, Cole grabbed J.T. by the shirt, and jerked him to his feet. "That's enough."

"The hell it is." At least he wasn't feeling dead anymore. Every atom in J.T.'s body was in full battle alert mode. "He never would've gotten that first hit in if he hadn't cheated and I'd been totally sober."

"Oh, we can take care of that problem." Cole grabbed J.T. under the arms. "You take the kid's legs," he told Sax. "A swim should sober him up quick enough."

He'd definitely lost his edge. There'd been a time when it would've taken a helluva lot more than two guys to pick him off his feet.

J.T. cursed and kicked as they carried him out the door and threw him unceremoniously into the bay, which was cold enough to have his balls rising up into his throat.

He had just sputtered to the surface, determined to take them both on, when he saw Sax's fiancée standing on the dock.

"I thought you boys would've outgrown this stupidity by now," she said.

"He started it," both Sax and J.T. said at the same time.

She looked up at the drizzling sky, as if seeking patience.

"Pitiful," she muttered. "You'd think three grown men, one of whom is about to become a father" — she shot a hard look at Sax — "would have better things to do than get into brawls. Want to give me one reason why I shouldn't run you all in for disturbing the peace?"

"We were only trying to sober the kid up," Sax said, sounding, J.T. thought, uncharacteristically chastened.

"That's another thing." She turned to J.T. "You've been drunk for six weeks."

"Not drunk. Merely not entirely sober," he amended when she gave a steely cop stare he imagined she used on perps when trying to get them to confess. Which, in this town, where hardly anything exciting ever happened, probably involved teenagers bashing mailboxes or spraying graffiti on the water tower. He boosted himself out of the water and onto the dock. "And I haven't been driving."

"I know. I've received reports. You're starting to scare tourists, the way you're constantly running around in those combat boots."

"I couldn't run if I were that drunk." Though standing upright on the floating, bobbing dock wasn't as easy as it should have been.

She shook her head. "You know the trouble with you, J. T. Douchett?"

"No." But he had no doubt the former Shelter Bay High School valedictorian was about to tell him.

"You need something worthwhile to do with your time." Her tone suggested she didn't consider running and drinking worthwhile pursuits. "And fortunately for all of us, the solution just came to me."

"What?"

"You may not have read the flyers tacked up all around town, or noticed so many of the store windows are painted with displays promoting it, but Shelter Bay's holding its first film festival. And I was just informed that none other than Mary Joyce is going to be the guest of honor."

"Good for Shelter Bay. And who's Mary Joyce?"

"Jeez," Sax said. "What planet did the Marines assign you to the past three years?"

"I've been a bit occupied."

"She's only the hottest actress in Hollywood," Cole said.

"She's an Irish movie star who plays the queen of the selkies in a blockbuster series," Kara added.

"And a selkie is?"

"A seal woman," Sax said, his tone thick

with disgust at having such an apparently boneheaded brother. "You know, like a mermaid."

"But hotter," Cole said.

"I'll refrain from telling your wife you keep coming back to that," Kara said dryly. "Anyway," she said to J.T., "she's also acquired a crazy following of fans who dress up like selkies and reenact scenes. I'm assured they're harmless, but since my department doesn't have the manpower to handle additional security, I'm asking you, as a personal favor, to act as her bodyguard and keep them at bay with that hard, mean stare they teach all you Marines in basic training."

"No way."

"Way." She folded her arms across the front of her stiff khaki shirt. "So much for trying to play the good cop and appeal to your friendship and family loyalty. So, let me put it this way, J.T. You may have been a big bad Marine, but do you really want to mess with a hormonal pregnant sheriff who's armed and carries her own handcuffs?"

"Plus, there's the fact that if you upset my woman, *I'll* have to shoot you," Sax warned on something close to a growl. Although J.T. didn't believe for a minute his brother would follow through on the threat, he thought back again on that pregnant woman he'd bought the sheets for and felt his resolve crumbling.

"Well," she asked, "do I hear a volunteer?"

Damn. He'd had drill instructors who weren't as tough as Sheriff Kara Conway. Knowing when he was outnumbered, J.T. managed, just barely, to stand at attention. Then he snapped a salute. "Aye, aye, ma'am."

5

As her chartered plane approached Newport, on the Oregon coast, Mary was pulling on the shoes she'd kicked off upon boarding when she caught sight of the uplift of tree-covered cliffs visible through the fog blowing in from the Pacific.

Mist was forming on the outside of the window. Mary pulled her champagne-colored angora shrug over the black tank top she'd tucked into a pair of wide-legged black pants, and wished she'd remembered to buy a Gore-Tex jacket. Which would undoubtedly give Leon, her stylist, who was originally from Atlanta, the vapors.

Three men and a woman were waiting for her at the bottom of the stairs as she left the jet. One of the men was dressed in a brown corduroy suit, a blue checked shirt, and a brown and yellow polka-dot bow tie. Another had gone with khakis and a denim shirt with suede patches on the elbows, while one had gone totally casual in a Hawaiian shirt designed to blind and well-worn jeans. The sixty-something woman had opted for a middle ground, with dark slacks, a fitted red jacket, and a white blouse.

A fourth man, clad in jeans and a smoky blue and gray plaid shirt open over a charcoal gray T-shirt, was standing next to the black Suburban, back as straight as a turf spade handle, arms crossed. Unlike the others, who were wearing wide smiles, he'd drawn his mouth into a tight line. Despite the gray day, he was wearing sunglasses, which kept her from seeing his eyes. Even so, she had the impression he wasn't a member of the Shelter Bay Welcome Wagon come here to the airport today to give her a fruit basket.

The woman strode forward, hand outstretched. "Good afternoon, Ms. Joyce. I'm Colleen Dennis, mayor of Shelter Bay." Her fingers were stained yellow, which went along with the cigarette rasp in her voice. Apparently not everyone in Oregon lived up to the state's reputation of being populated by physical-fitness buffs. "And it's an honor to welcome you to Oregon."

"It's Mary. And the honor's mine. I'm delighted to be invited, Mayor Dennis. I've known many people with the Dennis surname back home. Would your family have Irish ties?"

"They certainly do," the mayor said proudly. "My maiden name was McLaughlin, and John McLaughlin fought with the Jacobites at the Battle of the Boyne in 1690."

"As did my ancestors," Mary said, causing the mayor to beam to have something in common with the town's celebrity guest. "It was a sad time for many." The battle had established Protestant rule over the Emerald Isle, which lasted until the Anglo-Irish war in the 1920s.

"I can imagine. My husband's great-great-grand-father was born at sea while his parents emigrated during the mid-1840s potato famine. They were originally from Letterfrack, a small Connemara village few have ever heard of."

"I know it well," Mary said. "I filmed a few scenes of *Selkie Bride* at the village's Kylemore Abbey, as you'll be seeing when we premiere my new film the last day of the festival."

It had been the studio's idea to do a surprise sneak preview of the movie. An idea the committee had jumped to endorse, since it would bring the fledgling festival much-needed publicity and buzz that would help them build for next year. Which was vital when there were more than a thousand film festivals being held all over the world these days.

"I'm so looking forward to that," Mayor Dennis said. "I've visited the abbey, and being a gardener myself, I was blown away by the walled Victorian garden."

"A spectacular place," Mary agreed, always happy to talk about her home. "Though it always leaves me feeling terribly inadequate, given my own pitiful black thumb." Which was ironic, having grown up on a farm.

"We're looking forward to the honor of being the first to view your new film," bow tie man, who'd apparently decided Her Honor had gotten enough of their guest's attention, broke into the conversation. "While your appearance is decidedly last-minute, better late than never, and everyone's excited to have you partake in our little event." His grip as he shook her hand wasn't nearly as brisk as Colleen Dennis's had been. "Thomas Clark. I teach drama and musical theater at Coastal Community College."

His tone, at that announcement, was heavy with a self-importance that had Mary thinking it should properly have come with a flare of trumpets.

"I saw your name on the brochure," she said with a smile that ignored his little barb. She decided against repeating what the mayor had already been told about the letter going astray. "Teaching must be an extremely gratifying career."

His chest puffed out like a plump pigeon's. "I like to believe I'm helping create the next generation of thespians. Which is why we're so pleased you'll be speaking and answering questions after tomorrow's viewing of *The Lady of the Lake.*"

"I'm looking forward to it," Mary said.

It hadn't been that long since she'd been a student herself, and one of the things she missed about her university days was the passionate discussions of the art of filmmaking that often would last all night. In L.A. topics more often centered on the business aspect of filmmaking instead of on storytelling.

"I was a bit younger than your students when I appeared in that film, but it changed my life."

Which was definitely no exaggeration. When Quinn had arrived in Castlelough for the filming of the movie adaptation of his novel, she'd been an overly emotional, tempestuous teenage girl adrift after a breakup that she had been certain had shattered her heart. She'd been cast in the film, first as a walk-on extra, but when both Quinn and the director declared the camera loved her, her part had been expanded. By the time the film hit the theaters, she'd forgotten all about the sex-crazed boy who'd dumped her right before the spring dance, and had decided to become an actress.

It was later, while at university, that she'd become interested in screenwriting, and her first film, *A Secret Selkie* — a story of a motherless young child who discovers his selkie heritage, which his father's family has kept hidden from him — won the award for best screenwriting at the Jameson Dublin International Film Festival.

Her second was based on the old Irish fairy tale of a young man, son of Conn of the Hundred Fights, who fell desperately in love with a fairy maiden and, ignoring warnings from others, ran away with her over the sea to the Plains of the Ever Living, and was never seen in Ireland again. That film had surpassed her first, garnering numerous international awards.

When *Siren Song,* the first in her selkie queen trilogy, won an Audience Award at Sundance, a Toronto's People's Choice

Award, and the Heineken Audience Award at New York City's Tribeca Film Festival, topped off with a Best Screenplay award at the illustrious Cannes, Mary was, overnight, thrust from being a struggling, independent Irish screenwriter/filmmaker who'd originally starred in her films to lower the cast budget, to the big leagues of American cinema.

Which was when she'd come to realize the axiom her grandmother Fionna was always quoting was true: *Be careful what you wish for.*

She was shaking off the touch of pity party she had no business feeling, when the balding, ponytailed man in the Hawaiian shirt pushed forward to introduce himself. "I'm Bob Bodine," he said. "But everyone calls me Bodhi, after Swayze's character in *Point Break.*"

"Not because you rob banks wearing a president's mask, I hope." The movie was one of her brother-in-law's favorites. She'd enjoyed it, as well, though admittedly paid less attention to the plot than she did to Patrick Swayze surfing.

The laugh rumbled up from his belly. "No. Because when I'm not running the Orcas Theater, where we're going to screen your films, I surf."

It was Mary's turn to laugh. "No! Really?" she asked with mock surprise. The shirt's print featuring old woody station wagons with surfboards on their roofs had been her first clue. "Why, I never would have guessed that." She glanced over to where the ocean was hidden by a stand of fir trees. "Isn't it cold surfing this far north?"

"Like the Arctic." He winked. "But you don't have to worry about falling asleep."

"And here I thought falling asleep was one of the things that happen when you freeze to death," Mary said with a laugh, then turned to speak with the third man, who'd been patiently awaiting his turn. As she did, her attention was momentarily captured by the silent man still standing beside the SUV, his shielded gaze directed straight at her.

Refusing to be intimidated, Mary threw up her chin and stared back. Then tossed her head and turned toward the third man.

"You must be Reece Ryan." The editor and publisher of the *Shelter Bay Beacon*. "I've read some of your articles." Even as she could feel the driver's eyes on her, she forced a smile. "They were very good."

He lifted a brow as he shook her hand. His brown eyes, magnified by black Elvis Costello glasses, were friendly and intelligent. "Thank you. And since I doubt the

Shelter Bay Beacon is your usual reading material, you must have Googled the paper."

"I did. And, as I said, liked what I read. Especially the article on the 'Great Pacific Cleanup.' I use canvas bags for groceries, but realizing how many millions of sea turtles, seabirds, whales, and fish are strangled and suffocated by plastic pollution every year has definitely changed my shopping habits."

"Shelter Bay banned plastic shopping bags last year," the mayor said. "Once people realized that something they might use for five minutes lasts five hundred years in the ocean, they voted overwhelmingly for businesses to stop using them."

The man Mary assumed was the driver continued to stare at her. Hating that a stranger could prove so distracting, she forged on with the conversation. "It must be lovely to know you've made such a difference in the world. I assume we'll be doing an interview?"

"Our local paper hardly has the power to influence the world," he said, showing himself to have less of an ego than the professor. "Though I try to enlighten my little corner of it. And while I may have worked the political desk at the *Washington Post* before moving to the West Coast, I still enjoy entertainment news. And you, Ms. Joyce, are definitely the hottest celebrity ever to hit Shelter Bay."

"Hell, she's the only celebrity to ever hit Shelter Bay," Bodhi said.

Mary wasn't surprised the newsman had once worked at a larger paper. Not only had the stories she'd read been well sourced, but the content was exceptionally strong for such a small town, where news often tended to revolve around local gossip.

"Why would I be having the feeling that if you'd been editor of the *Beacon* back when my family visited Shelter Bay, my brother-in-law wouldn't have slipped under your radar, Mr. Ryan?"

His grin was quick and appealing. "Once an investigative reporter, always an investigative reporter. But, since I've never approved of paparazzi tactics to get a story, I would've waited until you all left town to run the story."

Mary smiled and wished that more reporters had such ethics. "I knew I liked you."

"Well," the mayor said abruptly, as an airport employee drove over a luggage cart with Mary's suitcases, "I'm sure you'd like to get settled into your hotel room and decompress a bit from the trip before tonight's events."

Having seen the schedule, which began with a reception that night, then a parade the following day with her as grand marshal, and ended with her giving out the Golden Whale award for best festival film the final day, Mary knew that this would be no laid-back holiday like the first time she'd visited the town. Promoting a film for the studio releasing it was part of any actor's job description. Having also written the screenplays, which had her even more invested in this new film's success, she wasn't about to complain.

Unsurprisingly, a line of spectators had formed outside the terminal. Given that her photo — or some badly Photoshopped version of it — was continually appearing on those tacky supermarket tabloids and online blogs, she'd reluctantly grown accustomed to being recognized everywhere she went.

Breaking away from the others, she went over to the crowd and spent the next fifteen minutes signing autographs and posing for photos. This was one advantage the small-town airport had over larger ones. She'd learned the hard way that if she even paused for a moment in a larger-city airport, she'd soon be mobbed.

But this gave her the opportunity to thank

some of the people who'd provided her with a very comfortable living. It also took her mind off that very rude driver.

"Would you mind holding my baby?" one woman asked, holding out an infant wrapped in a pink sweater and wearing a pink knit cap. "She's named after you . . . Muirenn."

Which was actually her character's name, which translated to "born of the sea." She'd begun receiving more and more mail that included photos of baby girls who'd been given the ancient Irish name solely because of her movies. While flattered that her work would touch someone enough to name a child after a fictional character she'd created, Mary also found it a little unsettling.

"She's lovely." Which was the truth, but understanding that all newborns are beautiful to their mothers, she would have said the same if the baby had looked like a hobbit.

Cradling the infant in her arms, she smiled for the woman's camera. Then asked Bodhi to photograph her with the mother and child.

"I'm going to put this in her scrapbook," the mother said. "When she gets a little older, I'll tell Muirenn all about the day she was held by the queen of the selkies."

Uncertain whether the woman was serious, Mary merely smiled again, and, having reached the end of the line, continued on to the waiting SUV where she came face-to-face with the scowling male wearing the aviator shades. Who, unlike the other Oregonians she'd met so far, wasn't proving the least bit welcoming.

Without a word of *hello, hi,* or *nice to meet you,* he began loading her bags into the back of the Suburban while the mayor shepherded everyone else into the SUV. Saving — oh joy — the passenger seat for Mary.

"J.T.'s going to be providing security," Mayor Dennis said when the silent driver joined them.

"Security?" Surprised by this announcement, Mary glanced over at him. "I seriously doubt I'll be needing any on this trip."

The studio typically arranged for a security detail when any of their stars were going to be thrown into a huge, uncontrollable event, but this was a small, quiet town.

"The sheriff thought it would be a good idea," the Sphinx finally spoke. "Since you seem to have a lot of . . . *enthusiastic* fans."

From his momentary pause, she suspected he'd been close to using another, far less flattering description. "They may be enthusiastic. But as I'm sure you could tell, they're not dangerous," she argued.

"Maybe those weren't," he allowed. "But there's no way of knowing about any others. Until it's too late."

"Well." Fighting back a flare of annoyance, Mary folded her arms. "And won't you be adding a festive air to these upcoming days?" Her voice dripped sarcasm.

"J.T. may be overstating the situation," the mayor jumped in before the negative man could respond. "Kara Conway — that would be our sheriff — is merely taking precautions. J.T.'s here to allow you to get from venue to venue."

"I've managed to walk on my own without assistance for several years."

"Although I'll agree that he might be overkill, there's no denying that he could prove helpful with running your gauntlet of fans," the theater professor allowed.

His tone suggested he had no more use for this J.T. person than she did. Which, perversely, almost had her changing her mind about the scowling male sitting next to her. Almost.

"They began arriving in town this morning," Reece Ryan volunteered. "Though less than we'd expected because somehow the word erroneously got out on the Internet that your flight was landing in Portland. According to the airport security officer I spoke with, there's a crowd waiting for you there.

"Others, for some unknown reason, also showed up at Eugene. Some apparently decided to skip trying to see you at the airport and came straight to Shelter Bay. Several have shown up at the tourist information office, asking where various locations from your movies can be found."

"While several of the sites were inspired by ones both here and back home in Castlelough, the films were shot on the northern coast of California," Mary said. "Which, in many ways, resembles this coast, which was why it was chosen." In between breaks in the stands of fir trees spearing into the silvered sky, Mary could see the vast expanse of the Pacific Ocean.

"It's not surprising that facts got twisted," she said. "I've discovered, since earning a bit of fame, that celebrity news is often like that old game we played as children. Where one starts a story and it continues until it no longer resembles the original statement."

"Gossip." Mayor Dennis nodded. "We always played it at Girl Scout camp on Rainbow Lake. But the lighthouse is definitely ours. You didn't shoot that in California."

"True. A second crew filmed some local color to edit in with the California scenes."

"They're good," Ryan said. "No one ever noticed them."

She smiled at that. "That's because the photographer blended in with the tourists. You'd be surprised what people are shooting with DSLR cameras these days," she said.

"What about the cave?" Bodhi asked.

"Those scenes were shot on a studio set," Mary admitted. "Even if we had wanted to film in the actual cave, the lighting would've been tricky and we would have been up against time constraints trying to time the light with the tide. But it *is* one I remember from when we visited. My nephew, Rory, thought it was made of diamonds."

"I remember thinking the same thing," he said. "So do my kids."

"Those fans at the airport seemed harmless," the mayor said. "And the ones who've shown up in town so far are very friendly."

"And enthusiastic," the Sphinx repeated. Once again, he did not make it sound like an attribute.

And wasn't he Mr. Sparkling Personality? Mary turned toward him. "Are you a sheriff's deputy?" He certainly didn't have the look of a small-town policeman.

"No."

"From a private security firm, then?"

"No."

"J.T.'s recently separated from the Marines," the mayor volunteered. "With multiple deployments under his belt, so you needn't worry. He's totally qualified to keep you safe."

"I wasn't worried to begin with," she said. Hearing that he was a military man brought that erotic dream crashing back. Surely it was only a coincidence that she'd end up with a former Marine providing security? And speaking of safety, who was going to protect her from him? "Unlike some of the other genres, my movies don't bring out the serious crazies."

"Just people who think they're seals," he muttered.

"Would you happen to have to have a last name, J.T.?" She was pleased her voice remained calm, without revealing the temper he'd sparked. "Or do you go by just one? Like Bono. Or Sting?" She racked her brain. Damn. Most of the ones who came immediately to mind were women. "Or Mr. T?"

"*Mr. T* happens to be two words."

"And isn't *J.T.* two letters?" Ha! Score a point for her side.

"Got me there." He shrugged shoulders as broad as ax handles. And kept his shaded eyes on the road. "It's Douchett."

"Is your family French?" Although growing up in the west had made her fluent in Irish, Castlelough had enough French tourists that she'd picked up some of that language, which had proved useful in Cannes.

"Cajun."

He wasn't a sparkling conversationalist. Then again, Mary reminded herself, the sheriff hadn't assigned him to this one-man security detail to keep her entertained.

She may have learned to control her temper, but her Irish stubborn streak went all the way to the bone. Which was why, although she'd never considered herself a glutton for punishment, because she could feel the mayor in the backseat desperate for things to go well, Mary found herself trying yet again to draw the man out.

"I first tasted Cajun food in New Orleans on a fund-raising visit after Katrina. Although it's much spicier than the plain Irish fare I grew up with, I fell in love with it at my first taste of gumbo."

"The Douchetts have owned one of the most popular restaurants on the mid-Oregon coast for two generations," Colleen

Dennis volunteered, in an increasingly desperate attempt to fill in the silence that settled over them when the frustratingly closemouthed Marine didn't respond to Mary's statement. "Which was why we decided to hold the private reception tonight at Bon Temps."

The city council, taking advantage of their position, had scheduled a cocktail and buffet party for the evening, giving them all an opportunity to spend personal time with her. Apparently, along with the contestants who'd entered films, local business owners and other citizens actively involved in the community had been invited.

Remembering the buzz in Castlelough when the movie people had arrived from Hollywood, Mary couldn't blame them for being excited.

"Good times," she translated the restaurant's French name. "I'm looking forward to it."

Which wasn't exactly a lie. Merely a polite white one. Having spent the last two days and this morning doing press interviews, which involved sitting in a room answering the same questions from entertainment reporters writing for newspapers around the world, she'd just wanted to escape to some desert island, without TV, cell phones, or the Internet.

Then again, desert islands weren't exactly known for their crawfish jambalaya or shrimp gumbo. Just the idea, after all those cheese and salad trays the hotel caterers kept sending up, had her mouth watering. She supposed a spicy Cajun meal would be an upside to having to play movie star for a few hours.

They were passing a sign declaring Shelter Bay to be the home of Navy Cross winner Sax Douchett. "I assume that's a relative?" Mary asked her silent driver/bodyguard.

"My brother." Another sign announced the town to be the sister city of Castlelough. He slanted her a look. "Though he'd probably appreciate it if you didn't mention that Navy Cross when you meet him."

Well, wasn't that more words than the frustratingly silent man had managed to string together thus far? Mary, who understood the complexities of families all too well, found it interesting that it was the mention of his brother that had him opening up just that little bit.

"I'll keep that in mind," she said mildly.

Going back into silent mode, he didn't respond. But he did nod. Slightly. Which, Mary thought, was at least acknowledgment that she'd spoken. Which, while progress of a sort, also had her thinking that it was going to be a very long five days.

6

J.T. could feel the annoyance from the others in the back of the Suburban and sensed that the mayor was second-guessing Kara's idea of assigning him guard-dog duty.

He knew he was behaving badly. Maureen Douchett had taught her three sons better manners. But the truth was that he'd spent so many months mostly listening to the families he'd been assigned to take care of, and being careful to try to always say the right thing, even when he knew there really wasn't anything he could ever say that would make the pain go away, he'd totally lost the knack of having a normal conversation that didn't revolve around death.

Since returning home, he'd found that the one thing that got him out of bed each day was having a routine. Okay, so maybe Kara didn't consider running and drinking a responsible routine, but it had been working for him.

guy who almost drove the luggage truck into the side of a tied-down Cessna as he'd driven out to the jet to retrieve her suitcases.

Although the bio information he found on the Web site said that she currently lived in — where else? — Malibu, instead of sporting a California beach bunny tan, her oval face was as pale as the porcelain his mother would bring out for special dinners.

The ruler-straight black hair that fell below her shoulders was as shiny as obsidian. Her eyes were nearly the exact same blue as the neon light surrounding the Orcas Theater marquee. But much, much warmer when she smiled.

Someone at the airport must've tipped off the people in the terminal, because by the time she'd begun walking toward the SUV, a line of lookie-loos had gathered. He'd watched as she bestowed that dazzling smile on the bystanders and waved; then, instead of going straight to the SUV to escape, she'd broken away from the delegation to personally greet the crowd and sign autographs.

When she'd held a baby wrapped in a pink lanket, and not only smiled for the wom-n's camera but asked the newspaper guy take a photo of her with both the mother d daughter, J.T. had decided that if she dn't chosen to be a movie star, she might

The only reason he'd agreed to babysit Mary Joyce — a job that had the potential for being far from routine — was that he hadn't wanted to upset Kara, who was not only a stand-up cop but a childhood friend and the woman his brother was going to marry. Which meant that she was going to be family. And family always backed up family.

He had made a commitment to her to take on the assignment and he needed to see it through. Although before coming home he'd been suffocating in duty to the point when there'd been times he could barely breathe, and had even wondered if a guy his age could actually have a heart attack, no way could he could turn his back on his responsibility now.

Then, if he'd needed any more proof that just when you thought things were really bad, they could get a whole lot worse, he'd woken up this morning with an all-too-familiar black cloud hovering over his head. And not the one that had begun drizzling rain along the coast, but the suffocating one that followed him around like his own personal damn albatross.

He'd wanted to go running, to clear the ghosts and his head, but after Kara claiming he was scaring the tourists, he decided to just put off any PT until the actress left town. It wasn't as if all those hours spent pounding the pavement and sand had helped make his depression go away.

However, he knew from experience that he could still function if he had to, even when he found himself stuck in this dark place. So, since Marines didn't hide beneath the covers just because life got a little tough, he'd dragged himself out of the bottomless void, downed about a gallon of coffee, and headed out to begin his day with the best of intentions.

He'd figured the others would be eager to talk with a bona fide movie star, so it wouldn't be as if anyone expected *him* to be chatty. He'd intended to be civil, though if given the choice between babysitting some spoiled, self-indulgent Hollywood sex symbol or having his spleen removed with a rusty chain saw, he'd have to say, "Start up the engine."

But proving yet again that missions never turn out the way they're originally planned, the moment Mary Joyce walked down the steps of that jet, J.T. had felt a faint, distant spark simmer. Making him think that maybe he wasn't all-the-way dead after all.

And just when he was trying to figure out whether that was a good or bad thing, she'd

glanced over at him while chatting up the delegation the town council had sent out to greet her. It wasn't a sexy, come-and-get-me-big-boy look. Merely a quick appraisal that had hit his gut like a grenade blast.

Since every mission depended on solid intel, he'd spent the past two nights watching DVDs of her movies. Cole had been dead-on when he'd said that Mary Joyce was really, really hot. The fact that she spent a great deal of time naked hadn't hurt, either.

But she wasn't naked today. And while she wasn't exactly dressed for a drizzly day on the coast, neither was she all dolled up like he'd expect a movie star to be. Those leopard-print high heels might be impractical, but it wasn't as if she were going to be jogging on the beach in them, and he'
known enough women to realize that, f
some unfathomable reason, they all seem
to go gaga over footwear. His own mot
who could never be considered high ma
nance, had an entire wall of shelves i
closet just for shoes.

So, while Mary Joyce wasn't deck
for the red carpet, damned if ther
something about her — a sparkl
field — that had captured the at
every person on the tarmac. In

have made a good politician.

During the drive up the coast road to Shelter Bay, he could tell that she was puzzled by his attitude. And growing frustrated. Hell, he wasn't exactly thrilled with it himself. He might not be the same fun-loving guy who'd left Shelter Bay so many years ago for adventure, but he wasn't by nature rude. Until now.

"Oh, except for so many of the windows being painted, it's just the way I remembered it," she murmured as he drove past the shops on Harborview Drive. Which, as the name suggested, provided an expansive view of the harbor, marina, and bridge. A sailboat was skimming across the blue water, reminding J.T. that there was a time, in what now seemed like another life, when he'd enjoyed sailing.

"The paintings were created by art students at Shelter Bay High School," Colleen Dennis chirped up from the backseat, proving that although she might be in her late sixties, there was nothing wrong with her hearing. "You'll be announcing the winner of the competition tomorrow after the parade.

"As for Shelter Bay seemingly being stuck in a time capsule, that's one of the things those of us lucky enough to live here love about our town," the mayor said.

"Castlelough's much the same way. Many towns experienced unprecedented growth during the Celtic Tiger boom, mostly from houses built by wealthy Dubliners or Englishmen wanting a country holiday home. But being off the beaten track as Castlelough is made it less attractive for developers. Plus, many of the residents, including my brother and sister, are active in the preservation movement."

"Another reason we're the perfect sister cities," the mayor said. "Our people have a great deal in common. At every annual town hall, our citizens vote to keep fast-food restaurants and the big-box stores out of town. It's not that we have anything against them, per se. Good heavens, I've been known to enjoy a Big Mac from time to time. But we'd lose our uniqueness, and if we became just another town, we could also lose our tourists. Who've been the lifeblood of Shelter Bay since it was founded back in the eighteen hundreds."

J.T. braced himself for a telling of the town's admittedly colorful history, which, he decided, would at least keep him from having to join in any lame conversation.

Fortunately, he was saved by the bell. Or, more accurately, by Bodhi, who pointed out the theater they were passing.

"Oh, that's so beautiful!" She actually clapped her hands. Which J.T. considered overkill, but hey, it wasn't *his* name up there in lights. "I love the neon around the marquee."

"The neon's a recent addition," Bodhi said with obvious pride. "Though it's merely replicating what was there originally. The Orcas is a grand historic theater. When it was built in 1935, the governor called it the finest cinema house in the Pacific Northwest, and I don't think you'd have found many who'd have disagreed."

"Your former governor was obviously a man of good taste," Mary said. "The detail is amazing. After our Independence, there were a few Art Deco buildings built, though many have since, unfortunately, gone into disrepair. Out in the west, we were too poor and lacked the population for the type of grand buildings Dublin is known for. But I've always admired the style."

"The frieze across the top depicts the town's history," Bodhi pointed out. "First you've got the Native Americans, then the fishermen and sailors, then next the timbermen who came to cut down the trees as the town grew, and, finally, of course, the train that changed everything."

"A train?"

Here it came, J.T. thought fatalistically. The story he'd heard so many times growing up he figured he could recite it by heart. Which he'd once had to, when he'd been narrator of his third grade's play performed at the Pioneer Days celebration.

"Oh, don't tell her yet," the mayor jumped in. "The children at the creative arts summer camp have been working on a skit that depicts the entire event."

J.T. figured it was the same play. And wow, wasn't that going to be fun? If it had been anyone but Kara who'd stuck him with this duty, he'd go AWOL right now.

"The skit's going to be part of tomorrow's events," Colleen Dennis continued. "After the art competition awards. I can't tell you how honored they all are to perform it for such a famous actress."

"That's lovely they'd be going to so much trouble, but I didn't start writing screenplays to become famous. I felt a need to express myself, and, well" — she shrugged — "events escalated from there."

"That's why you're such a perfect role model. I do hope you'll tell them all about when you were a child. It's always so helpful when children can identify with a role model."

"To be honest," Mary said, "I wasn't one of those children who knew what I wanted to do when I was young. My life's been more a series of fortunate events that put me on the path to get to where I am today."

"Then you must tell them about that. Because it's always good for them to realize that it's also okay to be a late bloomer."

Even J.T., who'd never claim to be bucking for any Miss Manners etiquette award, knew that wasn't exactly a compliment.

He shot a sideways glance toward Mary Joyce at the same time she looked over at him. The humor sparkling in her eyes suggested that not only was she not offended, but she didn't take herself all that seriously in the first place. Which was not at all what he'd been expecting.

As if she could read his mind, her lips curved and her challenging smile seemed to say, *Surprised, Douchett?*

Maybe, he thought. *But the jury's still out.*

"Since you're such a fan of Art Deco, wait until you see the inside," Bodhi said, breaking into the silent conversation taking place in the front seats. "The original theater didn't have a concession stand. Back then patrons purchased refreshments from rolling carts in the lobby. So we added two permanent stands built in the same style as the outside of the building. We have a special souvenir program from opening night in a glass case in the lobby. And framed photos in the lobby showing the restoration after the town nearly lost it in the nineteen eighties."

"A former administration felt we needed a parking lot for the tourists," Mayor Dennis said scornfully. "Fortunately more intelligent heads prevailed, we were able to get the Orcas put on the historical register, and with all the local businesspeople and citizens pitching in — the high school clubs even had car washes and younger children sent in pennies — we achieved the funding to restore it to its former glory."

"We Irish love our historic buildings. Even those crumbling away in the fields." Mary twisted in her seat to talk directly to the theater owner. "How many seats does the Orcas hold?"

"The original building had nine hundred and forty-five seats. Now, because we've expanded the stage and added an orchestra pit for live performances, it can accommodate six hundred and fifty, along with ten wheelchairs. Of course, although we're not taking advance reservations for the entry films, we sold out all your films in the first thirty minutes."

"Well, that's encouraging. I'd feel terrible if you changed your schedule on my account and no one showed up!"

"Oh, that would never happen," the mayor chirped.

"I know multiplexes are all the rage right now, but intimate theaters like the Orcas are where I first fell in love with the movies," Bodhi said. "It's also where I copped my first feel while necking with Betty Ann Palmer in the back row of the balcony during *Night of the Living Dead.*"

Mary laughed at that. It was a warm, seductively smoky laugh that slipped beneath J.T.'s skin and had him tightening his fingers on the steering wheel. It was also, he remembered, the same one her selkie character had used to charm the scientist as she'd made love with him on the beach.

"And isn't that an age-old teenage boy's ploy?" There was more of a lilt of Ireland in her voice when she was amused. "Taking a girl to a horror movie to get her poor frightened self to practically climb into your lap?"

"Hey." Bodhi laughed back. "When you're fourteen, whatever works."

"A guy's gotta go with whatever works however old he is," Reece said. "Isn't that right, J.T.?"

Less than thrilled to be dragged into the conversation, J.T. shrugged. "Works for me." No way was he going to admit that he'd done his own share of romantic fumblings in that balcony.

"Of course, J.T. wouldn't know about having to resort to ploys," the mayor said. "Not only is he handsome as homemade sin — those Marine dress blues don't hurt a man's chances."

The headache J.T. had woken up with this morning returned as maniacs began pounding at his temples with jackhammers. "I'm a former Marine," he said firmly, having no intention of ever wearing those blues again.

"My late husband always said there's no such thing as a former Marine," the mayor, who appeared to have never met a silence she didn't feel the need to fill, said.

J.T. privately agreed with that one, but he damn well had no intention of expanding this conversation into his time in the corps. First of all, given that the actress lived in Hollywood, she was probably one of those wine and cheese liberals who, unless they thought there was an audience for war movies, had never seemed real fond of the military men and women who allowed them to sleep safe and secure on their gazillion-thread Egyptian cotton sheets every night.

There was also the fact that he hadn't talked about the last eighteen months with anyone, and if he *were* to open up about it, it'd be with his brothers. Or his Marine dad, who'd done a tour in the final year of the Vietnam War and had been involved in the evacuation during the Fall of Saigon. Or maybe even his grandfather, who'd seen a lot of bad stuff during his time in Korea. But he didn't want to share. Especially not with some actress whose only views of military life — and death — probably came from movies.

He just wanted to be left alone. Was that too damn much to ask?

"*Night of the Living Dead* was originally written as a horror comedy." Mary Joyce returned the conversation to its original track, even as he felt her gaze drift back toward him. As grateful as he was to her for getting the focus off him, he kept his eyes on the road straight ahead. "It was titled *Monster Flick,* and was about a group of teenage aliens who visit Earth and become friends with human teenagers."

"I've never heard that," Clark said. The theater professor's tone was thick with skepticism. When they'd first met that morning, it was clear the guy didn't like J.T.

J.T. considered the feeling mutual.

"It's true. Maybe it's because my brother-in-law's a horror novelist, or due to his books always being around our house because my older brother devoured them like sweets, but I took a class on American fifties and sixties horror films at UCD. University College Dublin," she clarified her credentials. "The second version had a young man running away from home and discovering rotting corpses the aliens used for food scattered over a meadow."

"Yuck," said the mayor.

"You won't be getting any argument with me there. The film was widely criticized for being too graphic, but it's definitely become a cult classic. In fact, over a hundred artists from around the world created a reenactment, using everything from manga to Claymation, to puppets. It's foolishly grand fun."

Damn. This time the warm female laugh caused an unwelcome little sexual sizzle. As reassuring as J.T. might have found it under any other circumstances, with any other woman, he tamped it down. He'd kept his distance from women during his casualty-notification days, because dealing with that mission had proved so emotionally grinding, he didn't have anything left to give to a relationship.

Since returning home, feeling as if he'd

been hollowed out with a rusty machete, he'd kept to himself.

And how's that been working for you? a nagging voice in the back of his mind asked as the others enthusiastically discussed zombies and ghouls and other things that went bump in the night.

Just fine, he answered back.

Which was a flat-out lie. He was a long way from fine. Which was another reason not to even let himself think about this woman whose voice carried the lilt of the auld sod and who smelled like a green Irish meadow.

7

At least Mary Joyce's fans had added some color to the town, Kara considered, as she skirted around a woman wearing a sequined green skirt with a mermaid-tail train and matching bra. Since she'd seen bikini tops a lot skimpier, she decided that the outfit was a long way from breaking any decency laws. The woman was talking to a pirate, who'd accessorized his costume with a red bandanna with fake braids attached, a plastic cutlass, tall leather boots, and eyeliner.

She entered the Sea Mist restaurant, and wove her way through the restaurant out to the harbor-front patio where Sedona Sullivan, Maddy Chaffee, and Charity Tiernan were seated. It was their once-a-week lunch, and since so far things were peaceful, Kara had decided she could risk the hour off duty they'd spend catching up.

"Refresh my memory," she said, as she joined them at the round table. "Were there any Johnny Depp–type pirates in Mary Joyce's selkie movies?"

"Believe me," Sedona said, "I'd remember if there had been. The man's been mine since *21 Jump Street.*"

"I had him first," Kara said. "And a guy who looked a lot like a low-rent Captain Jack Sparrow was outside hitting on a mermaid when I arrived."

"Maybe he decided that dressing up like a merman with a fish tail wouldn't exactly make him a babe magnet," Maddy suggested.

"That's undoubtedly the case. Though I've got to tell you, very few men in this world can make eyeliner work. The guy on the sidewalk is not one of them."

The server arrived to take their orders. Sedona opted for the Dungeness crab Caesar salad, Maddy the fish taco, and Charity the shrimp and crab Louis, while Kara ordered crab cakes, coleslaw, and smoked corn chowder. With a side of fried clam strips.

"I'm eating for two," she said, hearing the defensiveness come out in her tone. "And we can share the clam strips."

"Did we say a thing?" Sedona asked.

"No. But it's embarrassing. I had morning sickness for months with Trey. But with this one" — she placed her hand over her stomach, which, while not sporting a true baby bump yet, had begun to press against the front of her khaki shirt — "I'm famished all the time."

"Admittedly, I've never been pregnant, but famished has to be better than throwing up," Sedona said. "And perhaps it's a sign that you're going to have a boy."

Preferring to be surprised, Kara and Sax had opted against learning the gender of their baby ahead of time.

"Is that some New Age thing you learned growing up on the commune?" Kara plucked a cheese muffin from the basket the server had left on the table. Not that she believed in woo-woo stuff. Then again, there were those who'd think that the way she'd once talked with her murdered husband wasn't exactly mainstream.

"No, merely logic and observation," Sedona said. "It makes a certain sense that a boy would take after his father. And Sax has always appeared to be a man of hefty appetites."

The double entendre, which was, indeed, true, had Charity nearly spitting out the drink of ice water she'd just taken. Maddy grinned wickedly, while Kara felt her cheeks turn hot.

"So," she said, deliberately changing the subject, "the reason I didn't cancel on this week's lunch, although I should probably be out patrolling our soon-to-be very crowded streets, is because I have news." She paused a beat. "I'm getting married."

"Well, of course you are," Maddy said as their server arrived back at the table with the clam strips appetizer and four small plates. "That's what that ring on your finger is all about."

"No, I mean like I'm actually, officially getting married."

Charity, who was reaching for a strip, paused, her hand over the basket. "You've set a date?"

"I have."

"It's about time," Sedona said. "Sax must be over the moon."

"He's definitely pleased." That was an understatement, since he'd been pushing for marriage even before she learned she was pregnant. More often since.

"When?" Maddy asked.

"That's the thing. It's this week."

"During the festival?" Sedona asked.

"I know the timing's insane, especially what with all I have to do, but my mom called, and I did what you advised me to do a few weeks ago," Kara said to Charity. "I told her about the baby. Since she missed Trey's birth, she was thrilled. She also told me that she and John were on the way to some island in the South Pacific that had suffered a tsunami, but because Doctors Without Borders are already on the scene, they're able to make a stop here. So we can have that double wedding we talked about."

"I guess you're going to have it at Bon Temps?" Sedona asked.

"I wouldn't mind, because it's a great place, and Cole and Kelli's wedding there was wonderful, but it's also where Sax already spends all his working hours since he reopened it. Which doesn't make it all that romantic."

And, although she felt it was a little foolish, after getting married at the civil registry office in Tijuana the first time, the romantic that Sax had unearthed lurking inside her wanted something more special.

Which was when she'd thought of Lavender Hill Farm. A Cooking Network celebrity chef who'd given up living in Manhattan after her marriage to her chef husband had dissolved, Maddy had returned home to Shelter Bay and had a new show in the works that would feature the cooking school she and her grandmother planned to open at her grandmother's herb farm.

Maddy had recently gotten married herself, to one of Sax's former SEAL teammates. The small beach ceremony had been celebrated with her grandmother, a close group of Shelter Bay friends, many of whom had attended high school with her, and her agent, who'd flown in from New York for the occasion. Lucas Chaffee's dog, Scout, who'd retired from the military after losing a leg to a bomb in Afghanistan, had served as ring bearer, carrying the rings in a basket.

Later, at the reception, Lucas admitted that since he'd fully intended to win his former summer love back, he'd begun training the dog to play that part the day after Maddy had returned to Shelter Bay from New York City.

Taking a deep breath, Kara asked her the question she'd been contemplating since her mother's call. "How close are you and Lucas to getting Lavender Hill Farm's restaurant completed?"

"Oh, wow." Maddy snagged a clam strip and chewed thoughtfully. Kara could see the construction punch list being ticked off in her friend's head. "How much time are we talking about?"

"Mom's only going to be able to stay for a couple days. So, I was thinking, possibly Thursday?"

"That's three days away."

"I know. And I'm sorry, but —"

"We'll do it," Maddy said decisively. "Somehow. After all, Lucas and I managed to pull off *our* wedding in a mere week and I have to admit there was something to be said about not having time to stress out about every little detail.

"We're really close to finishing, so with some long hours and maybe an all-nighter to get all the design stuff in place, we can make it work. Especially if we use the gazebo instead of the farmhouse for the actual ceremony."

"That's what I was hoping," Kara admitted. She'd imagined the lacy white structure, which overlooked the sea, festooned with flowers.

Maddy gazed toward the bay, deep in thought. "And you'll want a reception luncheon, or dinner, or some sort of food service."

"Nothing all that special," Kara assured her. "Certainly no formal sit-down dinner. If need be, Sax can provide the food from Bon Temps."

"Don't be ridiculous." Maddy waved away the suggestion. "As delicious as it would be, and I was so grateful when he got together with Gram for Lucas' and my reception, we are not going to have the groom cooking his own wedding meal.

"It's summer, so we can stay light. Make it buffet-style, which would save us from having to train servers at the last minute. You know Phoebe Tyler?"

"Of course," Kara said. Hadn't she arrested the woman's abusive husband after he'd tracked her to Shelter Bay and taken the residents of Haven House, a local shelter, hostage while trying to kidnap his pregnant runaway wife?

Although she was relieved the bully was out of Phoebe's life, having had her first husband away on deployment when she was carrying Trey, Kara knew how difficult it was to go through a pregnancy on your own.

Of course, Phoebe had the other residents of Haven House, but it wasn't the same thing as having a husband to provide emotional support. Still, having no husband would be preferable to the dangerous Peter Fletcher.

Although Fletcher's wealthy family had managed to bond the bastard out until trial, at least he'd been put under house arrest, so Kara didn't have to worry about him returning to Shelter Bay anytime soon.

However, she kept in contact with the Denver police chief. If Fletcher did break his house arrest and show up in town, she'd damn well be ready.

"Once she started getting her confidence back, Phoebe's proven to be a natural," Maddy said. "I've already promised her the job of sous-chef, so this will be a good hands-on learning experience for her. And now that she's not hiding from her rat bastard husband anymore, we can even include her in the new TV show."

During her years as a cop, first in Los Angeles County, then here, where she'd taken over her father's job as sheriff, Kara had learned to keep her thoughts to herself. Maddy was much more open; Kara could practically see the wheels turning in her head.

"Oh! I just had an idea. Now, feel free to tell me no, but what would you say to having the wedding taped for my new Cooking Network show?" she asked. "It would make such a great launch episode."

"It would also save you a bundle of money on hiring a wedding videographer," Sedona, the former accountant turned baker, who'd provided financial advice to more than one person in Shelter Bay, pointed out.

Kara was torn between wanting to keep the ceremony private and yet also wanting to help out a friend.

"I promise you wouldn't even know the camera's there," Maddy assured her. "In fact, the photographer would probably be more invisible than anyone you'd hire."

"I hadn't even gotten around to thinking about a video," Kara admitted. She knew Sax would go along with whatever she wanted, and now that he was no longer a SEAL, there wasn't any problem with his face appearing on television, but . . .

"I'll have to ask Mom, but I can't see any reason why she wouldn't go along with the idea. She always liked you."

"Really? Jeez," Maddy said, "I sure wish I'd known that back when we were in high school when I was afraid of her."

Kara laughed. "Would it help to know that I spent most of my life intimidated by her perfection?"

But that was all in the past. Ironically, it had been only after they'd both been widowed that she and her mother had finally found something in common. And from that foundation, although it hadn't been easy, and had required effort and forgiveness on both their parts, they'd established a strong relationship — of the kind Kara could only hope she'd be able to have with her daughter, if the child she was carrying turned out to be a girl.

"I'll make the cake," Sedona volunteered. "Unless you'd rather do that," she deferred to Maddy, the professional chef of the group.

"I've never been much of a baker, since it takes more patience than I have, so that would be great."

Sedona whipped out a notepad and pen from her bag. And as the three women got down to planning a dream wedding that would be taking place in three short days, Kara, an only child who'd always secretly wished for sisters, realized that when she hadn't been looking, she'd acquired some very special ones.

8

Since Shelter Bay wasn't overrun with five-star hotels, and Mary's acceptance had come at that last minute, the town council had voted to buy out a couple who'd already reserved the penthouse honeymoon suite at the Whale Song Inn. Not only did they offer to pay for their accommodations in another inn, local restaurants, including Bon Temps, had tossed in coupons for free meals, and shop owners had put together a gift basket of Shelter Bay souvenirs and yet more coupons as additional enticement. To the festival committee's relief, the two attorneys from Portland, who hadn't actually been on a honeymoon but were celebrating an anniversary, accepted the offer and surrendered the suite.

After dropping the others off at the town hall on Harborview Drive, J.T. drove up the hill to the Victorian inn.

"You travel light," he said, taking the two

bags from the back of the SUV he'd been renting.

"For a spoiled Hollywood starlet you expected to arrive laden down with a mountain of designer luggage, the Marine left unsaid," she responded dryly.

"*Former* Marine," he pointed out yet again. "And I hadn't given it much thought, to tell the truth. I was merely making conversation."

"I'm sorry." She looked up and flashed him a smile that, while dazzling, was every bit as phony as all those counterfeit somoni that had flooded into the Afghan monetary system while he'd been deployed downrange. "I didn't realize making conversation was in your job description."

"Touché."

Opening the glass door of the Victorian inn for her, J.T. knew his mother would be furious at him for his behavior. Or worse, he considered, remembering what his brothers had said about their parents worrying about him, she'd be concerned by his uncharacteristic behavior. If a guy was so deep down in a pit that a beautiful, sexy woman couldn't lift him up, he really was in a world of hurt.

He was trying to come up with an apology that wouldn't sound too lame as they walked into the lobby, which had nothing like the heavy, fussy style associated with Victorians. The floor was a whitewashed pine, the colors on the walls and furniture looking as if the sea, sand, and sky had all been brought indoors. J.T. didn't know much about decorating — hell, he didn't know *anything* about it — but he did recognize a place designed for comfort when he saw it.

Unfortunately, he had no time to get comfortable, because the moment they entered, it seemed an entire lobby full of Mary Joyce fans rushed toward her.

"No," she murmured, putting a hand on his arm when he stiffened. "It's okay."

"I took on a job," he said under his breath even as he found himself momentarily mesmerized by her slender hand on his sleeve, wondering if it would feel as soft as it looked on his skin.

"You have yours, and I have mine. So, stand down, Marine."

He felt the change in her. It wasn't that she suddenly became someone else. Or some larger-than-life movie star, but once again, as it had at the airport, whatever innate light he'd sensed burning in her became even brighter. And warmer.

Since no one in the place looked like a

threat — though the pirate guy with the eyeliner was kind of weird — he did as ordered and stood down. But that didn't stop him from continuing to scan the crowd, many of whom were in costume as characters he recognized from the films, even as he kept one eye on Mary Joyce.

A young girl, who didn't look quite in her teens, with a wild mass of carrot red hair surrounding a thin, angular though pretty face, thrust at her a glossy magazine with Mary's face adorning the cover. "Would you please sign this? To Erin?"

"Of course." Mary smiled, took the pen offered, and said, "Erin is my sister-in-law's name."

The freckled face beamed. Her grin showed a mouthful of pink and purple braces. "It means Ireland."

Although he wouldn't have thought it possible, Mary's smile rose on the wattage dial. "I know. Do you live here in Shelter Bay?"

"No. When I heard you were going to be here, my mom drove me down from Vancouver. Washington, not Canada."

"And aren't you fortunate to have such a lovely mother?" She handed the magazine back and looked at the small pink digital camera the girl was holding. "Would you like a picture?"

"Really?" The girl looked as if she had just been told she'd won *American Idol.*

"Well, you have come all this way, after all." Mary took the camera and handed it to J.T. "Would you mind?"

And what was he to say to that? That his mission was to keep this obviously awe-struck kid away? Besides, it wasn't really a question, but an order.

Thinking that he was becoming surrounded by bossy women lately, he took the camera and snapped the first of what turned out to be many, many photos. And, as at the airport, not only did her smile not waver for an instant, but Mary chatted with each and every person in the inn's small, cozy lobby, making them feel as if *they* were the stars, not her.

Even when a young man in flip-flops, torn jeans, and a maroon Reed College hoodie with a griffin on the front worn open over a gray grunge T-shirt tried to force the screenplay he'd brought with him on her, she politely turned him down, handed him a card from her purse, and suggested he send it to her production company in Los Angeles.

Rather than appear pissed, the guy acted as if she'd assured him she was going to produce, direct, and star in his movie herself.

"That's a good ploy," J.T. said, once they'd finally escaped and he was ushering her into the old-fashioned cage elevator.

"What ploy would that be?"

"Managing to turn that guy down, but making it seem as if you'd just handed him an Oscar."

"What makes you think I turned him down?"

"Like anyone's going to actually read his screenplay?"

"Actually, someone will. All right," she admitted, when he arched a brow after inserting the key that would take them directly to the honeymoon suite, "*I* won't be the one to give it a first read, because if I did that with every screenplay we receive, I'd never get anything else done. But I do employ several people to look for work they think might have potential."

"Why would you be looking for outside scripts? When you write all your movies yourself?"

"Ah." She glanced up at him, interest sparkling in those electric blue eyes as the elevator slowly cranked its way up to the fourth floor. "You've done your research."

"One of the most important things you

learn at boot camp is that the more intel you have going into a mission, the better."

"Would that be along the lines of knowing your enemy?"

"I didn't say that."

"No. Though you *do* consider me a mission?"

"Not exactly a mission." He'd once always known exactly what to say in uncomfortable situations. Which was probably why he'd been given more than his share of casualty families. If there was a particularly touchy family situation, hey, give it to Douchett to handle. But that was before he'd flamed out. He'd probably talked more in the past hour than he had since returning home. "And not an enemy. More along the lines of a job."

"Ah. Then you'd be getting paid to keep starstruck children and aspiring screenwriters away from me?"

She was like a damn terrier. Deciding she wasn't going to just let it drop, he said, "No, I'm not getting paid, and it's not how it sounds. In case you haven't noticed, Shelter Bay isn't exactly the big city, and Kara — the sheriff — isn't exactly running a big-city department here. She's concerned about your safety, so, since I wasn't doing anything all that important, she drafted me into making sure no crazies decided to kill you in her town."

"Well." The door opened directly onto a living room painted in sea glass blues and greens with a pair of French doors that led onto a balcony and looked directly out at the Shelter Bay lighthouse. "I suppose I should be thanking you. For making such a noble sacrifice on my behalf."

"I didn't sign on for you. I'm doing it for Kara."

Hell. He might be out of practice carrying on a conversation, but even J.T. could realize how that sounded. He scraped a hand down his face and considered just biting off his tongue. It wasn't as if he had any pressing desire to talk with anyone anyway. "Okay. I definitely didn't mean that the way it sounded."

"Don't worry. I'd have to be a *culchie* not to realize that you'd rather have pulled latrine duty than be stuck here with me." She held up a hand. "And to save you having to expend the additional words to ask, a *culchie* is a country person. Usually thought of as stupid or daft."

"You couldn't have achieved what you have by being stupid." Though it did cross his mind that a person would have to be crazy to go into the movie business in the first place. Especially if you needed to hire people like him to be allowed any privacy.

"Thank you. But you've no idea how many people attribute my success to having a famous author brother-in-law who's had movies made of all his books."

"I don't have a clue how Hollywood works. But I'd guess that while family connections might open doors for you, they're not going to get people to come to your movies."

So far, so good. Seeing that she was beginning to soften, he decided to forge forward through this conversational minefield. "And I'll admit that I wasn't looking forward to babysitting some Hollywood starlet."

Damn. He really should've just shut up while he was ahead. Although he was not above lying — there were times when his and his teammates' lives had depended on it — in opting for the absolute truth, J.T. knew he'd screwed up again.

"If you're concerned about me using my moviestar wiles on you, you needn't worry," she said silkily. "Because strong, silent, rude men aren't really my type."

That stung, but since he couldn't deny the description fit, he didn't argue. "You're not mine, either." *Hot, sophisticated, dangerous.* "Though you're not exactly what I expected."

"Ah." She nodded. "Just when I begin to think there might be hope for you, J. T. Douchett, I'm damned with faint praise. And would you mind doing me a favor?"

Like he had a choice? "What?"

"Would you please take off those sunglasses? Because it's proving very disconcerting talking to my reflection."

Although it wasn't his first choice, he pulled the aviators off and hooked the stems into the pocket of his shirt.

"Better?"

For some reason he couldn't fathom, she'd gone pale as sea foam. Before he could figure out what the hell he'd done wrong now, she merely said, "Yes. Thank you." Then turned away and walked over toward the balcony doors. "The lighthouse is just as I remembered it," she murmured.

"How long ago were you here?"

"I was seventeen. Which seems like eons ago. After my sister married Quinn, he brought us all to the States on an extended holiday. We started with tours at Ellis Island and the Statue of Liberty, then worked our way west. It was a grand trip." Her accent grew more pronounced, bringing to mind whitewashed cottages, stone fences, and fields painted in a thousand shades of green.

"I'd never been out of Ireland before, unless you count shopping trips to the North, which my grandmother would be the first to tell you is not a foreign country," she said. "So, all I knew of America was what I'd seen in your films or read about in books. It was so vast and diversified, I began to realize why so many Americans seem arrogant."

"Yet you've chosen to live in L.A." In what was probably one of the most ego-driven communities on the planet. But this time he managed to keep his thoughts to himself.

"For now," she said. "Though it wasn't necessarily my goal. In truth, since I was determined to succeed on my own, and was working on a shoestring budget, it was only natural to make my smaller, intimate films in my own country. But once *Siren Song* started winning so many awards . . ."

She sighed.

"Things changed," he said, finishing her thought for her.

"And wouldn't that be putting it mildly?" She glanced back over her shoulder, her neon blue eyes serious as they met his. "Yet, they always do, don't they?"

"Seems so."

He'd spent eighteen months waking up every morning hoping that would be the day he'd escape CACO duty. When he'd never have to be responsible for anyone else ever again. Then, once that wish had finally come true after he'd separated from the military, he'd ended up stuck in this recent drinking and running routine that wasn't getting him anywhere but going in circles.

"Why did you leave the Marines?" she asked abruptly.

"Because my tour of duty was up." And because he'd been on the razor's edge of flaming out.

She tilted that dark head, studying him as if he were a character she was considering putting in one of her movies. "But it wasn't your first tour?"

"No."

She turned around. Folded her arms beneath her breasts, lifting them in a way that had him calculating how long it had been since he'd even allowed himself to look at a woman's breast.

The Marines were the youngest branch of the U.S. military, with an average age of twenty-three. Which meant that during his time as a casualty assistance calls officer, most of the NOK (next of kin) J.T. had been assigned to were young. Even a couple of the mothers were in their mid-thirties, not much older than he. They were grieving, and, he didn't need to be told, vulnerable. And occasionally needy. For more than what a CACO was supposed to provide.

In the past, drawing the line between his personal life and professional life hadn't been all that difficult. When he was deployed, he was at war. Which meant he *had* no personal life. When he was stateside, while he still might be training for battle, once he left base, he could flip the switch and enjoy being a single guy who might not be the chick magnet his brother Sax had been, but had never had any trouble attracting women who'd enjoyed partying as much as he had.

But the manual he'd been given specified that the NOK should be notified within eight hours of the Marines learning of the death or serious injury. Which, during the surge, definitely cut out any weekend getaways, and after the third time being dragged away from some warm bed just as things were really heating up, J.T. had begun to realize that — except for the hours between 2400 and 0500, when notifications were no longer supposed to take place — juggling his Marine duty with a real life was going to prove difficult.

When, after notifying a pregnant mother of three whose parents were both deceased, he'd broken down and humiliated himself by crying like a baby while taking a shower with a wet and willing anthropology instructor from MiraCosta College, he'd thrown in the towel.

After a couple of months of self-imposed celibacy, J.T. had begun to worry whether he'd even remember what to do if an opportunity for a hookup did occur.

By the time he'd separated from the corps, sex had gone completely off the radar.

Until Mary Joyce got off that plane. And flipped a damn switch.

"Are you armed?" she asked, dragging his mind from wondering what she was wearing beneath that silky top back to their conversation.

"No." He'd had enough of weapons to last him the rest of his life. "But I'm more than capable of taking out any bad guys who might decide to get too close and personal."

"While I don't expect that to happen, it's encouraging. Do you always glower so? Or would you happen to have PTSD issues I should know about?"

"I don't glower. And here I'd always thought the Irish treated conversation as an art form. Are you always this direct?" he asked, dodging her question with one of his own.

"I wouldn't be, as a rule. And you'd be correct about our conversation, but I've always believed that if we Irish were supposed to think in straight lines, the Celts wouldn't have put all those pretty curves around the rigid lines of the cross when they converted from paganism.

"However, it appears that we're going to be forced to live in each other's pockets for the next few days. While you've obviously taken the time to research my life, you haven't been at all forthcoming about yourself, and since I'm not one to hand over control that easily, particularly to complete strangers, I'd like to know what, exactly, my studio and your sheriff have gotten me into."

"I don't have PTSD, so you don't have to worry about me going Rambo and shooting up the festival. If for no other reason than I wouldn't want to piss off the sheriff, who just happens to be engaged to my brother."

"The hero brother."

"Yeah, but —"

"I shouldn't be bringing that up."

"It'd probably be best you don't. Not that he has PTSD, either."

At least, from what Sax had said, his ghosts were gone since he and Kara had gotten together. As happy as J.T. was for his brother, getting engaged seemed like a radical way to get rid of his own.

"It's just that he's a former SEAL. And those guys prefer to keep their work in the shadows."

"Understood."

She studied him for a while longer. Then her lips curved, ever so slightly.

"Small towns," she murmured. "Everyone lives in everyone else's pockets."

"Pretty much so."

"And wouldn't I be knowing that well enough?" She sat down on the couch, kicked off her shoes, and began rubbing a narrow, high-arched foot. "I have no idea why on earth I allowed my stylist to talk me into wearing these heels," she muttered.

"You don't get to choose your own clothes?" Who'd have suspected the Marines and a Hollywood star would have anything in common?

"I spent the past two days and another three hours this morning doing a press tour. Well, actually, that's misnamed, since it isn't truly a tour. I was essentially held prisoner in a hotel suite at the Beverly Wilshire, while the studio PR people paraded reporters and the higher-profile celebrity bloggers in and out like a herd of cattle. Everyone gets ten minutes, including those television stations that can't afford to send someone to Los

Angeles, so they do satellite remote interviews instead.

"Because they all seem to ask the same questions, I've no doubt all the interviews will end up reading and sounding exactly the same. Which doesn't answer your question, so getting back to my choice of clothing, since my personal style is much more casual, for performances such as this festival, it's easier just to show up and let someone else dress me."

"Movie-star Barbie."

The words, once again, were out of his mouth before he could stop them. To his surprise, she didn't appear offended, but merely laughed.

"Isn't that the exact same thing my grandmother Fionna said when she visited Hollywood for the Oscars?"

He'd read that Mary Joyce had been nominated for best original screenplay, but hadn't won. Some of the Web sites whose links he'd followed while researching her claimed it was because she refused to play by Hollywood's old boys' club rules.

"At any rate, Leon, my stylist, assured me that since I'd be sitting the entire time, these would be fine. He also told me that if they only came in size twelve, he'd kill to have a pair himself."

She switched to rubbing the other foot. She'd painted — or had some minion do it for her — her toenails the color of ripe peaches. Although he'd never had a foot fetish, J.T. had a sudden urge to nibble on them. "Which is when, although they're not his size, I just should have handed these over and let him try to wear them.

"And, proving that I can, eventually, wind my way back to an original topic, to answer your earlier question about that young man's screenplay, the reason I started my own production company is because women, unfortunately, have a very short shelf life in the American cinema. I'm well aware that much of my appeal is that while women buy tickets to be told a romantic story, men go with them, or watch the DVDs, because I happen to look good naked."

Although J.T. had never blushed in his life, he knew his expression must have given him away when she laughed.

"I take it you watched my films." She paused a beat. "Solely as intel research for your mission, of course."

"I checked them out. You're a compelling writer. And you're very good in them."

The sparkle returned to sea blue eyes. "And if I were to give you a pop test on intricate plot details and selkie history, I'm sure you'd pass with flying colors."

He folded his arms. "Try me."

"Although I'm tempted, I'd best be hanging up my clothes to get the wrinkles out before this evening's performance."

She stood, picked up the high heels from the floor, then walked into the adjoining bedroom, assuming, he decided, that he was like that stylist who chose her clothes for her, yet another minion who'd handle her luggage.

Shrugging, and finding it interesting that she'd think of the festival as a performance — which made him wonder how he was supposed to tell whether the person he'd just finished speaking to was real or merely acting — J.T. picked up the bags and followed her.

9

Deciding that there was no way her fans could reach Mary Joyce as long as she stayed put up in the honeymoon suite at the inn, J.T. returned to Bon Temps, where his family was busy preparing the place for the reception.

"So?" Sax asked as he dusted all the bottles on the shelves behind the bar. Not that the place wasn't clean enough to do surgery on the floor, but it wasn't every day a famous Hollywood movie star paid a visit to the restaurant and dance hall. "How did it go?"

"Okay."

"Okay?" His sister-in-law, Kelli, turned and put her hands on her hips. "You've just spent all that time with Mary Joyce, who just might be the hottest name in Hollywood right now, and all you can say is that it was okay? We want details, J.T."

"Her plane was on time. She didn't have

as much luggage as I would've figured, and when I left her, she was hanging up her clothes so they won't wrinkle."

"I'll bet she has people to do that in L.A.," Sax said.

"I didn't ask. But some guy did pick out her clothes. And her shoes."

Unsurprisingly, being of the female persuasion, Kelli was quick to jump on that one.

"What kind of shoes were they?"

"I don't know." J.T. shrugged. "Shoes. They were high. With skinny metal heels and covered with some sort of leopard stuff."

"Did they have red soles?" his mother asked.

"I didn't notice."

"I'll bet they did," Kelli decided. "Dammit, think harder, J.T."

He thought. "Okay. Yeah. They did."

Kelli stopped polishing a table, turned to her mother-in-law, and both women said together, "Christian Louboutin."

"Not that I could ever afford more than a thousand dollars for a pair of high heels, but that leopard model is impossible to find," Maureen said.

"I know." Kelli nodded. "While I was getting my hair trimmed last week down at Cut

Loose, I read in *People* that even Oprah is on a wait list."

"A thousand dollars?" Lucien Douchett asked. "For a pair of shoes?"

"Closer to fifteen hundred," Maureen informed her husband. "I saw them on his Web site."

J.T. was wondering why, if she couldn't afford the stupid shoes, his mother was even surfing Internet shopping Web sites for them, when his two brothers both laughed.

"When you get married, one of the first things you'll learn," Cole told J.T., "is that women are hot on shoe porn."

"Even I would've known to come back with a more complete report than that," Sax said.

"Well, obviously, since I don't have a wife or a fiancée, I haven't slipped into embracing my feminine side," J.T. shot back.

"What about her clothes?" Kelli asked before one or both of his brothers could put him in a headlock for that comment.

"Pants, a top, and some sort of short sweater thing." Knowing that they'd demand more description than that, he tacked on, "The pants and top were black. The sweater fuzzy and sort of creamy beige."

"Honestly, J.T." Kelli blew out a frustrated breath. "You are absolutely no help at all."

"Sorry. I thought I'd been tasked with keeping crazy fans away. Not giving the two of you a Red Carpet report." Since they were his mother and sister-in-law, he struggled for some insider fashion bone to throw them. "But she was really glad to take her shoes off."

"If I owned a pair of Christian Louboutin shoes, I would never take them off," Kelli said.

"Well, you'd look damn silly wearing stilettos to help Cole scrape barnacles off his fishing boat," J.T. countered.

"I was speaking hypothetically." Her tone was that an empress might use to an annoying footman.

"Sorry." He held his hands up and found himself thinking that it might be easier being back in the Kush with bullets flying.

"Why don't you help me carry in the beer for tonight?" Sax suggested.

Ooh-rah. J.T. did not have to be asked twice.

"So," his brother said, opening the door to the walk-in cooler in the back of the kitchen, "how did it go? Really?"

He'd suspected Sax didn't need help getting the beer. What his brother wanted was a mission status report. "Like I said, it went okay. She seems nice enough. Not as much of a diva as I was expecting. Are we carrying in beer or giving me the third degree?"

"Just curious. I saw her once. In Iraq."

"Iraq? How come you didn't say that the other day when Kara stuck me with this detail?"

"It didn't seem all that relevant right then, since we were talking about you and I didn't want to sidetrack the conversation. . . . I was down doing covert stuff during the surge. She was on a USO tour. Apparently not her first."

"That's admirable. And dicey for a civilian, even in the Green Zone." Apparently Mary Joyce was tougher and definitely gutsier than she looked.

"This one wasn't in Baghdad. It was at FOB Warhorse."

Okay. He had to give the actress major props for that. Enclosed by fences and concertina wire, Forward Operating Base Warhorse had been one of the deadliest regions for coalition troops during the surge.

"What did she do?"

"It started out as the usual dog and pony show. She showed a DVD of outtakes from her movies, which were kinda funny. Of course, when you're stuck out in the damn desert, anything's going to be more entertaining than it might be back home. Then she sang with a country singer whose name I forget, because he's not all that famous."

"Famous ones tend to get the big stages and extra security."

"Yeah. Which was why I was surprised to see her at Warhorse, 'cause she's at a star level that usually travels with a lot of brass. She also did Normandy on that same trip."

Another FOB by the Iranian border, which hardly ever got any visiting entertainers.

"So, she can sing, too?"

Sax laughed at that. "Not worth a damn. Which was what made it really great. Because she seemed . . . real, you know? And not like some big Hollywood star who needed to look perfect. Then it was what she did afterward that was really cool."

"Which was what?"

"She just hung around the rest of the day, visiting everyone, signing autographs, posing for photos, oohing and aahing over baby pictures, wedding pictures, whatever anyone wanted to stick in her face.

"And although Cole's right about her being really, really hot, especially in those movies where she's naked a lot, she didn't give off all that many sexy vibes."

"I have a hard time believing that." She'd

certainly stirred up juices he'd put in cold storage.

"I'm not saying there probably weren't a lot of guys dreaming about her that night, but by the time she made her way through the camp, and even stayed for dinner, it was more as if she was all the guys' sister. And the women's BFF."

Having seen a little bit of that behavior at the airport, although it was a stretch to imagine the woman who'd gotten off the plane dressed in Kevlar and a helmet, strolling around the Iraq desert chatting up troops, J.T. could almost envision it.

"So," Sax said, "my reason for telling you this now is that she seemed like a nice woman who genuinely cared about people. And God knows, appearing at a small-town film festival no one's ever heard of damn well isn't going to do a thing for her career. You might want to keep that in mind over the next few days and attempt to be more hospitable."

J.T. wasn't surprised that Sax had already heard about his less-than-welcoming behavior. Gossip was the coin of the realm in small towns, whether they were in a Middle East desert or on the Oregon coast.

"I wasn't that bad," he argued, following his brother out of the cooler. "And who the hell snitched?" He'd put money on that pissy theater guy.

"Her Honor, the mayor, called Kara. Kara, in turn, called me. She's not happy."

"Sorry." It was true. He'd always liked Kara, a lot. In fact, there'd been a time, back in seventh grade, when he'd had a crush on her, which, showing that he hadn't lost all his brain cells, he was smart enough not to share. "I didn't mean to cause you any problems. It's just that . . . Shit."

He dragged a hand through his hair. "Does it ever get easy?"

Sax didn't have to ask *what.* "No. But I can tell you that it gets bearable. And there are actually days that it almost seems like all that shit happened to someone else."

He put the beer down on a counter and narrowed his eyes, giving J.T. a hard big-brother look. Having always been the town bad boy, he hadn't developed it as well as Cole, who'd been the "perfect" eldest Douchett brother, but it was not a bad imitation. J.T. figured Sax had probably gotten better at it while doing all that covert SEAL stuff.

"You sure you're okay?" Sax asked with serious concern. "Because if you need help —"

"You don't have to worry. Despite what

some of the people in town seem to be saying, I'm not a danger to myself or others," J.T. answered as he had on the questionnaire he'd had to fill out during his separation from the corps. At the time he figured most of the Marines did the same thing he did — tick off the boxes that would get them out with the least amount of hassle.

"But?"

"It's just hard, okay?"

"I believe we've determined that." Sax shook his head. Thrust a hand through his hair and looked conflicted as hell. "Look, if hanging out with Mary Joyce is that tough a duty, there's a bunch of jarheads down at the VFW hall who'd probably jump at the chance to take your place."

"No." J.T. drew in a deep breath. Squared his shoulders. "I just had a bad morning." After a mostly sleepless night. "But you can promise Kara that I'll be on my best behavior until the woman leaves town. Hell, I'll be so nice and polite, people will think I'm effing Mr. Rogers."

"You don't have to go that far. Just try to be civil. Because if you screw this up and make my bride-to-be unhappy before the wedding, then I may have to throw you back in the bay."

"There were two of you against the one of

me," J.T. said. "And yeah, though I didn't want to admit it at the time, I was sorta halfway drunk, which gave you the advantage." Something Sax had said sank in. "Wedding?"

"Yeah. Kara's mom is coming to town this week. We're getting hitched."

The grin on his brother's face did a lot to lift the cloud J.T. had woken up with this morning. "It's about time." He grabbed two bottles of the IPA from the carton and used his Swiss Army knife to pop the caps.

Then, after handing a bottle to Sax, he lifted his own in a salute. "Ooh-rah."

10

Phoebe Tyler couldn't remember the last time she'd indulged in anything as simply pleasant as a picnic. But after she'd gone to Blue Heron farm with a meat order for the shelter kitchen, Ethan Concannon had surprised her by suggesting they have lunch out by a small lake on his farm. When she called Zelda to tell her she might be a bit late getting back to Haven House, the elderly woman insisted she just go ahead and take the day off.

And what a perfect day it was! Warm, with a benevolent, buttery yellow sun casting diamonds over the blue water. Bees buzzed lazily over wildflowers while songbirds played musical chairs in the branches of the tree they were sitting beneath.

Apparently confident that she'd accept his invitation, he'd prepared a lunch. It wasn't fancy — a chicken Cobb salad wrap with the best smoked bacon she'd ever tasted, a grilled corn and tomato salad, and watermelon lemonade — but to Phoebe, because of the setting and the company, it was the best meal she'd ever eaten.

"This is wonderful."

"I'm glad you're enjoying it. You looked a little pale when you arrived."

"It's just morning sickness. Which is definitely misnamed. At least in my case. I have this looming fear that I'm actually going to end up throwing up on the delivery room table."

"I remember, from going to classes with Mia, that some women have it worse than others. Are you sorry you're pregnant?"

"Absolutely not." She pressed her hands against her stomach, which was feeling steadier now that she had something in it. She'd been too anxious about coming out here today to eat this morning. Which had been a mistake. Some days she still couldn't quite believe a baby was growing inside her. Until she was on her knees in the bathroom, which was always a vivid reminder.

"I was admittedly surprised when the home pregnancy test came out positive." When he hadn't been berating her for perceived mistakes, or blaming her for failures in his life, during their last two months together Peter had turned icily cold and distant. Except for that night he'd raped her.

The night their — no, her! — child had been conceived.

"But it was a good surprise." Which was an understatement. Her baby was a blessing, and not just because her pregnancy had provided the impetus to escape her dangerous marriage. "Though sometimes I'm worried I won't be a good enough mother."

If she were to believe her soon-to-be ex-husband, she certainly hadn't been an even adequate wife. And, although she was working with the therapist who visited Haven House every week, to overcome those false accusations that he'd wrapped her in — like a dark, clinging shroud — sometimes she felt an unbidden prick of fear that just maybe some of those painful words he'd attacked her with had been true.

"No one's perfect. And every parent makes mistakes," Ethan said. "I know I did. And I would have made a lot more if I'd gotten the opportunity."

His voice had turned as rough as tires on a gravel road. Too late she thought about his wife and child, who'd been killed in a tragic accident, and felt guilty about having caused this man, who'd been nothing but kind and gentle to her, renewed pain.

"I'm so sorry," she said. "This must be hard on you."

"What?"

"Being friends with me."

"What?" The pain she'd seen in his beautiful warm eyes turned to incredulity. "How could you possibly think that?"

"Because every time you're with me, you must think about your wife and son."

"I'd think about them anyway," he said mildly. "I loved them both with every fiber of my being, and they were, hands down, the most important people in my life." His gaze turned serious. "But I also know that Mia wouldn't want me to spend my life living in the past. And you, Phoebe, are proof that life does indeed go on.

"So, although I'm sorry for the circumstances that brought you to Shelter Bay, I'm not going to deny that I'm also grateful that you landed in Haven House, which, in turn, brought you into my life."

She felt the color, which had nothing to do with the sun shining down, warm her cheeks. Confused and wary, as her unruly pulse began to sprint — either from pleasure or anxiety, she wasn't sure which — Phoebe lowered her gaze and plucked at a wildflower, pulling off the petals.

He loves me.

He loves me not.

He loves me.

Loves me not.

No! Phoebe reminded herself. It was too soon to even think about love. She had so many other balls she was juggling — learning to cook so she could hopefully earn a living working at the new Lavender Hill Farm restaurant Chef Madeline was establishing. She needed to be able to stand on her own two feet and prepare to take care of her baby, because even if Zelda, who ran Haven House, let her stay on after the birth, no way was she going to bring her newborn home to a battered-women's shelter.

Which meant she also had to find an apartment. And furnish it with a crib, and all those other things infants would need. Although the courts were requiring Peter to pay child support, ever since his parents had bonded him out of jail for charges of assault and battery and attempted kidnapping, she hadn't seen a dime.

Which was just as well. This was *her* baby. All he'd done was provide the sperm. No way did she ever want to share her child with such an evil, brutal, manipulative man.

Ethan was nothing like her soon-to-be ex-husband. He was kind and gentle, and smelled richly of the dark earth he spent his days working.

But she still couldn't let herself become emotionally involved with him.

"My point," he continued, when she didn't, couldn't, answer, "is that despite our parents' mistakes, look how good we turned out."

His smile was warm and generous, earning one in return. A leaf from the tree they were sitting beneath, stirred by the wind, fluttered down and landed on her hair. With a gesture as natural as breathing, Ethan reached out and brushed it away. That simple touch — a broad, dark hand to her hair — sent heat shimmering all the way to her bare toes. When her baby turned a sudden somersault, Phoebe decided she must be carrying a girl.

Just a few more months and she'd be able to hold her child — son or daughter, Phoebe didn't care which — in her arms. That thought, which she continued to cling to like a drowning woman might cling to a driftwood log, had given her the nerve to escape her dangerous marriage in the first place. And it continued to provide strength during those times when her fledgling, reborn confidence would waver.

11

She'd been wrong, Mary realized as she watched J. T. Douchett during the cocktail party held in her honor at his brother's Cajun restaurant later that evening. He wasn't the rudest man she'd ever met in her life.

He was the saddest.

She'd discovered while honing her crafts of writing and performing that she possessed a natural gift of empathy. The ability to put herself in other people's shoes had proved helpful when creating characters an audience would hopefully identify with.

It had also helped during the military-base tours she'd been doing the past years. She was not naive enough to believe that she could — never in a million years — ever know what those troops she'd visited had gone through, but she *could* try to understand where they'd come from. When they talked about their loved ones — and wasn't that what every one of those men and women was so eager to tell her about? — her own family came to mind.

She'd think of her older sister, tragically widowed. Although Nora was now happily remarried, Mary remembered how difficult that time had been for her and dearly hoped that none of the pretty brides in the photographs the proud soldiers would show her ever had to suffer the pain of losing a husband.

Her thoughts would then shift to her older brother Michael, now a farmer and happily married family man, who'd risked his own life as a war photographer for so many years. She'd been a typical, self-absorbed teen girl when he'd returned home to Castlelough, but she'd never forget his distant, thousand-yard stare.

While preparing for her first USO tour, she'd read up on life in a war zone, and a quote that had stayed with her was one about how, by looking in the eyes of a soldier, you'd know how much war he'd seen. She'd witnessed that same battle-weary fatigue in too many eyes in Iraq and Afghanistan. Which was why, although the visits proved both physically and emotionally exhausting, she continued to return, because the pleasure she felt when something she said could coax a soldier or Marine out of that numbness, when the rigid muscles in a face would actually loosen enough to smile, was priceless.

J. T. Douchett had that look. Oh, on one level, he was alert, ready to leap into action if necessary. But that was instinct, developed by years of training and experience. Emotionally, he was as numb as many of those troops she'd met. As sad-to-the-bone as her own brother had been.

And, just as her family had fretted over Michael, who hadn't wanted their attention, surreptitiously watching J.T.'s family as she worked the crowded room with a practiced skill, Mary sensed they had the same concerns. Even as they chatted with friends and neighbors, their eyes would continually drift back to the former Marine. Who had cleaned up really well and was wearing a dark charcoal suit and white shirt. The only jarring, yet interesting, detail was the tie sporting a Tabasco red crawfish.

She'd been grateful that the schedule had allowed her some time to herself this afternoon. Because she'd been so shaken when he'd taken off those glasses, allowing her to look into those granite gray eyes from her dream, she wasn't sure she could have just jumped right into chatting everyone up this evening.

Not having wanted him to know how upset she'd been, she'd turned away, and on trembling legs walked over to the balcony, looked out at the lighthouse flashing its warning, and wished that she'd had some sort of advance warning before getting on that plane in L.A.

It didn't make sense. Despite what Kate had said about her mother sending her a man, despite the fact that she spent much of her time in make-believe worlds, Mary had discovered that, deep down, she was as levelheaded as her older sister. And her grandmother, who admittedly could be called eccentric, but certainly possessed more than her share of Irish pragmatism.

She'd have to think about how she'd come to dream of J. T. Douchett before she'd met him, later. When she had yet more time alone to sort it through, and his mere, overwhelming presence didn't have her mind turning circles, like a leaf caught in an eddy.

After doing her best to charm the members of the city council, the Rotary Club, the chamber of commerce, and the historical society, the filmmakers whose work had been chosen to be shown at the festival, along with a gaggle of red-hatted women all dressed in purple, she turned toward J.T.

"I could use a bit of fresh air. Would you like to come outside with me?"

He glanced out the windows. "It's raining."

"Just a mist," she countered. "And if you'd be concerned about melting, we'll stay on the porch."

"It wasn't me I was thinking about," he said, his shoulders stiffening.

She suspected that had been true for some time. "Just for a moment."

"Your call." He shrugged and followed her out onto the front patio.

"This is lovely," she said as they stood beneath the purple, green, and gold neon BON TEMPS sign. The lighted arched bridge leading across the bay looked like a picture postcard. A plaintive air, played by the Celtic musicians Sax Douchett had hired for the occasion, drifted out an open window.

"Yeah. I guess it is." He sounded surprised.

"Ah, and wouldn't you be taking such natural beauty for granted?" she teased gently. "As we Irish often admittedly do."

The sun had set and a cool breeze was blowing in off the water that had her wishing Leon had chosen something warmer for

the reception than this short, shoulder-baring midnight blue dress. If she'd given the matter any thought, she'd have realized that her clothes were entirely wrong for both the weather and this small coastal town. Though she had seen a flash of something that looked like lust in J.T.'s eyes when she'd opened the door to the suite earlier. It had come and gone so quickly, if she hadn't been drinking in the sight of him, she might have missed it.

She'd noticed a boutique on the drive to the inn. She'd have to make time tomorrow to drop in for some quick power shopping.

The cell phone she'd forgotten to turn off played Celtic Woman's "Beyond the Sea" from her satin evening bag. She took it out, looked at the caller ID screen, then closed it.

"If you want privacy," J.T. began to say.

"Oh, no." She put the phone back in her bag. "It's merely business. And none I'd be wanting to deal with at the moment."

Or ever, for that matter. Tammi Newsome, the executive assistant to Aaron Pressler, the head of the studio that had spent a great deal of money to release her movies, was relentless in her zeal to climb her way up the ladder into a VP's office. Whereas Mary had no interest in Hollywood politics, and

there was no way she was going to make the changes Pressler was suggesting to "beef up" what he kept insisting on referring to as her selkie *franchise.*

"Aren't you going to introduce me to your family?" she asked before he could question her about the call. The mayor, who'd been dragging her around from person to person for the past hour, hadn't yet made it over to the Douchett table at the far side of the room.

"Why?" He shrugged off his suit jacket, and put it over her shoulders, revealing that he'd caught the faint shiver she'd tried to hide.

She'd watched him watching everyone else, even as he continued to keep her in his vision during the reception, and suspected very little got past him.

Again, that was much like Michael had been. When her brother had first returned to Castlelough, after the injury that had nearly claimed his life, he'd played hermit on his farm, never going into the village to talk with people he'd known all his life. Many of whom were like family.

"Thank you." She pulled the edges of the suit jacket, which held his body heat, closer together. "Because I'd like to meet them. And, although I don't want to sound con-

ceited, since you obviously have your own ideas about my celebrity, I suspect that one of the reasons they've come here tonight is to meet me." She did not share her belief with him that they were also here to keep an eye on the youngest Douchett son.

"You'd undoubtedly make their night. Hell, week. Month. Year. But," he said, confirming her belief, "I suspect another reason they've shown up in force is to make sure I don't make more of an ass of myself than I already have."

Rather than the annoyance she might have expected to hear in his tone, Mary heard resignation.

"You're overstating it." When he shot her a skeptical look, she said, "You weren't all that hospitable, true. And even, I suppose, a tad rude, which makes sense, since I'm sure there are other things you'd rather be doing. But you were a long ways from being an ass, J. T. Douchett.

"As for your family, if they do have concerns, it would not be because they're afraid you'll offend me as much as the fact that they care about you."

She put a hand on his arm and felt the muscle tense beneath the starched shirtsleeve. A toucher by nature, she'd made the gesture unconsciously. But his reaction had her wondering how long it had been since any woman had placed her hand anywhere on his body.

Which, in turn, had her wondering when he'd last touched a woman. When her unruly imagination brought back memories of her dream lover cupping her breasts with his long dark fingers, reminding herself that this Marine was trouble with a capital *T*, she forced the erotic fantasy to fade to black.

"And, I suspect, they worry."

He moved his shoulders, clearly uneasy with the topic. And although he didn't rudely jerk his arm away, he did take a step back, breaking the light contact.

"I told them the same thing I told you. That there's no damn need to worry, because I'm fine."

"And isn't that what my own brother said, when he came back from war?"

His gaze had been directed toward the bridge, but her words had him looking down at her with renewed interest. "There aren't that many Irish troops serving in the NATO forces. Are you saying your brother was one of them?"

"Oh, no." She realized how he could have misunderstood. "He was a civilian war photographer, and although he hasn't covered these recent ones, he did spend a great deal of time in Afghanistan during the time the Russians were fighting there. You've undoubtedly never heard of Michael Joyce, but —"

"I've not only heard of him — I was assigned one of his books at the War College. I have an MA in history," he clarified at her surprised expression. "With an emphasis on military history. Since the guy wasn't working for the government, his photos weren't colored by any nationalistic red, white, and blue flag waving. They were probably the closest I've ever seen to capturing what people who live in countries that have become a war zone experience. I should've made the connection from your last name."

"Well, now." She felt a flush of family pride even as she was pleased that she'd managed to learn something about the man, who, thus far, had not been an open book. "I'll be telling him you said that. Although we don't often talk about those days, as I'm sure you can appreciate, I know your compliment will bring him pleasure."

"It's not so much a compliment as the truth."

"Well, won't he be happy to hear it, just the same? These days his photos have become much more centered on family and farming." The calendar of Irish scenes was on the wall of her home office in Malibu, which only somewhat eased her homesickness.

A not entirely uncomfortable silence settled over them.

The fog that had been blowing in from the sea had lifted. As Mary looked up at the vast, star-spangled sky, she thought how long it had been since she'd been far enough from city lights to actually see stars. And how much she'd missed them.

As soon as her release appearances for *Selkie Bride* were finished, she'd have to schedule in a trip home.

But at this moment, in this place that reminded her of the village that had played such a vital part in the woman she'd become, for the first time in ages, Mary felt herself beginning to unwind. A feeling that was, unfortunately, to be short-lived.

"Ready to go back in?" he asked as the musicians switched from "The Rising of the Moon" to the more sprightly "Emily's Reel."

"I suppose I should."

It wouldn't have been her first choice. She was a bit surprised, and pleased, by the way J.T. had slightly lowered his barricades, giving her a bit of insight, and even as Mary reminded herself that she should keep her distance, another, stronger part of her would have preferred they stay out here by themselves.

She handed him back his jacket, took a breath, and made the mental shift into public movie-star mode. Something that was far more exhausting than it looked to outsiders.

As difficult as her first meeting with J.T. had been, her introduction to his family was the first truly enjoyable part of the evening.

Good looks obviously ran in the Douchett family. His grandfather Bernard, who — she did the math — had to have been in his seventies though looked a decade younger, and his father, whom Mary guessed to be in his late fifties, both were still ruggedly handsome men and gave her an idea of how the youngest Douchett son would age.

The oldest brother, Cole, obviously doted on his wife, smiling down on her as she'd assured Mary that she'd seen every one of her movies.

"More than once," Kelli said breathlessly. "I can't wait until this new one's available so I can have them as a boxed set."

"I could get you a copy before it goes on sale, if you'd like."

"Really? Oh, wow!" She pressed a hand against the front of the Barbie pink dress, as if to still her excited heart. "That would be so wonderful! Wouldn't it, honey?" She beamed up at her husband before turning back to Mary. "Cole's a huge fan, too. He usually doesn't watch a movie more than once, but whenever I have yours on the Blu-ray player, he comes and watches with me again. I swear, he's watched *Siren Song* more than *Iron Man.*"

J.T. tried to smother his laugh, but Mary heard it just the same. As she glanced up at him, she saw something that looked like humor in his eyes. But it came and went so quickly, she wondered whether it could have been merely a trick of the light.

"I love your shoes," Kelli gushed. "I never would have thought to wear hot pink with midnight blue. But they so work."

"Thank you." Definitely not a Rodeo Drive fashionista, Mary wouldn't have chosen the combination, either. But Leon had pressed, and although she still thought the dress was overkill for the occasion, she couldn't deny that he'd nailed the shoes.

"My wife could have been a Hollywood star," J.T.'s father, Lucien, announced.

"My husband exaggerates," Maureen Douchett, who bore a striking resemblance to Maureen O'Hara, demurred.

"You would've been famous," he insisted.

"With a star on the Walk of Fame in Hollywood. She was second runner-up to Miss Oregon," he informed Mary proudly, "which got some big-shot agent from Hollywood calling. But she turned down his offer, to marry me." The way his eyes gleamed as he gazed down at his wife revealed that he still couldn't believe his luck.

"It was a very small offer," Maureen told Mary. She lifted a hand to her husband's dark cheek. "While Lucien's was impossible to resist."

The chemistry between them was palpable, somehow shutting out everyone else in the restaurant, making Mary feel a bit as if she were intruding on a private moment. She also wondered how many women could ever hope to be as fortunate as the Douchett women appeared to be.

"I remember you," Adèle Douchett, J.T.'s grandmother, spoke up suddenly. "You were that pretty girl J.T. dated for a while back in high school. The one who had the pregnancy scare."

Silence dropped like a stone over the group.

"This is Mary Joyce, *Grand-mère,*" J.T. said, his gentle tone, which was far different from the guff one she'd heard thus far, revealing none of the embarrassment Mary knew he must be experiencing. "She's an actress. Who plays the selkie queen, remember? You really like those movies."

"Oh." She looked up at Mary, squinting a little, as if to study her more closely. "Well, of course I remember those films. You're a very good actress and my grandson's right. I do enjoy those selkie stories."

Mary smiled. "Thank you."

She could feel J.T., standing beside her, begin to relax. A moment too soon.

"I suppose the reason I didn't recognize you right off the bat is that you're wearing clothes tonight."

Touching her for the first time, J.T. put a hand on Mary's waist. "The mayor's trying to get your attention," he said evenly. "As much fun as this has been, I guess you'd better get back to work meeting and greeting folks to keep the festival committee happy."

"I suppose so." Mary wished she could just sit down and spend the rest of the evening with the Douchetts, but unfortunately this trip wasn't a personal one. "You must be very proud of your sons," she told Maureen. "And it was a pleasure meeting you, Mrs. Douchett," she said to his grandmother.

"The pleasure was mine," the older

woman said. She looked up at J.T. "If you're as smart as your grandfather and I have always known you are, you won't let this one get away."

"I'll keep that in mind. . . . Hell, I'm sorry," he said to Mary as he practically pushed her across the wooden floor.

"You needn't apologize for her." Didn't Adèle Douchett remind Mary of her own grandmother? "I like your family." She glanced back to where J.T.'s grandfather Bernard Douchett had crouched down in front of his wife and taken her hands in his. Both love and concern were etched into his sea-weathered face. "And it's obvious that both your parents and grandparents are still very much in love," Mary said as she blinked back an unexpected misting in her eyes.

"There were times, growing up, when we were kids, that my brothers and I were embarrassed by the way our parents sort of made out while slow dancing here at Bon Temps," J.T. said, revealing yet another personal tidbit. "No one else's mom and dad were anything like that." He shook his head. "But now that I'm older, I guess they set the bar for what I'd want if I ever get married."

"It's a high bar." With her own father never having remarried after her mother had died, and the Irish not being all that publicly demonstrative, Mary hadn't witnessed that type of deep and abiding love until her sister Nora had fallen in love with Quinn. "But I know exactly what you mean."

He paused briefly to look down at her. He was, she thought, a bit surprised. "I may work in Hollywood," she said. "But I have my own marriage role model in my sister and her husband. And I've never believed in settling for second-best."

He gave her another of those long, inscrutable looks. Just when she thought he might be about to say something personal, Mayor Dennis was standing in front of them.

"There's someone over here who's dying to meet you, Mary," she said. "He's a state legislator who's planning a run for the U.S. Congress, and a huge fan." Taking Mary by the arm, she dragged her away.

Mary heard J.T. curse beneath his breath; then he followed.

12

Two hours later, they were back in the Whale Song honeymoon suite. "Can I get you anything?" Mary asked with the hostess manners her grandmother had taught her early in life. "Some wine? A beer, perhaps? Apparently people feel the need to drink while on a honeymoon, because the bar's well stocked with just about anything anyone would want. Including champagne. Which makes sense, given this is supposed to be the honeymoon suite."

J.T. didn't need any reminder of that huge bed that had seemed to take up the major part of the bedroom. The bed he had, when he'd taken her luggage in, momentarily fantasized about dragging her down onto.

"I wouldn't turn down a beer." He hadn't drunk anything at the reception, just in case he'd be called to leap into duty. And although he could hear Kara reminding him that he was still technically on duty, it wasn't as if he were going to chug down a six-pack.

"But you've been entertaining everyone for the past three hours," he said. And, except for that brief time out on the porch, she'd worked every minute of it, succeeding in charming everyone in the place. "So sit down and I'll get it. And whatever you'd like." She had, he'd noticed, stuck to club soda with a twist of lime.

She didn't argue but, going over to the built-in music system, pushed some buttons, then sank down onto the sofa that overlooked the bay, kicked off the strappy pink heels that were even higher and spikier than the leopard ones, and sighed in what sounded like relief.

"I'd love a glass of chardonnay."

"You got it."

Having been living in Bon Temps for the past six weeks, he recognized the haunting Irish tones coming from the ceiling speakers as Enya. His mother had long been a fan, which was one of the reasons why the album was on Bon Temps' jukebox, and as he remembered that the singer had garnered a number of stalkers, he hoped to hell that Kara was right and he wouldn't have to worry about that problem with this Irish star.

He could feel her eyes on his back as he got the beer and wine out of the cooler.

"I love your brother's restaurant."

"I do, too. My mom first opened Bon Temps shortly after marrying Dad — as a take-out joint in a building about the size of a broom closet, to hear them tell it. Since it was the only Cajun restaurant on the coast, it took off, and by the time Sax was born, it was bringing in enough income our dad was able to quit fishing and they ran the place together. They also provided all the entertainment. We kids grew up there and I still remember falling asleep listening to Mom singing like a nightingale on the big stage that used to be there."

"That's a lovely memory," she murmured. "Some would consider running a restaurant, as good as your family's is, a step down from being offered a movie contract."

"You saw them together." He poured the wine, opened the bottle of beer, crossed the room, and handed her the stemmed glass. "Did you notice any signs of regret?"

"Not a one." She took a sip of the wine. "Perfect, thank you."

"Hey, it's your wine," J.T. said with a shrug as he sat down in a blue striped wing chair, putting the white coffee table between them. "Thanks again for not saying anything to my grandmother when she brought up you being naked in those movies."

"Actually, for the record, I wasn't naked. In those beach and bedroom scenes when it looked as if I was, I was wearing a flesh-colored bodysuit. But you needn't worry about me being offended. Your grandmother reminds me a lot of my own. Who can be more than a little outspoken, herself."

"*Grand-mère*'s always spoken her mind. But after she hit her head in a fall, the doctors diagnosed her with dementia, which seems to have done away with any filters."

"I'm sorry."

And didn't that make two of them? J.T. also decided it wasn't his place to tell her that it hadn't actually been him, but Sax, who'd had that high school pregnancy scare.

"The doctors don't believe she'll get any worse. But they also can't guarantee she'll get better."

"It's troubling to have someone you love have health problems," she said. "I lost my mother when I was very young. And then my father when I was sixteen."

"That's rough." He'd read that family history in her bio, including the fact that her mother had died giving birth to the youngest Joyce sister when Mary had been nine years old. But seeing the statement online wasn't the same as watching the shadows darken her blue eyes at the memory.

"It wasn't easy. Fortunately, my sister had returned home from the convent to step into our mother's shoes. Nora's always been the Joyce family rock."

"Mom's pretty much the Douchett family anchor," J.T. said. "Though Kara's one tough cookie, too."

He told her an abridged version of how Kara's Marine husband and high school sweetheart had been killed on a domestic call as a cop after surviving multiple tours in Afghanistan and Iraq. How she'd been a detective in California, then come back to take over her dad's job when he'd been killed. And how Sax, who'd fallen in love with her back in high school — but hadn't said or done anything about it, since she'd been in love with his friend — had won her over and now they were having a baby and getting married.

She ran a fingernail around the rim of her wineglass. "That's a very bittersweet story that definitely says a lot about your brother. Not all teenage boys would've been that honorable."

"There was a time, back in the day, when Sax was doing his best to play the town hellion. But he never was, deep down."

He took a drink of beer, felt the cool slide down his throat, and, being that he was technically on the job, vowed this would be his only one of the day.

"The problem was that Cole, being the straight-arrow oldest brother, was a tough act to live up to. So, Sax pretty much quit trying during middle school and started carving out his own reputation."

Of the two of his brothers, although he'd looked up to Cole, Sax was the one J.T. had envied. Even if he had spent a lot of time in hot water. Until his senior year, when he'd promised Jared Conway, who'd gone off and joined the Marines, to watch out for Kara and keep her from being lonely.

"What about you?"

He dragged his mind from those days when it was more than obvious to everyone but Kara that Sax had fallen hard. And, as it turned out, his feelings had been strong enough to survive all those years apart.

"Me?"

"Well, if Cole was the straight arrow, and Sax was Shelter Bay's bad boy, what role did you take on?"

"Why, can't you tell?" He flashed a grin. "I was the smart, handsome, charming Douchett brother."

Hell, where had that come from? The past,

he realized as he watched her baby blues open wide with surprise. Before he'd gotten so deep in the pit that even this morning he hadn't been certain he was ever going to be able to climb out.

"I could tell that from the tie."

He glanced down at the cartoon crawfish. "The suit and shirt belong to Cole, who, as I mentioned, was the respectable brother and insisted tonight's occasion called for something more than flannel or leather over a T-shirt. I got the tie from Sax."

"I like it. Though I suspect the leather jacket would've made most of the women in Bon Temps tonight happy." She took a sip of the wine, studying him more deeply. "I feel as if I'm watching that old black-and-white TV quiz show. Would the real J. T. Douchett please stand up?"

He shrugged. Stretched out his legs and realized that since she was going to be in town for the next few days, she'd be bound to hear gossip.

"I liked being a Marine," he said. "A lot. It felt like home from the first day. But I was living with even more brothers than I had been back here."

"A band of brothers," she murmured.

"Yeah. That was a great series, and although our war was different from that generation's in a lot of ways, whenever you're out there getting shot at by bad guys, you bond pretty tight. I always figured I'd stay in until they forced me out."

He smiled, just a bit, at how naive he'd been. While he'd been able to handle the battle stuff, damned if it hadn't been his last, far tougher stateside assignment that had lit the torch that led to his burnout.

"And although there's nothing like the adrenaline rush of battle, I sure didn't intend to do that the rest of my life. My plan was to move on to teaching fulltime at the War College or maybe the Academy."

"The Naval Academy at Annapolis?"

"Yeah. Like I said, I already have my BA and MA. And I just need to finish writing my thesis for my PhD in history."

"Your thesis?"

"I got started on it while I was deployed, then got sidetracked. It's on the role of Special Operations in low-intensity combat, unconventional warfare, and the increasing use of the military, including Special Forces, as on-the-ground diplomats with local populations going forward into the future."

"I'm impressed."

She also sounded surprised, making him wonder if she'd stereotyped him the same way he had her. Of course she had.

"I taught some classes at the War College which touched on the topic, and really enjoyed training the next generation of warriors. It's important to know how to shoot, but the way things are changing, wars are going to be fought more with brains than brawn. And since I don't see the world holding hands on the mountaintop and singing 'Kumbaya' and the Coca-Cola song anytime soon, military men and women are going to have to be prepared for new challenges."

"Well," she said again. She crossed her legs, leaned back, and gave him another of those long looks that had him feeling as if he were on a Hollywood casting call and she was trying to decide what role he'd be testing for. "A warrior-scholar. Aren't you just one surprise after another?" she murmured, as much to herself, J.T. thought, as to him.

Yep. She'd definitely pegged him as just some jarhead with nothing between his ears.

"So, what changed your plans?"

"Let's just say the idea lost its appeal."

"Why?"

"What does it matter?" he countered. "It just did."

"Humor me."

"Now it's my turn to ask why."

"Because it's obvious that the festival

committee wants you to help keep the famous movie star happy. And because I'm a writer. Digging beneath the surface of characters is what we do."

"Don't look now, but I'm not a character."

She smiled at that. With those luscious full lips and eyes that had gone from sad and suspiciously misty when talking about her mother's death, to teasing. "Not yet, maybe," she agreed. "But the night, and the festival, are still young."

13

Day segued into evening. Then night, as Phoebe basked in the glory of the day off Zelda had insisted she deserved. Although Ethan had prepared their lunch, after an impromptu trip to the fishmonger's booth at the bay-side farmers' market, she insisted on trying out her newly discovered talents in the kitchen, something she'd never been allowed while living with Peter.

At first she was a little nervous, afraid of not getting all the diced potatoes for the clam chowder thc same size, or the oil the right temperature for the breaded Dungeness crab cakes, but not only was Ethan not the least bit critical, as Peter would have been under the same circumstances; instead of impatiently waiting to be fed, he pitched in on making the meal with her.

Yet again, unlike her husband, he didn't brush her aside and insist on doing things his way, but worked easily as he took on the role of her assistant, gathering the ingredients she asked for, setting the table. And, amazingly, after declaring her supper of clam chowder, crab cakes, and grilled asparagus with a medley of fresh berries for dessert the best he'd ever tasted, he wouldn't let her even clear the table, and insisted on loading the dishwasher himself.

She'd never — ever! — had a man wait on her. It felt strange. Yet, as relaxed as she was from the day, and the company, it also felt wonderful.

Which was why Phoebe was floating on air as he walked her up the steps to the door of Haven House.

"Thank you," she said. "For lunch and a lovely day." They were standing there on the pretty porch, only inches apart, she looking up at Ethan, he looking down at her, emotions swirling in the air between them.

"I had a great time." Although the night had grown cool, his deep voice wrapped her in a warm velvet embrace. As he ran a hand down her hair, she watched the desire rise in his eyes.

"Me, too." Over the past weeks, she'd prided herself on becoming strong and independent. So how could such a simple touch have her sounding so breathless?

He leaned closer. "Tell me," he said, as

that hand on her hair moved lower, to caress her collarbone, which until this moment she never would have expected to be an erogenous zone, "if I'm making a mistake."

"I don't know." Having lived a lie for so many years, Phoebe had promised herself never to fall into that trap again. "I can't always think straight when I'm with you."

"I know the feeling, all too well. . . . Okay, how about this?" That work-roughened hand skimmed down her side, and when she didn't automatically tense up, as she would have when they'd first met in the shelter's kitchen, it slipped around to her lower back. "I've spent all day — hell, weeks — trying to be patient, but if you don't tell me to back off now, I'm going to kiss you, Phoebe."

Phoebe was not at all surprised that Ethan, who had been so understanding and supportive since the day they met, would give her fair warning, rather than take what he wanted. What they both knew, deep down, that she wanted, as well.

But life was so complicated. She was still technically a married woman. Legally separated, true, but from everything she'd read, everything the counselor who came to the shelter for group sessions said, women in her situation should take their time, get to feel comfortable in their own skin, before entering into another relationship.

And then there was her baby to think of. Even if she did sometimes, late at night, lying alone in the dark, think about what it would've been like if she'd met Ethan that night at the Grand Canyon instead of Peter and wish that it was this man's child she was carrying.

She should tell him, politely, that she wasn't ready for the next stage in their relationship, that it would be better for all concerned if they remained friends. She should put on her big-girl panties, and back away from the temptation he was offering.

That was what she *should* do. It was the practical, safe thing. But she was so weary of always trying to take the safe way, and at this frozen moment in time, after a perfect day, as the sea sighed in the distance, and stars whirled overhead, Phoebe was finding it very difficult to take her own advice.

"Time's up." His hand pressed against her back, drawing her closer. As his mouth roamed over hers, slowly, softly, her lips trembled beneath his tender, nibbling kisses.

Murmuring something she couldn't hear over the blood roaring in her ears, he drew her closer yet, stroking her back, creating a trail of heat up to the nape of her neck, before retreating again to her waist.

Oh. My. The pleasure was liquid. As warm as a tropical sun. Her senses swimming, Phoebe clung to him, enjoying the stolen kiss for the sheer, bone-melting pleasure it was bringing her.

"Phoebe." His lips skimmed up her cheek.

"What?"

"Just Phoebe." His lips lingered at her temple before returning to hers. She could feel his smile against her mouth. "You're so sweet."

The teasing, tantalizing lips moved down her throat, warming her blood to the temperature of a beach bonfire. When he touched the tip of his tongue to the hollow at the base of her throat, she knew he could feel her pulse leap in response.

"So soft."

And he was so tender. Ethan Concannon was, in every way, the man a little girl who'd believed in Prince Charming had spent so many days and nights dreaming of. The same man whom a woman cruelly betrayed by the husband she'd foolishly trusted had come to believe did not truly exist.

But he did. This organic farmer with the clever mouth and slow, sure hands was wonderfully, exquisitely real.

His lips brushed over hers, again and

again, leaving warmth from one corner of her mouth to the other, inviting her into a warm, gilded world of sensation. Murmuring his name as she framed his face between her palms, Phoebe went willingly.

It was as if he intended to kiss her endlessly. Demonstrating the same patience he had for weeks, as they'd grown closer and she'd come to trust him, he didn't rush. Nor did he make any demands. There were only shimmering sighs, soft murmurs, and a glorious golden pleasure that seeped into her blood-stream.

Her head began to swim as, without surrendering the gentleness, without passion or fire, he took the kiss deeper. Then deeper still, drawing a trembling breath from her that shuddered into his mouth.

"Excuse me."

The woman's voice, coming from behind Phoebe, shattered the exquisite mood like cold water thrown on smoldering flames.

When she would have jumped away, Ethan put his arm loosely around her waist and looked over her head. "Hey, Kara. What's up?"

Although Phoebe no longer had any reason to be afraid of Shelter Bay's sheriff, a foreboding rose up like ice, flowing over the warmth that had, only a moment earlier, been glowing so gloriously inside her.

"I hate to interrupt." Kara Conway's face was set in what Phoebe had come to recognize as her professional cop expression. "But I need to talk with Phoebe."

The ice chilled all the way to her fingertips. "Is it about Peter?"

The sheriff didn't answer directly. Which, Phoebe thought, could only mean bad news.

"Let's go inside," she suggested.

Her tone was too gentle. Her amber eyes too apologetic.

Which was why Phoebe knew that Sheriff Conway hadn't come here tonight to tell her good news.

14

Damn. J.T. would rather be back in the Kush, battling the bad guys, than answer questions about his life. But possessing a fair bit of tenacity himself, he could recognize it in others. Realizing that the Irish movie star was going to keep picking away, he decided that this situation was a lot like pulling off a Band-Aid. He could peel it off, bit by bit, allowing her to gradually see the wound over the next few days, or he could just let it rip.

Deciding to go for it, to get it over with once and for all, so they could move the hell on and get through this damn festival, he said, "I spent the last eighteen months as a CACO. A casualty assistance calls officer."

"What I know about the American military could fit on the head of a pin and still leave room for a thousand dancing Marines," she said. "But is that what it sounds like?"

"If it sounds like the guy who has the responsibility — and honor — of informing families that they've lost a loved one, you'd be right."

There was a long pause as she processed his answer. J.T. could practically see the wheels turning in her writer's imagination.

"That must be both the worst and best job in the military," she decided.

"Yeah." Now it was his turn to be surprised when she nailed it so perfectly. Polishing off the beer, he resisted the urge to get up and open another bottle, knowing that would lead to another. Then another. And still another. Until he'd drunk enough not to be falling down trashed, but to numb the scenes that ran in a nonstop loop through his mind night and day. "I'd say that about sums it up."

"I wouldn't imagine they assign such a delicate job to just anyone."

Since it wasn't directly a question, and there wasn't any way to answer that, J.T. said nothing.

"No," she said, again seemingly to herself. "They wouldn't. They'd have chosen someone with not only a great deal of self-control but empathy, as well."

Another silence settled over them as Enya's evocative voice floated through the suite like a balm, managing to somewhat smooth the jagged edges of his mind.

Once again J.T. was struggling to reconcile this perceptive woman with the glamorous movie star who'd opened the door to him when he'd arrived to drive her to Bon Temps.

The dress, if you could call the short, slick tube of silk a dress, bared one smooth shoulder and skimmed down her toned, athletic body like rainfall. The deep blue color was a vivid contrast with porcelain flesh that looked as if it had never seen sunshine, and the fabric fit like a second skin. Pearls and diamonds dripped like glittery rain from her ears and more diamonds blazed on her wrist.

She'd put her hair up, in a loose twist that had his fingers itching to pull out some of those pearl pins, and she'd done female things with powders and pencils that made her blue eyes appear to be surrounded by smoke.

The ice pick heels she'd kicked off accentuated legs that went on forever.

Long-dormant embers stirred. Dammit, he wanted his hands on that long slim body. Then his mouth. And that was just for starters.

Dangerous thinking, that.

"Do you know how many women in this country make scrapbooks?" he asked.

"I have no idea."

"Neither do I. But sometimes it seemed like every damn one of them."

"And you'd have to sit in their living rooms and stoically listen to their stories of their dead loved ones while bits and pieces were being torn off your heart."

The woman was too perceptive for comfort. Even his brothers had focused more on the battle stuff he'd gone through than what, to outsiders, might look like a safe stateside assignment.

"It wasn't that bad." At least not in the beginning. But as the days and weeks and months went by, and the unrelenting sorrow seeped first into his blood, then deeper, into the very marrow of his bones, he'd begun to suspect that he might be as dead as the Marines whose families all had stories they needed to tell him. *Dead man walking.*

"Yes, I suspect it would be," she corrected quietly. "There was a time, in ancient days, in the British Isles and Ireland, when people believed in the shamanic tradition of sin-eating. Sin-eaters were always outcasts in a community, living on the very fringes, both literally and figuratively, of society. The Catholic Church also executed them, for the excess of sins darkening their souls. And, of course, because they were infringing on the priest's performance of last rites, and sin-eaters were given a few coins for their work, they were also depriving the church coffers of income."

"There was a sin-eater in some old Spider-Man comic books," J.T. remembered. A gunnery sergeant he'd served with in Iraq was constantly buying comic books online. Although they weren't as popular as the porn books and magazines a lot of guys managed to get past the censors, since beggars couldn't be choosers, J.T. had read them all.

"He was a minor villain who turned out to be a homicide detective who'd undergone drug experiments when he'd been a member of S.H.I.E.L.D. — Supreme Headquarters, International Espionage, Law-Enforcement Division," he explained at her questioning look. "Though later it was changed to Strategic Hazard Intervention Espionage Logistics Directorate. Then, when the movies started coming out, it was changed again to Strategic Homeland Intervention, Enforcement and Logistics Division."

"What would governments do without acronyms? And what would an espionage division be needing with a sin-eater? Although," she tacked on, "given how most such covert agencies appear to work, I may have just answered my own question."

"The guy didn't really eat sins. The drug treatments were supposed to increase strength and stamina, but the experiments were called off when people started having violent episodes and personality changes.

"When the detective's partner was killed, he snapped and went on a murder spree, determined to wipe away the sins of humanity. Spidey finally caught him, and he spent a year in a mental institution and was supposedly rehabilitated, but he was haunted by his crimes until he was finally gunned down in a hail of bullets."

"Well, isn't that far more dramatic than the situation I was speaking of? In the case of which I were speaking, the person would arrive at the home, where the family would feed him or her some salted bread and wine, which would be first passed over the body, which was laid out in the center of the room. It was believed that the food absorbed all the deceased's sins."

"Which, when consumed by the sin-eater, eased the person's way into heaven." The heaven J.T. no longer believed in.

"So it was thought. It would seem that your role as counselor to all those grieving families must have been much the same. Because, while bringing them what comfort you could, wouldn't you also, in turn, be absorbing their pain and sorrow?"

Bull's-eye. Since she'd hit too close to home, J.T. decided that it was past time to call it a night.

"That's an interesting take on it," he said. "I can see why you're a writer." He stood up. "Well, I guess I'd better get going and let you get your beauty rest."

The problem was not that he wanted to go. But that he wanted to stay. Which, of course, was exactly why he should leave. Now.

He dumped the empty beer bottle into the recycling tub beneath the bar, and after assuring her that he'd be back to pick her up in the morning, J.T. made a tactical retreat.

15

When was she going to learn? It hadn't been easy drawing J. T. Douchett out of the Kevlar shell he'd constructed around himself, but just when he was starting to lighten up, she'd let her heart run away with her head and wanted to know everything about him. Not just because she'd never known anyone like him, nor because he exuded testosterone the way other men might expensive aftershave, but because Mary had felt something stir inside her. Which, of course, could be from having dreamed about him.

Which was impossible. Wasn't it?

She knew that one of the draws of her series was the absolutely uninhibited nature selkies had toward sex. The hunger to mate was no different for their species from hunger toward food or the need of a safe place to dwell. There were times, after she'd lost herself in the sensuality of a scene, Mary had wondered if her fantasies were partly in response to the far more inhibited Irish Catholic religion in which she'd been raised.

She'd grown up with the selkie myths, of course. You couldn't live in the west of Ireland without someone claiming to either be a selkie or know of someone who'd made the fatal mistake of falling in love with one.

Although those stories hinted at the sexuality behind the stories of the seal women shedding their skins — which she'd later come to realize was a metaphor for shedding those inhibitions that had been drilled into her from the cradle — her first encounter with eroticism was when, while attending university, she'd been researching the myths for a screenplay idea when she'd stumbled across an ancient, leather-bound book hidden away in a dusty corner of a Dublin bookstore. The stories, all written by some anonymous author more than a century ago, stimulated fantasies she'd never known were lurking in her subconscious.

Once they were set free, it was as if a dam had burst inside her and she'd poured those yearnings into her stories. Having never met anyone she'd been tempted to risk indulging those unruly passions with in her real life, she'd kept them confined to her work.

Which hadn't stopped her from dreaming about them. And, as impossible as it seemed, about J.T. Douchett.

Although she wasn't nearly as sexually experienced as some who were drawn to her work might suspect, she had no doubt that J.T. would be a grand lover. She'd also felt that spark he'd tried, unsuccessfully, to hide when she'd opened the door to him when he'd come to pick her up earlier this evening.

Since she'd been the first to admit that her fashion sense wasn't up to those high-maintenance women who seemed determined to outspend one another in those fancy Rodeo Drive designer boutiques, she'd been more than willing to allow her stylist to choose her wardrobe for this trip. And when she'd suggested that the small coastal Oregon town wasn't exactly fashion forward, he'd assured her that was exactly the reason she should pull out all the stops.

"They didn't invite the small-town Irish farm girl to their little festival, dearheart." He'd brushed off her concerns. "They invited the drop-dead gorgeous, rich and famous movie star. If you show up in your usual jeans and sweater, you'll disappoint."

He'd opened up the suitcase he'd brought to her house with a flourish that suggested he was gifting her with the glittering contents of Aladdin's cave.

"Now, this," he'd assured her as he held up that scrap of midnight blue dress she'd worn tonight, "will definitely wow them. There won't be a woman in the room who wouldn't kill to be you. And every man at the reception will want to drag you off to bed on the spot."

While she continued to be skeptical of Kate MacKenna's claim of her possessing the sight, Mary knew enough about men to know that was exactly the thought that had flashed through J. T. Douchett's head when he'd gotten his first look at her wearing the dress. But then he'd determinedly tamped down the flare of hunger and gone even deeper into that dark, lonely cave where he seemed to dwell.

And now that she'd heard the story of his last assignment, she fully understood why his beautiful eyes, which in his case were definitely windows to the soul, were so tragically sad.

She'd never been the type of woman to be attracted to dark and brooding wounded males. That had been her sister Nora, who was a natural-born caretaker. When Quinn Gallagher had first come to Castlelough, even the teenager she'd been had realized that he was cynical, bitter, and disillusioned. Although she wasn't that aware of others in those days, being caught up in the throes of romantic disappointment, even Mary had realized that the rich American boarder their da had brought home from the Irish Rose pub had been a man who believed in nothing.

But Nora had believed in him. And while, to those who didn't know her well, she might seem all soft and maternal on the outside, she had a steely core of Joyce stubbornness and had refused to give up on him. Although their road to a happy ending had been a difficult one, what she'd told J.T. earlier was true: Whenever she thought about the type of marriage she might someday want, the bond shared between her sister and her brother-in-law remained the gold standard.

J.T. reminded her a great deal of the guarded man Quinn had once been. As unfriendly as he'd been in the beginning, she sensed that he was a good man. Something about his kindness and patience toward his grandmother, the way his eyes warmed when he talked about his family, and didn't the fact that the Marines had seen fit to assign him to what had to be the most delicate task in the military tell her that he was a very special man?

A man whom, although it was foolish to think about, she'd like to introduce to her own family.

And isn't that getting ahead of yourself?

She was undoubtedly romanticizing their entire situation. The tug she felt — the pull of a woman toward a man, and not just any man, but a hot, hard, and handsome-as-sin warrior — was merely chemistry.

Unfortunately, she'd never been any good at chemistry. In fact, if it hadn't been for Devon Cassidy's tutoring, she would have failed that part of her high school leaving test. Which was why she'd bestowed his given name on the human her selkie queen had given her heart to. And in doing so, the selkie had risked not only her warm and generous heart, but her kingdom and her life.

"That's fiction. This is real life." Unfortunately.

Because, despite Nora and Quinn's success, only a very foolish woman would give her heart to a man who was unable, or unwilling, to give anything back.

16

They went into the sunroom, which was usually Phoebe's favorite room in the house, with its large windows, pretty wicker furniture, and so many plants it felt like being in a rain forest. When she'd first arrived at Haven House, it was where she'd felt the most calm.

Not tonight.

Because her legs felt horribly unsteady, she sank down on the flowered cushion of the love seat. Ethan, who'd come into the house with her, sat beside her. She hadn't realized she'd been squeezing her hands so tightly together, until he pried them open and began smoothing out the indentations her fingernails had made in her icy skin.

"It's about Peter, isn't it?" Her throat burned.

"Yes," the sheriff said. "He's gone."

Gone. If only that were true . . . But like Freddy Krueger from all those *Nightmare on Elm Street* movies, he just kept coming back.

"Gone as in dead?" She'd imagined that scenario too many times over the years not to consider it now. As it always had, the idea brought relief rather than grief.

"No, I'm sorry." Kara frowned. "Bad choice of words. He's missing."

Zelda, who'd just brought in tea and cookies, gasped at that announcement. But did not drop the pretty china tray.

"He was wearing an ankle bracelet," Ethan said.

"Unfortunately, while accurate in an ideal environment, they're not always reliable. The GPS signal can get lost by walking into a building, or dense urban environments, or even during weather interruptions, like a snowstorm."

"It's summer. Even in Denver."

"There's a safe room in the house," Phoebe said. "It's hidden behind a fake wall in Peter's den. He worried about a home invasion. It's built out of some sort of armor-plated metal that's bulletproof." She did not add that he'd often threatened to lock her in there and leave her to die.

"Do the police know about it?"

"I'm sorry." Tears burned at the backs of her eyes. "I never thought about telling them." The truth was she'd tried to forget everything about her years spent in the nightmare that was her marriage.

"That explains why they kept getting so many false alarms. Just like cell phones, ankle bracelets can drop signals. Your husband was on his third."

"But once he'd leave the room, wouldn't it come back on again?" Ethan asked.

"I'd guess so. But there's also the point that even the best ones only work if the person wearing them keeps them on. He didn't."

"Which means that the Denver police don't have any idea where he is?" The others in the room had no idea how much it cost Phoebe to keep her voice calm and controlled as her world tilted, teetering precariously on its axis.

"I'm afraid not. I also suspect that all those false alarms were how he managed to escape before they made it out to his house. They probably were expecting another error, so didn't move as quickly as they might have, which makes me think he'd been setting up an elaborate escape scenario all along. Then there was an additional glitch. . . .

"The sheriff was off mountain climbing in the Rockies, and whoever was on duty dropped the ball calling me right away."

"How long ago did he escape?"

"Two days ago."

"You're coming back to the farm," Ethan announced.

"What?" Unable to think clearly, Phoebe rubbed her forehead with the hand he wasn't holding. "Why?"

"Because he knows where you are. And although you all stopped him once, you can't count on succeeding a second time. And because, as good as Sheriff Conway is, there's no way her small-town police force can offer you twenty-four-hour protection."

"Unfortunately that's true," Kara allowed. "And also unfortunately, it would be true in a larger city, too."

"I can take care of myself," Phoebe said as her head, which had been whirling ever since she'd turned around and seen the sheriff standing on the sidewalk, began to clear. Wasn't that what all the therapy sessions and working so hard to escape Peter in the first place had been about? Winning back her independence?

"Of course you can," Ethan said quickly. Too quickly. "In any normal circumstances. But there's nothing normal about this, Phoebe. If he was crazy determined to get you back and 'punish' you for running away the first time he showed up here at the house, think how he's going to feel now. After all his dirty laundry's been hung out in the press."

Oh, God. She hadn't even thought of the media. She looked up at Zelda. "The reporters are going to try to find you."

The elderly woman stiffened a spine that was already rod straight from decades of ballet training. "They can try."

"No." She shook her head. "I already almost got you killed. I'm not going to risk putting anyone in such a horrible, life-threatening situation. Never again."

She'd known, the first day she'd walked around Shelter Bay, that she wouldn't be able to stay. But she'd let herself fall in love with not only the town but the people. Zelda and the other women at Haven House, Chef Maddy, who had helped her regain her confidence and given her a job that she once never would've dared dream of, and, yes, maybe even Ethan Concannon. Each and every one of them had helped her make her way out of the dark shadows where she'd been fearfully hiding, into the warm sun of acceptance.

During the years of her marriage made in hell, Peter had battered away at her ego, eroding her self-confidence the same way the Pacific Ocean unrelentingly turned the cliffs to sand.

For the first time in years, in Shelter Bay she woke up each morning, not dreading the hours ahead of her, but feeling truly alive, willing to embrace whatever the day might bring. Since meeting Ethan in this very house, she'd even remembered how it had felt to be a woman. A woman who wanted. And, from what she'd guessed, and Ethan had confirmed earlier, was wanted in return.

If only . . .

Refusing to wallow in regrets, unwilling to give way to the tears she felt stinging at the backs of her lids, she tugged her hand free and stood up. "I need to pack." Now. Quickly.

"I'll be waiting," Ethan said.

"No. I'm sorry." And wasn't that an understatement? Although this was nearly as hard as when she'd escaped Denver, Phoebe knew she was doing the right thing. The only thing. "I need to leave. It's one of the first things they teach." She looked at Zelda for confirmation. "Not to ever plan to remain in any one place very long."

"I know." Zelda's eyes misted, reminding Phoebe that she'd started Haven House because her best friend had been killed by an abusive husband. "And normally it's how it's done in the shelter railroad and probably good advice. But you're no longer alone, Phoebe darling. And you're building a good life. A wonderful, new, exciting life for you and your child. You can't let that damn *svoloch'* take it all away from you. Again."

Although the former ballerina was born in the Ukraine, she'd been taken to Moscow as a young girl to train for the Bolshoi Ballet. So, when she was excited, or agitated, as she obviously was now, she tended to slip into the language she'd grown up speaking. Phoebe didn't need a Russian/English dictionary to know that the word, nearly spit with such harsh scorn, was no compliment.

"She's right." Ethan stood and put both his hands on Phoebe's shoulders. Not in any harsh, threatening way, but to hold her attention. "The police are going to know the same thing we do. That he'll be coming here. The problem is that although he's a bastard who deserves to be locked up until he forgets what a woman looks like, he's not stupid. He'll know that they know. So, he's undoubtedly spent the past weeks while on home arrest devising a plan to get around that."

"He probably read about the festival," Kara said. "What better time to blend in than when the town's going to practically double in size from the tourists coming for it?"

"All the more reason to leave," Phoebe insisted. Her heart was racing in a way that was all too familiar. And she was breathing too fast and too shallowly, but she couldn't seem to make herself stop.

"You must see that," she said fervently to Kara, who'd told her, after the Denver police had arrived to take Peter back to Colorado, about how Kara's police officer husband had been killed when he'd responded to a domestic abuse call. "If it was just myself I'd be putting in danger, I might take the risk. Just to keep him from winning."

She put her hand over her stomach, which had tightened into a knot. "But we're talking about my child. And Zelda and all the other women who live here. And perhaps one of your officers. Or even yourself."

"We're cops," Kara said briskly. "We'll worry about ourselves. The question on the table is what *you* should do." She looked thoughtfully between Ethan and Phoebe, then back to Ethan. "Do you have any weapons out at that farmhouse?"

"I was a Marine before I turned farmer," he said. "I do have guns and I know how to use them."

The sheriff was silent, studying him with a hard look that Phoebe thought had probably worked well in the city. Not that she was intimidating him. For the first time, Phoebe had a glimpse of the warrior Ethan Concannon had been before leaving the military to work the land.

"I completely understand the appeal in this case," Kara said finally, "but I'm not going to allow anyone to go vigilante in my town."

Ethan nodded. "Understood." He looked down at Phoebe. "Why don't you go pack? I'll wait here."

She hesitated, torn. There'd been a time, not very long ago, when her existence, perhaps even her life, had depended on the ability to read every nuance in a man's commanding voice. Every expression to cross his face.

Ethan did not push. Nor demand. He merely waited with the patience she'd come to expect from him. That same patience needed to nurture the tiniest seeds to beautiful vegetables that appeared to have washed off a painting by Cézanne or van Gogh.

As if they were the only two people in the room, he skimmed the rough pad of his thumb over her lips. Lips that only earlier had been warmed by his exquisite kiss, but were now stinging from her teeth sunk deeply into them.

"There's no one in this room who won't give you props for being a strong, independent woman," he said. "You've already proven that you have the heart of a lioness. But even big macho Marines like me know the value of working in teams." Despite the seriousness of the subject, he smiled down at her to let her know he was kidding about the macho Marine thing.

But it was true.

Peter wouldn't stand a chance against this man. So, why was she hesitating? Perhaps, a little voice in her mind suggested, this was the first place in a very long time where she'd felt safe? Which was why she was, on some level, afraid to leave it?

"Do you trust me?" he asked quietly. The smile had faded and his expression was as serious as she'd ever seen it. His eyes reassuring.

"Yes." Of that she had not a single doubt. "Of course."

He held out a hand. "Then come out to the farm with me. If it proves too much, too soon, we'll work something else out. You're not in this alone anymore. There's not a person in Shelter Bay who won't be watching out for the bastard. And your friends will all have your back."

Her friends. She'd once had friends, a very long time ago, until Peter had gradually cut her off from everyone, causing the map of her world to narrow to just the house where she'd been a physical and emotional prisoner.

Now she realized that she truly did have friends. And although she'd never want to risk being responsible for their being harmed, she also knew that if Zelda, Maddy, or Sedona, from the bakery, were in the same situation she found herself in now, she'd want to help any of them.

She blew out a breath she'd been unaware of holding.

"All right," she said. "And thank you."

He shrugged. "No thanks needed. And, although you didn't ask, there are four bedrooms in the house. One with your name on it."

As she went upstairs to pack, Phoebe couldn't decide whether his assuring her that they wouldn't be sharing a room had her feeling relieved. Or a little disappointed.

Hormones. That was what was causing all

these crazy, conflicted emotions she'd been having lately. That was all it was. It was all she could allow it to be.

17

"I can't believe I said that," Adèle said as she lay on her back, staring up at the bedroom ceiling, watching the lighthouse beacon flash on the plaster. "Bad enough I didn't recognize that lovely actress Mary Joyce, but then to bring up the part about her being skantily dressed in her movies . . ."

"It's the truth," Bernard said, drawing her into his arms. "No point in beating yourself up over it."

"It may be the truth, but it was also rude. And horribly inappropriate." She sighed. "I'm beginning to wonder if I should even be allowed out in public anymore."

"Don't talk such foolishness." He kissed the top of her head. "If you stopped going out, everyone in town would be showing up at our door because they'd miss you so."

"You're just saying that because you love me." Knowing how he hated it when she wept, Adèle struggled against the tears that were filling her eyes and blurred the light.

"I always have." He put a palm beneath her chin and lifted her gaze to his. "And I always will. But I've never lied to you, Del, darlin'. And I never will. You're part of the fabric of Shelter Bay.

"Think of all the people you've got knitting to make those blankets for those Project Linus kids. And all the other volunteer work you've done over the years. Why, after we lost our library to the Columbus Day storm back in the sixties, don't forget, you were the one who spearheaded the campaign to fund a new one.

"And didn't you and Sofia work together to get Second Harvest started here? And it was your idea to open a Kids' Café here so kids who might otherwise go hungry have not only a nutritious snack at the end of their school day, but somewhere to hang out while their parents are working, so they're not left on their own."

It was true she'd always needed to keep busy, and the café was her newest project. She'd been going along full force when that stupid fall had slowed her down, but fortunately, Sofia, Dottie, and Doris had stepped in to keep up the momentum.

"And how about that Army vet Sax introduced us to last week?" Bernard continued to press his case. "You can't say that you didn't make a difference there."

When she'd heard her three grandsons were playing basketball with an Army veteran turned teacher and coach at Shelter Bay High School, she'd asked to meet Dillon Slater, so she could hopefully coax him into teaching a basketball clinic. She'd been surprised and more than a little excited when it hadn't taken any coaxing at all. In fact, not only had he immediately agreed; he'd also offered to help get momentum going for a tutoring program for the kids.

"There you go with your exaggerating again," she complained without heat. "You're making me sound like Mother Teresa." Which she definitely was not.

"Not Mother Teresa, but Adèle Douchett, the woman everyone in town adores. So, how can you even think about turning into a recluse?" He linked his fingers with hers and lifted their joined hands to his lips. "Shelter Bay needs you, Del." His mouth, which after more than fifty years of marriage still possessed the power to thrill, moved up her arm, across her shoulder, and began nuzzling at her neck. "*I* need you."

Although she knew his words were meant to reassure, they inadvertently brought up another concern. Bernard Douchett was one of the strongest, most independent, hardworking men she'd ever known. And the most optimistic.

Hadn't he assured her, as Hurricane Audrey had wreaked devastation on their small bayou community, wiping Petit Chenier off the map, that they'd survive?

Although she might not remember what she had for supper last night, and had failed to recognize a famous movie star earlier this evening, Adèle's mind clung to the memories of that seemingly endless dark night as tenaciously as hanging Spanish moss had clung to the ancient oak trees surrounding their home. As stubbornly as she'd clung to the roof after the small wooden house had been washed off its piers and sent floating through the bayou.

When she'd checked in on Lucien before going to bed that night, the weather bureau had been predicting that the storm would hit Texas. Unfortunately, as they'd discovered at one in the morning, the weather bureau had been wrong. Since there was no way to leave the island of Petit Chenier, they'd gone to the attic, hoping the additional height would provide protection.

But then the house had washed away, and one wall had been knocked apart when it had rammed into a half-sunken fishing boat. Which was when Bernard had strapped their toddler son to his broad chest, looped a rope between his waist and Adèle, and led them onto the roof. Where they'd huddled together as the storm raged around them.

When morning broke, Adèle had been crushed as she viewed the destruction that went as far as the eye could see. As bad as that had been, it had gotten worse over the next days as recovery efforts were undertaken to locate the nearly five hundred dead. Including Bernard's parents, who'd lived in Grand Chenier and were among those never found.

Tragically, the storm had not only taken the shrimp boat Bernard had saved for years to buy, but also left both of them without any family except for each other.

Rather than sit around bemoaning their fate, her husband had gotten busy looking for work to get them out of that shelter. When he'd heard they were hiring men to catch crab up in Oregon, he'd cashed out their very small bank account, bought a used pickup to replace the one that had washed away with the house, and moved the three of them to Shelter Bay.

Life still hadn't been easy. They'd both worked hard, but they'd always been a team.

Adèle knew she'd be lost without this man who'd won her heart so many years ago. And, she feared, as tough as he was, he'd be equally devastated if *he* was the one to be left alone.

"What if the doctors are wrong?" She finally gave voice to the fear that had been bedeviling her for weeks. "What if I don't get better?"

"Then we'll stay just the way we are." He bent his head and brushed a light kiss against her quivering lips. How was it, she wondered, that he could still create a spark with a single look? Or a tender touch. Or a soft-as-sea-foam kiss. "Which, from where I'm lying right now, isn't such a bad thing, *chère.*"

His deep voice was like velvet — rough and smooth at the same time. It was also the one he'd bring out whenever he was in the mood for seduction.

"But what if I have the Alzheimer's?"

"We'll cope. As we have with everything else."

His lips skimmed up her face to linger at her temple, where, if you looked carefully, you could see the scar from the blasted fall that had stolen so much of her memory.

"What if I forget who *you* are?"

Adèle had a dear friend, Betty Jenkins,

whose husband had stopped recognizing her six months ago. Even having been warned that such a day was coming, Betty had been heartbroken when Ralph Jenkins had told her that she couldn't possibly be his wife. That his wife was young and beautiful. And Betty was old and fat. Those were, tragically, the last words he ever said to the woman he'd come home to marry after defeating the Germans in World War II.

"Then I'll simply have to court you every day to remind you that I'm the man who loves you to distraction," he said easily. "Which, believe me, would be no hardship, Del. . . .

"And speaking of courting."

He leaned her back against the snowy sheets and, with an expertise that came from more than fifty years of practice, began making slow, beautiful love to her.

As warmth began to flow through her veins, and her limbs turned to water, putting aside her worries for now, Adèle wrapped her arms around his broad back and allowed herself to be drawn into the mists.

18

After another night of erotic dreams starring the wickedly hot warrior who now, inexplicably, had a name, Mary dragged herself out of bed, ordered room service, then took a shower. As she stood beneath the streaming warm water, she tried to keep her mind from imagining it was J. T. Douchett's hands smoothing the fragrant bar of oval soap over her wet and distractingly needy body.

Oh yes, it was going to be a very long four days. And she wasn't certain she'd helped her case last night when she'd realized she'd pushed too fast. After he'd left the suite, she belatedly remembered that a storyteller's innate need to dig beneath the surface, to know everything about both real people and fictional, could often be viewed by others as being intrusive.

"You should have taken a page from Nora's book," she muttered as she dragged a comb through her wet hair. Hadn't her sister taken four long weeks to draw Quinn out of his life-hardened shell? What made Mary think that she could prove equally effective in a mere day?

Then, it had also been obvious to everyone in the family that Quinn had been attracted to Nora from the start. If J. T. Douchett was interested in her, except for his reaction to the dress she'd worn to the reception, he'd certainly done a very good job of hiding his feelings since she'd gotten off the plane. And couldn't that flash of lust be explained away by a knee-jerk response to any woman in a short, tight, skimpy dress? Especially a woman he'd already seen nearly naked on his TV screen. Like so many men she'd met, he'd undoubtedly been attracted to her sexually free character. Not her.

Not that she cared what the man thought of her personally.

Liar. Whether she was being influenced by those dreams, or merely because he was the most interesting man she'd met in a very long time, Mary did care. Too much for comfort.

She'd just snuggled into a thick, terry cloth robe with the inn's whale logo embroidered in blue on the front when the phone on the bathroom wall rang. Since the operator had been instructed not to send calls through unless they were from someone on the committee, she assumed it was a schedule update or perhaps room service calling to confirm something with her order, and picked up the phone.

"Finally!" the frustrated voice of the studio executive assistant said on an exasperated huff. "If I were a paranoid person, I might think you were ignoring my calls."

"I haven't had a minute to even breathe, so I turned my phone off." That part was true. Well, mostly.

"Have you given any more thought to the idea?"

"As I said last time we spoke, I've been busy, but I have been thinking about it, and honestly can't see where I could fit a vampire into my story."

"I was thinking about that last night," Tammi, who could make a bulldog look indecisive, said. "You already have a romantic triangle going on with your selkie queen, the scientist, and the queen's fiancé. So — now, just go along with me, here — you could have a female vampire claim your scientist."

"Why would she do that?"

"Well, because, for one, he's really, really hot. And second, it sets up another conflict when the heroine has to battle the vampire for his eternal soul."

"A real battle? He's thinking of turning my film into a summer special effects movie for adolescent males?" Although her stories might be set in fantastic realms, Mary had always held firm about not letting the tech-crazed FX guys get their hands on her scripts.

"Don't worry." Mary had heard that soothing tone before. Usually when Tammi's boss was pushing for changes in the script. Changes that he believed would make it even more commercial. "Given the state of the economy, Aaron wants to keep the budget down, so going with big FX isn't even being discussed."

"I'm glad to hear that."

Mary's relief was short-lived. "Instead, he's considered something more basic we both feel would be even more effective than computer-generated content."

"And that would be?"

"A fight scene. Between you and the vamp character over the scientist."

"Aaron wants to bring in the mud-wrestling audience now, too?"

"Of course not!"

Thank God.

"He was thinking of using the ocean for a

venue. Well, not actually the ocean, because an underwater fight scene would be more expensive to shoot. He's thinking in the surf."

Sand and surf wrestling? "He wants my heroine to roll around in the surf with a female vampire?" Forget the FX; this would get those adolescent males to buy tickets.

"Exactly!" Excitement shimmered in the other woman's voice. "Can't you see it, Mary? You naked, because you've been celebrating the summer solstice on the beach, so you've shed your sealskin, revealing your human form. There's a full moon shining down —"

"Wrong genre. Unless you and Aaron also are thinking of adding a werewolf."

"Aaron doesn't find werewolves sexy. All that fur and strange shape-shifting stuff. And this would work because vampires also go out hunting for blood during full moons." There was a pause. "Don't they?"

"I have no idea. Nor do I care, since I have no intention of writing a vampire into my scripts. And you know as well as I do that what Aaron's suggesting is gratuitous sex shoved into the story solely for the titillation factor, hoping to pull in a younger male demographic —"

"Exactly! I told Aaron that you'd understand his reasoning."

What? "I wasn't saying that. Okay, maybe I do understand, all too well, what he wants to do, but what I meant was —"

There was a knock at the door. Then someone called out "Room service!"

Saved by the bell.

"Look, Tammi, the festival committee has me on a killer schedule, there's someone at thc door, and I've got to run. Why don't I get back to you on this?"

"You promise you'll call?"

"Absolutcly."

"Because you know how Aaron is when he gets an idea into his head. He's just not going to let go of it, so if you don't get back to me, I'll have to keep calling. Or fly up there myself."

"Oh, you needn't do that," Mary said quickly. "I promise, as soon as this morning's activities are over, I'll call."

"All right." She sounded hesitant. "But I'm letting Aaron know that we can expect to hear back from you this afternoon."

"Absolutely," Mary repeated. "Now I really do have to run." She ended the call before she could be drawn deeper into an argument she was in no mood for. An argument she had no intention of losing.

19

On to the room service ruse that had been tried by more than one fan over the past few years, before opening the door, Mary looked through the peephole to where the object of her restless sleep was standing, holding a tray.

"I ran into the waiter getting into the elevator," he explained, as he walked through the door she held open, as if he had every right to be invading her privacy. Which, of course, he did.

"And ended up costing him a tip," she pointed out.

"You don't have to worry. I took care of that for you. You'll be glad to know that you're a very good tipper."

"I already know that." Having worked at a Dublin pub while in college, she always overtipped.

"I figured you did. Which is why I knew you'd want me to uphold your image." He put the tray down on the coffee table. "Coffee?"

"Oh, please, yes." As he poured a cup from the carafe, she kept the fact that she'd have been willing to beg to herself. As yet another reminder that there weren't any secrets in small towns, there were two cups on the tray. "And feel free to help yourself."

"Thanks. I will." After handing her a cup, he poured the second. The pretty flowered cup looked tiny in his broad hand. He skimmed a look over her. "Bad night?"

"I have trouble sleeping in strange beds," she said, not about to share her dream with this man. Especially since he'd played a starring role. "And then this morning I got a call from the studio. . . ."

She shook her head. "Never mind."

"Bad news?"

"I suppose that depends how you feel about vampires."

He took a drink of the coffee. Considered. "I've never given them any thought."

"Well, you and I appear to have something in common. Which may make us the only two people on the planet who don't talk about them as if they're real."

"So why are we talking about them now?"

"Because although I conceived the selkie story as a trilogy, I recently wrote a fourth script, because, given the choice, Hollywood would rather go with a proven franchise than attempt anything new."

"Yet you were new once."

"True. But I had buzz. Which is nearly as good. Sometimes even better, since everyone's also always after the next new thing. I received attention because I began garnering festival wins, which had me becoming the flavor of the month, and, although I don't see it, because I'm certainly not the least bit curvaceous, males in the sought-after demographic groups apparently think I look good naked. Not that I actually was," she felt obliged to remind him. "Naked."

"Yeah. You mentioned the bodysuit, which you've got to know doesn't detract from the fantasy," he said. "Besides, although guys may admittedly have a response to breasts built into our DNA, when it's hard to tell what's real anymore, they begin to sort of lose their appeal. You're a lot like your heroine — sleek and built for speed."

Mary shouldn't have been so pleased by that. But she was. Too much.

"Thank you." She picked up a strawberry from a fruit plate of berries, melon, kiwi, and mango slices, which had been arranged to resemble a flower. It was, she thought, almost too pretty to eat. And speaking of eating . . .

"I could call down for something more substantial if you'd like breakfast."

"Thanks, but I already ate at Bon Temps before coming over here."

"I didn't realize the restaurant served breakfast."

"It doesn't. But I'm staying there, in the office, for the time being, so I raided Sax's refrigerator and made up a mess of grits, red beans, and poached eggs."

"That's very ambitious." She also found it curious that he'd be camping out in his brother's office, but, after last night, didn't want to pry. "And I'm impressed you can cook."

"Cooking's pretty much a guy thing in the Cajun culture. Our dad taught us, and his dad taught him. I was never as much into it as Sax was, but months on end eating MREs bring home the importance of being able to feed yourself."

"Nora and Gran were always the cooks while I was growing up. During college, and now, in California, I'm afraid I've become a whiz at dialing for takeout."

"Too bad you're not going to be hanging around longer. Maddy Chaffee, who used to be Maddy Durand, is opening up a cooking school here in town at her grandmother's farm."

"Chef Madeline lives here?" Just because Mary didn't cook didn't mean she wasn't addicted to the Cooking Network. "I'm a huge fan. But I thought she lived in New York."

"She did. But there was this scandal —"

"I heard about that."

"Yeah, you and it seems everyone else on the planet. So, she dumped the cheating French chef husband and married a guy she dated when he'd spend summers here. We all hung out together growing up. She's catering Sax's wedding in a couple days."

He drained the cup and put it back on the tray. "Want to go?"

The question, tossed out so casually, confused her. Did he mean leave the suite for the parade? Or was he actually asking her to the wedding?

No. He *had* to be talking about the parade.

She glanced down at her robe. "I realize Shelter Bay has a more casual dress code than some cities, but I doubt they'd be all that pleased for their grand marshal to show up in a robe."

"I was talking about the wedding."

Okay. That was a surprise.

"You want me to go with you?"

"It only makes sense. Since I'm supposed

to be watching out for you. It's not a big deal," he assured her. "Just a few close friends and family. The only reason they're rushing it is Kara's mom's a doctor with this medical relief organization, and with all the stuff happening in the world, this was the only time window she had open."

"Are you certain Kara won't mind?" Mary had met her briefly at the reception last night, before she'd been called away.

"Like I said, she's the one who hooked us up in the first place. Why would she mind?"

"I wouldn't want to intrude on a family situation."

"They like you. You like them. Makes sense."

When he put it that way . . .

"I'd enjoy sharing your family's special day. Thank you."

Mary's mind sped into overdrive. She'd have to find a gift, since no way was she going to show up empty-handed. And she'd need something to wear, because she refused to wear Leon's movie-star clothes, which would look as if she were trying to upstage the bride on her big day. But first there was something even more important she needed to do.

20

"About last night," she said. "I need to apologize."

J.T. dragged his gaze from the droplets of water on that little V of fragrant skin revealed by the neckline of the bulky white robe. "For what?"

"About sounding as if I were prying into your life. As I said, I have this flaw of wanting to know everything about people. I suppose it's something we writers do instinctively. Gathering little bits and threads to weave into the tapestry of our stories.

"If it helps, it wasn't anything personal. I've never met a Marine before. Let alone someone who was tasked with as gut-wrenching a mission as death notification must have been. So I apologize if, in my interest to know more, I overlooked any No Trespassing signs."

Hell. She appeared honestly chagrined. It wasn't as if she'd waterboarded him. For some reason, although he'd never discussed his last assignment with anyone, even his brothers, he'd given up the information, including those damn scrapbooks and photo albums, voluntarily. Which, J.T. reminded himself, as he suddenly found himself thinking of sirens and temptation, made this sweet-smelling Irish actress even more dangerous.

"Don't worry about it. It's just that I don't usually talk about those days." Usually being never.

"People are always telling me things," she said mildly. "I've no idea why, though Kate, who's my sister Nora's best friend, insists it's because I have a touch of the sight."

"So, you're saying you're clairvoyant?"

He damn well hoped she hadn't been able to read his mind when he'd been thinking about stripping that short tight dress off her, carrying her into that honeymoon suite, and doing what millions of guys probably all fantasized about while watching her movies. Even knowing that she'd been wearing a body stocking in the nude scenes didn't make her any less desirable.

Like it or not, they were stuck with each other until the end of the festival. If she knew that at this moment all he could think about was what she was — or wasn't —

wearing beneath that thick white robe, she might be uncomfortable.

Which, in turn, would upset Kara.

Which would have Sax throwing him into the bay again.

"No. I don't believe so, though I do get a sense of people from time to time." She frowned into her coffee. "And occasionally have dreams that seem very real." A bit of color rose in her cheeks, making him wish he could read *her* mind. "But that's more women's intuition than any powers of clairvoyance. I'm nothing like Kate MacKenna, who's an actual druid witch."

She lifted her gaze again and smiled. A smile that he noted didn't quite reach her eyes. "If I could foretell the future, I wouldn't be such a nervous wreck whenever I had a film coming out."

"I have a hard time believing that."

She tilted her head. "And why would that be?"

Because he doubted if she'd ever had an insecure moment in her life. And why should she? When you looked like Mary Joyce, and were rich, intelligent, and talented to boot, the world was probably pretty much your oyster.

"You've got to know your work is good."

"Ah. If it were only that simple." She

sighed, glanced down at her watch, and stood up. "I'd better get ready. Hopefully we'll be able to run by that boutique I saw yesterday between the parade and the first showing."

"We're going shopping?"

Just when he was thinking this might not be the mission from hell. Why didn't they just take him out and keelhaul him?

She patted his cheek. "Don't worry, Marine. I've been told I shop like a man. We'll go in, I'll bag some more suitable clothes, and we'll be on our way."

She was laughing as she left the suite's living room.

21

Although it had taken a herculean effort, Ethan had managed to conceal the anger that had surged through him when Kara had told him and Phoebe about her abusive husband's escape. He'd seen for himself, that day he'd met her in the kitchen of Haven House, the mark the man's hand had left on her face.

And he knew, from the way she'd first behaved, like a nervous, wounded bird, that as bad as the physical abuse must have been, the beating her psyche had taken was much, much worse.

Although the transformation hadn't been overnight, she'd begun to rediscover the girl she'd once been. He'd watched her blossoming like a wildflower opens to the sun. And now the bastard was going to try to take that away.

Over his dead body.

But Phoebe didn't need his anger. What

she needed, he'd reminded himself, was his support. And, even though she'd argued against it, his protection.

He'd already lost one woman he'd loved. In that case, there'd been no way to protect Mia against that SUV whose driver had taken a curve on the winding coast road too fast, crossed the center line, and, in that one moment of recklessness, cost him both a wife and a son.

This time, he vowed, he would do whatever it took to keep Phoebe safe. Which meant making sure he stayed calm and collected enough that she wouldn't pick up on any vibes that would make her feel uncomfortable staying with him until the cops caught the bastard.

So, he'd driven her to the farm, made her some chamomile tea from a collection Sofia De Luca had given him last Christmas, shown her the guest bedroom and adjoining bath, and managed to escape without embarrassing either one of them by dragging her down onto that mattress and doing what he'd been fantasizing about for too many weeks.

He'd waited until he heard her soft breathing and knew she had gone to sleep. Then went outside to the small office he'd built in the barn, and put his fist through the wall.

■ ■ ■ ■

After a mostly sleepless night, during which time Ethan was all too aware of Phoebe sleeping in the next room, he pushed himself out of bed at dawn and went out to tend to the milking. Although the dairy operation was fully automated, which was a big change from when he'd been a kid and was expected to milk by hand, he'd always found the early-morning routine a relaxing way to begin the day.

Not this day.

He'd reminded himself of those guys who came home from the war and couldn't stop prowling their yards looking for bad guys. In their cases, the bad guys were in their heads, which was tough enough.

His bad guy was all too real. And he was coming after Ethan's woman.

And she *was* his woman. Just as he was her man. It was just going to take more time for her to realize that. And possibly longer to feel okay with it.

Which he could live with.

After all, any guy willing to work hard could make it through the good times. But any farmer who wasn't both optimistic and patient wouldn't last a season when things got tough. As they always did.

He was on his way back into the house when Kara called.

"How's Phoebe doing?" she asked.

"When I left, she was sleeping."

"Good . . . I called this woman I know. She's a former FBI agent married to one of Sax's old teammates. Cait McKade worked with me on helping solve my father's murder. Anyway, she's done a lot of profiling work, so I ran our situation by her."

"And?"

"And she thinks as long as someone's always with Phoebe, she'll be okay. Fletcher's driven by power and gets off by control and seeing her fear. She doubts he'd do anything like get a rifle and take a shot from some hidden location. He's undoubtedly after her, even more so since she got him arrested. But his intentions are the same as they were the last time he came to town. He wants things up close and personal."

"If he makes the mistake of getting too close, it could well be the last mistake the bastard ever makes."

"I understand your feelings but —"

Knowing she was about to repeat the warning she'd given him while they were in that pretty sunroom in Haven House, not wanting to waste time promising to remain reasonable when he felt anything but, Ethan cut off the call.

Apparently realizing the futility of arguing, she didn't call back.

He took off his boots in the mudroom, and, figuring that after last night's news Phoebe needed rest, he walked as quietly as a guy his size could to the kitchen.

Where he found her, already dressed, standing at the counter, taking eggs out of the refrigerator.

She looked up, and offered a tentative smile, revealing she was uncomfortable with their situation.

"Good morning." Before he could go over to the Mr. Coffee, she'd poured him a mug and held it out to him. "I realized, since we've never eaten breakfast together, I didn't know how you like your coffee. If you'd like cream, or sugar —"

"This is great. I usually drink it black."

"Good." When she seemed more relieved than pleased to have guessed right, alarm bells sounded.

"I also didn't know what you usually eat, so I thought I'd make a western omelet. I found a ham in the fridge, though if you were saving it for something else, or if you don't like omelets, and would rather have pancakes, or maybe waffles, or I could fry some eggs with hash browns —"

"Phoebe." She was so wound up, he was afraid that if he touched her, she'd jump through the ceiling. But on the other hand, the way she was flying around the kitchen, from the counter, to the stove, to the coffeepot, and back to the counter, once again had him thinking of a skittish bird. This time trapped in a room and trying desperately to escape.

Risking making things worse, he took hold of her upper arms. Not tightly, just enough to stop her frantic movements. "It's okay."

"I know." Her smile, after that automatic wariness, was bright, strained, and totally fake. "I'm always up early, so I wanted to pay you back for inviting me to stay here."

"You don't have to pay me back for anything. And like I told you, I'm not him. I don't need you to rush around waiting on me, and I'm damn sure not going to get angry if you decide that you'd rather make an omelet than waffles. Not that I need you to do anything," he stressed. "You're not here to be a housekeeper or cook."

"But —"

He touched a finger to her lips, cutting her off in midsentence. "You're here as a friend." He shook his head and realized that if he stood half a chance getting past the barricades she was putting up between them again, he needed to be entirely honest. "More than a friend," he admitted. "You're a woman I've come to care for. Deeply. A woman I admire."

"You admire me?" She seemed surprised by that. Christ, the guy really had done a number on her.

"Hell, yes. I can't begin to imagine what your life was with that guy you were married to, but you not only had the guts to escape a dangerous situation — you're starting a new career. I don't just want you, when you're ready, but I respect you for that. I've witnessed a lot of courage during my time in the military. But you, sweetheart" — he moved that finger to her chin and lifted her wary gaze up to his — "are every bit as brave as any Marine I fought with."

She bit her lip. "I don't always feel brave."

Her vulnerability, even after all she'd managed to achieve, pulled at him.

"Join the club."

After skimming a fingertip against that soft bottom lip her teeth had worried, he coaxed her closer, until her cheek was against his chest. He looped his arms loosely around her, not caging her in, just letting her call the shots as he rested his own cheek on her hair. When her coconut-scented shampoo had him imagining making love to her on a hidden tropical beach, since she was already trembling like a new planting in a coastal wind, he viciously throttled back the sudden burst of hunger that was threatening to make him hard as a rock.

"I can't believe you were ever afraid," she murmured into his shirt as her arms crept around his waist and held on.

"If you're not afraid during a battle, you're not paying attention," he said. "And after Mia and our son died, there were days I was afraid I was going to die from grief. And even more days I was afraid I wouldn't."

She lifted her eyes, which were bright with tears. "I hate that you had to go through such a terrible thing," she said, with a flare of the strength that had first attracted him to her. Even when he'd known she was nervous around him, from somewhere deep inside, she'd kept pulling up the strength not to let her fear overwhelm her.

Because he could not look down into that lovely, sweet face without touching, he cradled the side of her face in his palm. His dark, calloused hand looked the size of that ham she'd been about to take from the fridge against her pale, soft-as-silk skin, and made him feel huge and clumsy, like an oafish giant daring to touch a princess.

Or, he thought, like the Beast daring to fall in love with Beauty. Which, in that story, had worked out, but it was hardly a model being that it was only a fairy tale.

This wasn't the first time he'd felt that way around her, but apparently she didn't feel threatened because she reached up and put her hand on his.

"And I hate like hell that you had to go through what you've suffered." Especially since he suspected he didn't know the half of it. "And someday, maybe you'll feel comfortable enough to tell me more, but for now, I promise that, together, we can work through this."

Because he didn't think he could fight back the damn erection that was threatening to rise against her belly in another minute, he carefully put a little distance between the two of them.

"But for now, what do you say we go out for breakfast?"

"Out?" She glanced around the kitchen at the eggs, and flour, sugar, bowls, and pans she'd gotten out. "Like a date?" A flush like a ripe persimmon rose in her cheeks. "I'm sorry. It just popped into my head. I mean, I know you didn't mean that —"

"Actually, that's exactly what I meant." He leaned down and touched his lips to hers. The kiss was short, but from the way he felt her tremble, he knew it was potent. "One step at a time," he promised her. "But we'll never know where we're going if we don't take that first step."

"I've heard about the Grateful Bread's waffles. I've been wanting to try them."

This time her smile was warm and real. And still shy, which he considered could actually be the person she'd been before that coward prick had tried to his damnedest to break her.

"Terrific. Just let me shower up, and we'll drive into town. Have some breakfast, then maybe hang around and watch the festival parade. And you don't have to worry — I just finished talking with Kara, who consulted with some former FBI profiler she knows, and it's both of their opinion that you'll be safe as long as I'm with you." He touched his hand to her check. "And I'm not going anywhere."

It was only once he was alone, standing under the hot stream of water, that Ethan allowed the full heat of last night's anger to return. He'd promised Kara that he wouldn't turn vigilante on her, even though the urge to just get out his sniper rifle, wait at the outskirts of town, and double tap Fletcher right in the forehead was hugely tempting.

But, while getting rid of a problem, it would only make things worse for Phoebe, and since he'd sworn off violence when he'd taken off his uniform and taken up farming, he was going to try like hell to stick to his word.

But if Fletcher actually was stupid enough to dare to return to Shelter Bay, to get to his wife, he'd have to go through Ethan first.

And there was no way in hell that was going to happen.

22

Fortunately, the sun had broken through the early-morning clouds and the temperature had climbed into the mid-seventies, making it a perfect day for a parade.

"Oh, I'm so glad you're wearing red," the mayor said, taking in Mary's scarlet jacket with the satin lapels, her white blouse, the same black slacks she'd worn yesterday, and her short red boots. "You'll match the fire truck."

"Fire truck?"

"Oh, didn't anyone tell you? Instead of a typical convertible, you'll be riding atop one of our two Shelter Bay fire trucks."

Which, Mary realized, explained the two firemen clad in navy blue SBFD T-shirts standing beside the mayor.

"You've just made my day." The fire truck in question, parked not far away, had been washed to a brilliance that had the sun glinting off the hood. She shook hands with the men.

"The feeling's mutual, ma'am," the older firefighter said, his ruddy cheeks above his mustache turning a bit darker when she gave him her warmest smile.

"Oh, please, call me Mary. Will we get to sound the siren?"

"You want a siren, you'll get one," the younger and more outgoing one said with a bold wink. Then backed up a step, which had Mary casting a glance up at J.T., whose steely eyes could've blistered the paint off the truck. Intrigued, she studied him more carefully. Surely he couldn't consider the friendly fireman dangerous. Could he actually be jealous?

"Are you going to sit up there with me?" she asked him.

He looked as if he'd rather be back in a war zone at that idea, but shrugged. "I'm supposed to watch out for you. Kinda hard to do that inside the cab." He moved his shoulders in that gesture she was getting used to. At first she'd thought it was a sign of nonchalance. Now she realized it revealed a discomfort with the situation.

"Don't worry, Marine," she murmured, as he gave her a boost up onto the ladder. "From what I could tell by Googling the map of the town, the route's not that long.

And I'll do my movie-star best to keep the attention off you."

"It's that obvious?" he asked as she settled down on the wooden platform.

"That you'd rather be anywhere than here, with me?" The platform wasn't as large as it looked. They were thigh to thigh. Which she wasn't finding any hardship. "Yes, but I'm trying not to take it personally."

"It's not you." He rubbed the back of his neck. Yes, he was clearly uncomfortable. "It's just that, to hear my family tell it, I've sort of freaked people out since I got back."

"Oh?" Although he'd denied it, once again Mary wondered about PTSD.

"It's not what you're thinking. I didn't go around armed or screaming like a girl at loud noises."

"While I'm willing, for now, to overlook that sexist description, what *did* you do that freaked people out?"

"I ran."

"Ran?" She glanced over at him. "That's it?"

"That's it. Well, maybe I ran a lot."

"Define *a lot*."

"Is this really germane to our situation? I'm not running now, okay?"

"Okay." Although she could have pointed

out that she hadn't been with him 24-7, Mary decided, as the firemen climbed into the cab, that since this was neither the time nor the place, she'd table the discussion for now.

Behind them came a group of older cars, among which was Sax, sitting behind the wheel of a tough-looking white car with orange hood stripes. A small, freckle-faced boy sat in the passenger seat, while a huge dog seemed to take up the entire backseat. Mary noticed that everyone who passed by seemed obligated to pat the huge head stuck out the rear window.

"I like your brother's car."

Although more modern, it reminded her of the movie *American Graffiti.* She'd been thirteen when she'd first seen it on television and even as she'd identified with the small-town setting, she'd envied the American teenagers' freedom, which was very different from Castlelough's stricter social mores.

"It's a 'ninety-seven anniversary Camaro that used to be a Mustang killer in drag races. Dad kept it in shape for Sax the entire time he was in the Navy. He said he didn't want to see a classic car rust, but we all knew the reason was that he believed that as long as the car was waiting for my brother to come home, he'd make it home."

"That's so sweet of your father." She wondered if he'd realized he'd offered her another glimpse into his life.

"I wouldn't mention that at the wedding," he suggested. "Being that Marines don't usually consider *sweet* a compliment."

"I won't. But it is." Someone in a clown car shouted out to her. She smiled and waved. "I'm also wondering if perhaps you ought to make me a crib sheet."

"For what?"

"For all the things I'm not supposed to bring up when I'm around your family."

She turned and waved in the other direction when a person dressed as a tortoise carrying an oversized clock without hands and wearing a sign reading SLOW DOWN! YOU'RE NOW ON SHELTER BAY TIME! shouted out that he loved her movies.

"Point taken."

The engine started up. As it began to move along the waterfront, behind the color guard of veterans carrying the American flag and various flags of their services, the truck lurched, throwing her a bit off-balance. Which, in turn, had J.T. putting his arm around Mary's waist to steady her. He kept it there as the truck lumbered down the first block, and when he finally removed it, she felt a twinge of loss.

Although from the crowd at the starting point it appeared everyone in town must actually be *in* the parade, the sidewalks were still lined with people. Some had brought folding chairs, others sat on the curb, while still others stood, many fathers holding children on their shoulders.

The mood was universally festive as fans, many of whom had come dressed as characters from her movies — her third movie was just about to come out and she was still amazed by the variations on the mermaid theme — waved and called out to her.

The float behind her, which Mayor Dennis had told Mary had been built by volunteers, was pulled by a green John Deere tractor. Riding on the float, featuring huge posters of each of the films entered in the festival, were the ten contestants, along with members of the high school glee club, who were already belting out movie soundtrack songs. One, unsurprisingly, was "Under the Sea." Librarians, wearing costumes made to look like book covers, walked alongside, handing out bookmarks printed with the titles of books that had been made into movies currently in circulation at the library.

The local restaurants the floats passed along the way had set up booths in front of their stores, providing free food and drinks.

The Sea Mist was giving out clam chowder, while the Crab Shack had petite crab cocktails in foam cups, the Grateful Bread was serving cinnamon rolls the size of Mary's hand and cups of steaming coffee, Take the Cake had unsurprisingly opted for cupcakes, and although Sax was in the parade, his grandparents were manning the Bon Temps booth, handing out popcorn shrimp and Adèle's famous Come-Back sauce.

Although being in the parade prevented her from viewing it while the fire engine was moving, as soon as they pulled up into the parking lot of a green park atop a hill, she was able to watch the other participants as they arrived at the lot, where even more spectators were waiting.

Along with the glee club, the high school marching band — decked out in their royal blue and white uniforms — played Sousa, while Native Americans from the Siletz reservation, in ceremonial regalia, danced to the beat of their drums, and people dressed like whales (the town mascot) stood atop another float, throwing out pieces of candy to the kids.

"An enterprising dentist would follow them handing out toothbrushes with his name on them," J.T. observed as he helped her down from the platform.

Although she thought of herself as an independent woman, Mary couldn't deny that the supportive hands on her waist felt quite nice.

"Spoilsport." She slapped him lightly on the arm. "This is turning out to be such grand fun, I'm not going to let you put a damper on it."

"Easy for you to say. You're not the one who's going to be paying to have those kids' cavities filled."

"No, but I can also tell when someone's putting me on. Admit it, J.T. For a few minutes you were having a good time."

"It wasn't as bad as I thought it was going to be. But we haven't made it through the pageant yet."

Taking hold of her arm, he swept her through the crowd toward the white Victorian bandstand where the committee was already waiting for her to take the seat of honor. If she'd known she'd be walking across grass, she wouldn't have worn the heels that kept sinking into the wet turf.

"Don't you own any practical shoes?" he said as he put his arm around her and practically lifted her entirely off the ground. At least he hadn't slung her over his shoulder and carried her up the steps.

"Why should I?" she shot back, unable to

decide whether she was embarrassed or annoyed. "When I have minions, such as you, to drag me to where I'm going."

"If you expect me to start picking out your clothes, like Leonard —"

"Leon."

He blew out a frustrated breath. "Leon," he said through set teeth. "If I'm going to be forced into minion duty, then you'd better develop a liking for cammies and combat boots."

She tossed her head like the diva she knew he'd been expecting when she'd arrived in town. "Army chic," she drawled. "It just might catch on." She glanced at the bandstand, which was now less than ten feet away. "They're waiting."

"Last chance," he said. "We can blow this pop stand, put you back on a plane, and you could be drinking bubbly on your deck in Malibu by sunset."

"And miss all the fun we're going to have? Besides, no way am I going to miss your brother's wedding. Though we do have to stop by the boutique on the way to the theater," she reminded him as she began walking again. "And does Shelter Bay have a gift shop? Is Kara registered?"

"This is a tourist town." When her heels sank nearly to the soles of her lovely suede boots, he hoisted her out of the damp lawn again. "Every other store is a gift shop. And registered for what?"

"For wedding gifts."

"How would I know?"

"I take it that's a negative." She sighed. "Never mind. I'll think of something while I'm learning about Shelter Bay's founding."

"If you don't go to sleep first," J.T. muttered as they reached the steps.

23

Peter Fletcher stood in the shadow of a copse of trees, watching as Stephanie — he would *not* think of her as that fake name she'd taken on when she'd dared to run away from him — drove away with that hayseed farmer.

He waited until the truck was out of sight. Then, using the same set of lockpicks that had gotten him out of that ankle monitor, he opened the door to the farmhouse.

Instead of the one-of-a-kind imported Italian and French furnishings he'd paid a fortune for in their Denver home, this place had a random bunch of cheap, mismatched pieces, some obviously manufactured, others looking hand hewn. There was a woodstove against a brick wall, split logs stacked up next to it. As he imagined Stephanie lying on the rug in front of it, naked, while the hick farmer pounded into her, there was a throbbing behind his eyes, an intense, blinding pain that always came when he allowed the fury boiling in him to break its chains.

Knowing that if he trashed the place like he wanted to, he'd only give himself away, he took several deep breaths, reining in his temper.

Then continued wandering through the rooms, taking in the paperback books, the rental DVDs in their red and white envelopes, the beer and cheap wine in the refrigerator, which, like the living room furniture, didn't match any of the other appliances. The wine was domestic. He unscrewed a bottle of chardonnay, took a sniff, and grimaced.

There were four bedrooms. He went into the master, opened the closet, and saw a woman's clothes hanging there next to the farmer's. But they couldn't be Stephanie's. These were tacky, casual jeans and T-shirts — one actually a horrid bubble gum pink with cupcakes printed on it — that if she'd dared try to wear when she'd been with him, he'd have burned.

If the clothes were hers, it was obvious his wife had lost her mind. How else to explain that she'd leave him, and the wealthy, privileged life he'd given her, to shack up in this dump for some guy who mucked around in the dirt all day and undoubtedly had pig shit on his boots?

How had she managed to forget all her training? He'd taken away her romance novels because they weren't just brain candy; they gave impressionable women false expectations of relationships between men and women.

He'd skimmed through the colorful paperbacks she'd brought on their honeymoon and found that not only were the women dangerously independent; the men eventually turned out to be pushovers, even to the point of groveling for forgiveness when everyone knew that a strong husband was always in the right, so there was no need for apologies.

He'd taught her to appreciate the theater. Along with the ballet, and the opera, where he'd enjoyed showing her off in her tasteful, designer gowns. The pride he felt when other men had openly envied the way she'd behaved with deference, unlike their mouthy, opinionated, ballbuster wives, was a better high than any drug.

And now what was she doing for entertainment? Eating microwave popcorn and watching DVDs of romantic comedies?

When he first met her that night when she'd been waiting tables in the dining room at the El Tovar lodge at the Grand Canyon, he'd instantly been attracted to her shyness and lack of sophistication. Unlike the women he usually dated — rich girls who were spoiled bitches and needed to have every thing their way — the little rancher's daughter had been like a lovely bit of clay, just waiting for the right man to come along and properly mold her.

Which he'd done. It hadn't been at all difficult. All it had taken was some pretty words and she'd gone back with him to his room. He would have preferred a virgin, but since everything else about her was perfect, he'd been willing to overlook that flaw.

She'd totally surrendered to him, letting him do things to her she could never have imagined. It hadn't been the first time he'd had rough sex, but usually the women from his own world he played with knew the game, enjoyed it, but only as recreation and an escape from the more stultifying social circle they all existed in.

For those times when he didn't have an available partner, well, that was why call girls existed. But what had excited him at twenty had begun to pale over the years, becoming boring and predictable.

He'd been growing more and more frustrated, causing his attorney to write more and more checks to pay girls who hadn't lived up to their billing and had threatened him with exposure. Which was when, after writing a mid-six-figure check for an overpriced hospital bill, his father had told him if he didn't settle down with a proper wife within the year, he'd be cut off. Without a penny.

He'd been planning to travel to South America in search of a suitable candidate. Or, better yet, Asia or Indonesia, where women knew their proper place, when, after a rafting trip down the Colorado with friends, he'd walked into the lodge's dining room and there she was.

He'd tested her — not too harshly, but enough to get a sense of her limits. Then he'd pushed her further.

And still, instead of running away like a scared rabbit, the next morning she'd agreed to stay. And just like that, he'd owned her.

Until suddenly, out of the blue, she'd taken off, foolishly believing she could escape him. He'd once been behind a truck with a bumper sticker reading: *If you truly love someone, let them free. Then hunt them down and kill them.* The memory had him smiling.

Once he got her back home where she belonged, he'd give his wayward wife one last chance to behave. And if she didn't . . .

There was always the final option.

24

Kara needed a dress. Although she knew it was foolish, part of her, since she'd eloped the first time she'd gotten married, wanted a fairy-tale gown. But, having to plan a wedding in three days, and needing to stay in Shelter Bay in case there were any problems with the film festival, she was never going to have time to drive to Portland, or even Eugene, to check out a bridal shop.

So, with Charity and Maddy along for moral support, she entered the Dancing Deer Two with hopes of finding two halfway suitable dresses — one for herself and one for her mother, who'd left all her nonessential clothing behind when she'd taken off to save the world.

"After all," she told them, "it's not about the dress."

"I think we can both agree with that," Charity said dryly.

"Amen," Maddy agreed.

Since Charity had been a runaway bride, and Maddy's first marriage to that French chef had crashed and burned, Kara figured they knew what they were talking about.

But still . . .

As it turned out, she wasn't the only one who had a weakness for wedding gowns.

"We have some lovely dresses," Doris, one of the elderly twins who owned the shop, said as she led them to the rack in the back of the store that featured a limited supply of formal wear, mostly, she told them, purchased for proms. Which wasn't exactly what Kara had in mind.

Though it did have her thinking back to that night of her own prom. She'd found out that day that she was pregnant, and when Sax had arrived to take her to the prom, as Jared had asked him to do, she'd already cried herself a river.

And, although she'd tried to beg out of going, Sax had informed her that neither of them had a choice. "Jared told me to make sure you have a good time," he'd said. "Which is what we're going to do." He'd grinned that sexy bad-boy grin that had caused nearly every girl in the school to have a crush on him. Even though Kara had been madly in love with Jared, she'd been able to appreciate its effect. "Even if it kills us, I figure it's the least we can do for a guy who's off serving his country."

As he had always been able to do, he'd made her smile. Just a bit. And instead of commenting on her red-rimmed eyes, he'd assured her that she "looked a picture" in the lavender tulle vintage fifties dress she'd found at a local resale shop.

Later that night, when she'd confessed she was carrying Jared's child and burst into tears again, he'd taken her to the private spot on the beach, where they'd all hung out together, and, rattled at being stuck with a sobbing female, in a desperate attempt to make her feel better had impulsively kissed her.

Despite the kiss momentarily spiraling dangerously out of control, Kara had known that even if she'd begged him, he wouldn't have taken it any further. Because the man she'd been given a second chance with was not only even hotter than he'd been at eighteen; he was, hands down, the most honorable individual she'd ever known.

These dresses may not have been lavender tulle with three layers of starched petticoats, but they definitely screamed *prom!*

"Maybe a lovely cream suit," Doris suggested. The more restrained of the elderly twin sisters, it was more than apparent she agreed that the sequined and taffeta gowns were all wrong for an intimate late-afternoon ceremony and reception held at Lavender Hill Farm.

"Sister," Dottie said, "I suddenly had the most scintillating idea!"

They exchanged a look and in that brief glance, Kara could tell they were reading each other's minds in that sometimes spooky twin connection they had.

"It would be perfect," Doris agreed without Dottie having had to speak a word. She turned back to Kara.

"How do you feel about vintage clothing?"

"It depends. If you're talking sixties minis covered with daisies —"

"No. This would be late nineteen fifties," Dottie said.

"My prom dress was from that period. But I look back on that ruffled lavender tulle now and wonder what I was thinking."

"Oh, I'm sure you were lovely," Doris said.

"Lavender's one of my favorite colors." Dottie told them nothing Kara didn't already know. While Doris favored earth tones, Dottie had always gone for brighter colors and feminine pastels. "And lavender would have looked lovely with your auburn hair. But the dress I'm thinking of, while originally white, is a lovely ivory now. And it does have some satin tulle, but I promise, it's not at all fussy. In fact, it's feminine, fun, and very classic."

"That sounds like a possibility," Kara said carefully, exchanging a concerned glance with her friends, who appeared as under-whelmed by the prom dresses as she was.

"It would be perfect," Doris agreed.

Maddy glanced around the room. "It sounds wonderful. But I don't see it."

"That's because it's not here." Both women spoke at once.

"It's at home," Dottie said. "In the back of my closet."

"It's *your* dress?"

"Yes, and you don't have to worry, because while I certainly don't have the figure I once did, I was about your size when I married my Harold." The twins had married another set of identical twins. The elderly woman's eyes warmed in a way that suggested she was remembering her own wedding.

She wasn't alone. Although Kara had always told Sax everything, the one thing she hadn't told him was that while she knew that Jared would want her to be happy, he would have been even more pleased that she was going to be spending the rest of her life with their close friend.

And while Kara had written a letter to her

husband after falling in love with Sax, she couldn't help experiencing just a bit of what she recognized as survivor guilt. The same guilt she'd realized that Sax must have felt when he returned from being the lone survivor of his last battle in Afghanistan.

"Oh, I couldn't take your dress —"

"Don't be foolish." Dottie brushed Kara's concerns away with a wave of her plump hand. "It's just been packed away for years, doing no one any good. In fact, I was seriously thinking of giving it away to charity when we moved down here from Washington. But for some reason, although our home is much smaller, and I don't have nearly as much closet space, I held on to it."

She dimpled prettily, giving Kara a glimpse of the young woman she'd once been. "Obviously it was meant for you. You girls just stay here while Doris helps you find a dress for your mother, and I'll be back in two shakes of a lamb's tail."

She was off and out the door before Kara could say another word. After exchanging a look with the others, she shrugged and let Doris lead her over to another rack of more tailored dresses. Which would, Kara thought, suit her mother much better than tulle. In fact, she thought it said a great deal about how their relationship had changed that Shelter Bay's style icon was even allowing her daughter to choose her attire for such an important occasion.

Kara didn't know exactly how long it took for a lamb to shake its tail, but apparently Dottie had been optimistic concerning her timing. Kara chose a sheath knee-length dress with a matching bolero jacket in a lovely shade of teal, which Doris assured her would complement the natural silver her mother had mentioned her formerly ash-blond hair had turned to while she'd been traveling the world on emergency medical missions. Then Kara, Charity, and Maddy were served tea, made with herbs from Lavender Hill Farm, and the fresh-baked cookies that the women always seemed to have available for their customers.

"I'm back," Dottie said, her cheeks flushed as she raced back into the shop. "I'm sorry I took longer, but I got caught at the railroad crossing by a train that seemed to go on forever. However . . ."

She unzipped the white plastic garment bag. When she held up the gown, Kara could've sworn she felt her heart stop.

"Oh. My. God. That's Audrey Hepburn's gown. From *Funny Face.*" Only the most iconic wedding gown ever. "The one she wore dancing with Fred Astaire."

The beaded dress was sleeveless, with the bateau Sabrina neckline the actress had inspired, a tight dropped waistline, and full, tea-length skirt. If a fairy godmother had suddenly shown up and offered her the wedding dress of her dreams, this was the one Kara would've chosen.

"Well, it's not the actual dress," Dottie allowed. "But it was a very popular copy. In its time."

"It's obviously a classic," Maddy said.

"It's as fresh and modern as it looked in that movie you've only made us watch about a dozen times," Charity added.

With hands that were uncharacteristically unsteady, Kara took the hanger, held it against her chest, and stood in front of the three-way mirror, turning left and right. Okay, admittedly the starched khaki uniform she was wearing didn't help, but it still was the most perfect, most romantic gown in the world.

"Sax isn't going to know what hit him when you walk down that white satin runner," Doris said.

"Good thing Lucas is a former medic," Maddy said. "Because Sax might just keel over."

"Or, more likely, swallow his tongue," Charity said.

Feeling like Hepburn herself, despite the fact that, along with her uniform, Kara was also wearing her ugly black cop shoes, she twirled, hugging the dress tight.

"I love it." It was the understatement of the year. Decade. Century. "How much are you asking for it?" It didn't matter. She'd max out every one of her credit cards if that was what it took. After all, it wasn't as if she was ever going to get married again.

"Oh, I couldn't sell it!" When Dottie sounded honestly shocked by that idea, Kara thought she'd meant to loan it to her.

She was wrong.

"It's a gift."

"I couldn't." Even as she said it, she stroked a hand over the beaded top. "A wedding dress is so personal."

"After sixty years of marriage, I certainly don't need a dress to remind me that I married my soul mate," Dottie said. "Besides, as I said, Harold and I downsized when we moved here from Washington, and quite honestly it's been taking up a good portion of my closet I could use for clothes I actually wear."

She put a hand over Kara's. "Please, dear. Not only would you be doing me a favor clearing out space, but it would do my heart good to see you wear it when you marry your handsome groom."

Kara seldom cried. And she'd never, ever cried while in uniform. That was the first thing she'd learned at the academy from the more experienced policewomen trainers. Never let them see you sweat. And above all, never let them see you cry.

But that didn't stop her eyes from misting up as she thought how, once again, Shelter Bay had woven its own brand of magic.

25

Proving J.T.'s prediction wrong, Mary didn't fall asleep during the short play. According to the story acted out by the children, Shelter Bay had begun as a scattering of fishing shanties that had been built around a small railroad station.

Then one day, during the nineteen hundreds, a fortunate — for the town — derailment on the Oregon-California border stopped all train traffic up the coast. The fortunate part had been that a shirttail relative of Charles Crocker, one of the founders of the Central Pacific Railroad, happened to be traveling in his private Pullman car.

While he was stuck in the small town, the stationmaster had mentioned that native Indians and fishermen claimed that the springs out at Rainbow Lake held strange curative powers, so, having suffered debilitating headaches all his life, he sent his manservant out to get him some of that supposedly miraculous water.

"Ten minutes after he drank it," a little blond girl with Orphan Annie curls informed the audience, "hith headache was all gone!" The exaggerated emotion, along with her pronounced lisp, had the audience, most of whom undoubtedly knew the story well, laughing.

Knowing he'd struck gold, the mogul built a grand hotel in town and a lodge at the lake, then, using his family ties to reporters in newspapers up and down the coast, started a promotional campaign touting the hot springs as a miracle cure-all.

"I guess that proves that if you bottle it, they will come," Mary said as J.T. drove back down the hill toward Harborview Drive.

"There were a lot of snake-oil salesmen in those days," J.T. said. "But people continue to buy the stuff, so who knows? Maybe it does really work. One thing I noticed they failed to mention is that along with all the Victorians built by rich people coming here for the cure were others built as brothels for the sailors and fishermen. Cole's best friend's fiancée lives in that one." He pointed out a lovely yellow home with a wide front porch and flower boxes in the windows. "She's a vet."

"It's lovely." Mary read the sign in front. "Oh, she's a veterinarian vet. Not a military one."

"Yeah. She'll be at the wedding, but you'll probably want to keep your distance."

"Why?"

"Because she's stuck nearly everyone in town with one of her rescued dogs or cats. Word is she's as relentless as a Marine sniper when she gets you in her sights."

"I'll keep that in mind." Though, Mary considered, she wouldn't mind having some companionship other than her imaginary characters.

"Good idea. That little girl, the one with the lisp, is hers. Well, she and Gabe adopted her and her brother."

"Oh, I already like her."

"Everyone does," he said as he pulled up in front of the Dancing Deer Two boutique. "Which is how she slips beneath your radar and the next thing you know, you're at the pet store buying dog toys and kibble." He cut the engine and turned toward her. "You sure you want to do this? We've only got twenty minutes." Skepticism that she could pull off a shopping trip so quickly showed on his face.

"O ye of little faith." Not waiting for him to come around and open the door, she was out of the SUV and headed toward the store with the cheerful blue and yellow striped awnings.

A bell jingled as she opened the door, J.T. on her heels.

After entering, he turned the sign to CLOSED and twisted the lock.

The front of the boutique was empty, but knowing that she'd need some help for speed shopping, Mary followed the voices coming from the back of the store.

"Oh, wow." She stopped when she saw the sheriff standing in front of a three-way mirror holding an ivory beaded dress up against her body. "That's the wedding gown from *Funny Face.*"

Kara spun around and, on seeing J.T., spread her hands over the front of the dress, the same way she might have done if she'd been stark naked.

"J.T.! What are you doing here?"

"Apparently shopping," he said. "And I'm sorry, ladies, but I've been tasked with keeping enthusiastic fans away so Ms. Joyce can get in and out of here in time for the showing of her movie. In" — he looked down at the wide steel watch he wore on a tanned wrist — "nineteen minutes. And counting," he said with a warning look at Mary. "I hope you don't mind, but I closed your store for a few minutes."

"Oh, don't worry about that," the twins said. "We love being able to help." Doris held out her hand. "Doris Anderson," she said. "This is my sister Dottie and we're honored to have you visit our little shop."

"It's lovely," Mary said. "The window display drew me in."

"Why, thank you. We spent a great deal of time planning those. Our husbands, Harold and Henry, built those pretty platforms for the shoes for us."

"They did a great job," Mary said, hoping that the conversation would move on, since as much as she'd like to be able to chat, as J.T. had insisted on pointing out, the clock was ticking.

"You shouldn't be here," Kara complained to J.T.

"Why not?"

"Because you can't see the bride in her wedding dress before the wedding."

"I may not have ever been married, but I thought that rule was for the groom."

"Same idea," Kara said, shoving the dress into Charity's arms and placing her hands on her hips, just below her heavy gun belt. While movie actress cops often looked more like cover models than police officers, somehow, Mary considered, Kara managed to pull off both looks. With that red-gold hair and tall, slender figure, she brought to mind Nicole Kidman.

"It's only natural for your loyalty to be with your brother. But" — she wagged a finger at him — "if you dare say one word to him —"

J.T. threw up both hands as if she were about to put him under arrest. "My lips are sealed, Officer. Please don't bring out the bright lights and rubber hoses."

As Kara visibly relaxed and laughed, Mary was surprised by the J. T. Douchett she'd caught only a rare and fleeting glimpse of. Despite his feigned fear, it was obvious that he was not only more relaxed with his soon-to-be sister-in-law but genuinely fond of her.

"Just don't tell him you saw me and you can avoid arrest. Which is just as well, since I only have two jail cells. One is currently occupied by Marvin Miller, who fell off the wagon again and is sleeping off last night's drunk." She shook her head. "And a bald insurance man dressed up like a mermaid —"

"Merman," Mary heard herself saying. *Good move, idiot. Contradicting a police officer.* Even in Ireland, you didn't talk back to the Garda.

"Well, whatever you call him, I had to take

him in on a drunk and disorderly after he attacked another mer*man* during an argument over which of them was actually the true prince regent to the selkie queen."

She dragged a hand through her bright hair. "His hearing is this afternoon, during which time he'll probably be let go after he apologizes to the court and pays for the chairs he broke at the Stewed Clam and the hospital bill for the other alleged prince, who had to get stitches for the cut on his forehead."

"I'm sorry," Mary said.

"Why? You didn't do anything."

"They're only here in Shelter Bay because of me."

"Oh, don't worry about it. We have our own share of crazies and the tourist season brings even more. Don't even get me talking about the people every year who have to be rescued after they get the great idea that it'd be cool to go swimming with our resident whales.

"And, to be perfectly honest, after being a cop in the city, stuff like this makes my job more interesting than handing out citations for expired tags or investigating bashed mailboxes."

She turned back to J.T. "Now. You — go away."

"Sorry. But you told me to stick to Ms. Joyce like a barnacle. Which is what I'm doing."

"I didn't put it that way," Kara assured Mary. "But I did tell him to stay with you. However," she said to J.T., "I believe I'm capable of handling things. So, why don't you grab yourself some cookies and go outside and guard the door while Ms. Joyce finds the clothes she needs?" She made a shooing gesture with her hand.

Looking like a man who'd just gotten a last-minute reprieve from the electric chair, J.T. didn't hesitate to take her advice and leave.

"That's very good," Mary said.

"I've known him forever," Kara said with a quick grin. "It helps. Especially since he had a crush on me when he was in middle school. Not that either of us ever mentions it."

"I won't say a word. And the name, by the way, is Mary." She took in the gown the other woman was holding. "That truly is a beautiful dress and you're going to look beyond gorgeous in it."

After telling her a shortened version of how it belonged to one of the two owners of the boutique, who had rushed off and were back with cookies for their movie-star guest, Kara introduced the women with her.

"You probably get tired of hearing this," Mary told Maddy, "but I am a major fan girl."

"Thank you. That's lovely to hear," the celebrity chef said. "Especially since I'm a huge fan of your work."

"Thank *you.*" Mary felt a burst of pride that someone whose shows she never missed watching on TV enjoyed her movies. She smiled at the other woman. "Hi."

"Hi yourself. I'm Charity Tiernan."

"The vet J.T. told me about. Who's engaged to his brother's best friend."

"That would be me," Charity said. "And I'll bet he also warned you to stay away from me if you didn't want a dog."

"Or a cat," Mary said.

Charity laughed. "I can be a little driven. But you can relax, because I never push any animal on anyone who doesn't really want one. And wouldn't be a good fit with it." She tilted her head and studied Mary. "How do you work?"

"Excuse me?"

"I mean, do you go to a studio all day? Or do you mostly write at home?"

"At home, but —"

"Enough," Kara said on a rich laugh. "Give Mary a break. I'm sure there are lots of dogs in Los Angeles that need adopting. But she's got to get to her next event and we're holding her up. . . . Just tell Dottie and Doris what you're looking for, and they'll have you fixed up in no time."

"In two shakes of a lamb's tail," Doris said.

"That's true," Charity said. "I've never been much for shopping, but they're wonders at finding me exactly the right thing."

"Well, I need some more casual clothes to wear during the day. And something to wear to the wedding," Mary told them. Then, as they began rifling through the racks, she said to Kara, "If you're sure you don't mind J.T. inviting me."

"Are you kidding? Everyone will be so excited. Including my mother, who told me she watched *Siren Song* in Japanese when they were there helping after the tsunami."

"J.T. told me a bit about your mom's relief work. That's quite a second career."

"Isn't it? I worry about her, of course, but she's so thrilled to be having this grand adventure at this point in her life, I also can't help being excited for her."

Doris and Dottie lived up to their promise. In less than five minutes, they had a stack of shoes, bags, and jewelry on the counter and clothes hanging on the door of one of the dressing rooms. In another ten minutes, Mary was out the door, having exchanged her Leon-selected parade outfit for a pair of jeans, a red sweater, and red canvas sneakers.

"Done," she said.

J.T. swept a glance over her, from the top of her head, which, since it had begun sprinkling again, she'd covered in a baseball cap — which had the town's name above the whale logo and, below that, *A Whale of a Town* — down to her feet.

"Except for the touristy hat, you look a lot more like a native than you did a few minutes ago."

"I'm going to take that as a compliment."

"Which is how I meant it. From the looks of all those bags, you've probably equaled that store's yearly sales. I don't think I've ever met a woman who could snag so much stuff in ten minutes."

"They had a lot of great stuff. And know their customers."

"You do realize you're now going to have to buy another suitcase."

"Easier to just FedEx the stuff back to California." She grinned and handed over the bags for him to put in the back of the SUV. "I told you I'm a champion hunter-shopper. And not only did I bag this outfit

— I scored a lot of other terrific ones, as well. Including a dress to wear to the wedding, a lovely one-of-a-kind blown-glass piece of a bride and groom from this little gift nook they have at the back of the boutique, and running shoes to wear on the beach tomorrow morning."

He'd just closed the back of the SUV and climbed into the driver's seat. "What are you talking about?"

"Apparently they've been buying sea glass jewelry from a California designer who's expanded into blown glass, so since the jewelry sells so well, they decided to stock a few of her other pieces, one of which was perfect for a wedding present."

"I wasn't talking about the wedding present. I was referring to the running shoes."

"Oh, them. I run on the beach every morning in Malibu."

"Don't look now, sweetheart, but this isn't Malibu."

"Aw." She fluttered her lashes at him. "I knew I'd wear you down eventually. But I never expected to get to the romantic point where you'd be calling me sweetheart this quickly."

He looked up at the sunroof as if garnering strength. But learning to act for the big screen, where everything is magnified, had taught her nuances. Enough that she could see the faint smile trying to break free at the corners of his mouth.

"A beach is a beach," she said when he didn't respond to that teasing statement. "I like to run. And so, apparently, do you. So, I figured we could get out early, before everyone's up and about, get a few miles in, have breakfast; then I'll still have plenty of time to get to the first screening."

"What if it's raining?" He pulled into traffic, managing to avoid a young woman on roller skates, inexplicably turning circles in the middle of the two-lane street.

"Got that covered. Literally, with a slicker in one of those bags. So you're going to have to come up with a better reason to get out of it." She sobered a bit when she realized that for some reason he really seemed against the idea. Surely he didn't seriously believe she was in danger. "If you're worrying about protecting me —"

"That's not it. What I'm concerned about is . . . Oh, hell. Just forget it."

He pulled up in front of the theater, where a long line snaked down the sidewalk and around the corner. "Seems it's time for your close-up."

The smile was gone. And although the sky

had turned the color of tarnished silver, he'd stuck on those damn sunglasses again, keeping her from seeing his eyes.

She wanted to ask him what his problem was. But then people spotted her and began calling out her name, so, straightening her shoulders, she put on her best movie-star smile.

Showtime.

26

The clouds, which had held off until after the parade, began weeping again as Sax drove down the winding drive lined with fir trees from which gray moss hung like ghostly veils. As happy as he was that Kara had agreed to marry him — even knowing that they were perfect together and that "till death do we part" line in the vows didn't even begin to cover how long he intended to stay with her — when he'd awakened this morning, he'd realized there was something he still needed to do.

He pulled up outside a high iron gate that had been pitted and rusted by years of Pacific storms and rainy weather. The last time he'd been here to Sea View Cemetery was when he'd first gotten home. At the time his ghosts had accompanied him. Although he was relieved — for his sake and theirs — that they'd moved on to wherever ghosts go in the afterlife, at the moment he could've used some backup from his former battle teammates.

He sat in the Camaro his father had kept up for him while he'd been away for a long time, hands draped over the steering wheel, listening to Billie Holiday's "Willow Weep for Me." The blues singer's soulful tones brought to mind small, smoky rooms and half-empty whiskey glasses. It also reminded him how much his life had changed since Kara and Trey had enriched it.

Which, occasionally and unexpectedly, would cause a sharp stab of guilt he knew, on an intellectual level, his friend would tell him was misplaced.

He grabbed a bag from the front seat. "Might as well get it over with."

The tall gate creaked when he pushed it open, causing some birds in the branches of a century-old western hemlock to take to the leaden sky in a wild flurry of wings. The front rows of rounded headstones dated back to when the town was first founded, many of the dates worn away by the salt air and age.

Fog curled around his boots and the damp earth squished beneath his feet as he walked past a stone angel who'd lost a wing to a tree downed by the great Columbus Day storm of 1962. Because he'd been young and crazy, and only Cole may have been bucking for sainthood, bittersweet memories of coming to the cemetery to get drunk with the guys flashed through his mind. Including the night shortly before he'd taken off to the Marines, when Jared had belted out a drunken version of Willie Nelson's "Angel Flying Too Close to the Ground."

A weeping willow arched graceful green branches over the grave he'd come here today to visit. Which, he thought, made the Billie Holiday song that had come onto the jazz station just as he'd arrived at the cemetery both appropriate and ironic.

There was a small display of wildflowers, their petals damped by the misty rain, next to the granite stone. Although he couldn't name the flowers, since Jared's parents had left Shelter Bay after his death, he suspected they'd been left by Kara. Proving that once again they were on the same wavelength. Sax had never had any problem with her having loved another man so deeply. On the contrary, her ability to give her heart so fully and so freely was one of the reasons he'd fallen for her so many years ago.

Sax had no problem with Jared having been her first great love. Because she'd chosen him to be her last.

Unlike many of the earlier graves, which

bore elaborate epitaphs for the departed, the gray stone had merely been carved with his name, Jared Conway, the dates of his birth and death, and beneath that the words *Semper Fidelis* — "always faithful."

Which Sax, who may have been a Navy SEAL, not a Marine, had tried his best to be.

He took a deep breath. In the distance, the sea, which had given the cemetery its name, was draped in a thick blanket of fog.

"Kara's pregnant, Jare." He thought about his ghosts and how they'd made vague references to life after death. "But I guess you know that. Although it wasn't easy, since you're a really tough act to follow, I finally managed to talk her into marrying me."

Even now, with his child growing inside her, and her son, whom he couldn't love more if he'd been Trey's natural father, Sax couldn't quite believe his luck. Which, he reminded himself, was possible only because of this man's very bad luck to have survived multiple deployments, only to be killed when, as a cop, he'd responded to a domestic abuse call that had gone south.

He pressed his fingers against his eyes. Hard. Took another breath. Damn. Although he'd practiced what he was going to say, it was proving more difficult than he'd ever imagined.

"It's not that she doesn't still love you." He forced himself to speak past the lump in his throat, as Jared's words, the day he'd climbed onto that bus headed for basic training, echoed from beyond the grave. *Take good care of my girl while I'm gone, Douchett.*

And then him calling from Oceanside, asking him to take her to their senior prom. *Make sure she has a good time. We can't have her sitting around like a wall-flower, feeling sorry for herself.*

Which he'd tried his best to do, which hadn't been easy, since when he'd arrived to pick her up for that prom, her eyes had been red-rimmed from crying when the home pregnancy test she'd taken that morning had proved positive.

Sax wondered now if Jared knew about the impulsive kiss they'd shared on Moonshell Beach later that night. When she'd sobbed in his arms and, in a misguided attempt to make her feel better, he'd kissed her. And she'd kissed him back, and sealed his fate forever.

Not that he would've done anything about it. Because although he'd discovered that night that forbidden fruit really was the sweetest, no way would he betray a pal.

"She'll always love you, and hey, I'm okay with that. It's just that, believe it or not, she loves me now. And I want you to know that I'm going to continue to work every day to be worthy of that love.

"And that as honestly happy as I am that we're going to have a baby, and we're both going to make sure that Trey never forgets his father, and that you'll always be his hero, I'm going to do my damnedest to make sure I'm a good dad. Because he may not be son of my blood, but" — Sax put his hand on his chest — "he's the son of my heart.

"I hope you also know that I never tried to take advantage of the trust you put in me. I didn't mean to fall in love with Kara. But I did." Major understatement there, but he figured that if Jared, wherever he was, could actually hear him, he'd also know how hard and how deep his friend had fallen. "Though if you'd lived, I would've kept my mouth shut and this marriage wouldn't be happening.

"But you didn't, and now it is, and I want you to know that you don't have to worry about her. Because I swear it's going to work out. We can make each other, and our kids, happy."

He opened the bag, took out one of the bottles of Budweiser Jared had always brought out here when it was his turn to score the alcohol, unscrewed the cap, and poured the beer on the ground in front of the stone, next to Kara's pretty flowers. Then opened a second bottle and stood there drinking while the surf roared in the distance and birds sang in the trees overhead.

As he drank, Sax felt the nagging little guilt he'd been feeling since Kara told him about the pregnancy drift away.

"*Semper Fi,* Jare."

That said, Sax finally left the last of the past behind him and walked back through the iron gate toward his future with the incredible woman he loved.

27

Since the local video store hadn't carried the DVD, J.T. hadn't been able to watch *Lady of the Lake,* the first movie Mary had appeared in, but viewing it while sitting next to her in the Orcas Theater, he could see the beauty she would grow up to be.

Her expressive eyes had looked huge in her much thinner Irish milkmaid's face. Although she hadn't seemed as comfortable with her body as she was now, she was as graceful as a ballerina and there was a sweet, small-town innocence about her that reminded J.T. a bit of Kara, when his brother's fiancée had been sixteen.

It was no wonder she'd become a star. Her face was heartbreakingly expressive, the camera flat-out loved her, and although J.T. remembered that the teenage girl had appeared on only a few pages, having read the book years ago, he realized why either the director or writer, or more likely both, would've decided to expand her part.

J.T. also knew that if he'd grown up in Castlelough, or she in Shelter Bay, he would have fallen in love with Mary Joyce.

The movie was longer than most, running a full two and a half hours, but as much as he'd dreaded this duty, he wasn't finding sitting next to her in the darkened theater any hardship.

When the heroine, Shannon McGuire, played by Laura Gideon, one of the hottest actresses on the planet ten years ago, pulled a tarp over the baby sea creature, hiding it from the team of ruthless hunters determined to trap it for scientific examination, Mary unconsciously reached out for his hand. Her skin was soft as silk and brought up unbidden thoughts, yet again, of what that delicate, long-fingered hand would feel like on his body.

He heard her sniffle a bit as the heroine began rowing toward the island of Inisfree, determined to save the small green infant its brave mother, the mythical Lady of the Lake, had died protecting.

When the lights came back on again, she reclaimed her hand, reached into her bag, took out a tissue, and dabbed at her moist eyes.

"It's foolish," she murmured. "I know that

story by heart, but every time I see the film, it makes me cry."

"It's not foolish. It's an emotional story. There's no shame in being affected by it."

"Still, I'm supposed to be the professional."

"You wouldn't be such a good actress if you didn't absorb the feelings of the characters. Sort of like a sin-eater."

The theater professor, whose name J.T. hadn't bothered to try to remember, was now up on the stage going into a long-winded introduction, which began, unsurprisingly, with his own biography. Because, hey, this festival was all about him, right?

But neither J.T. nor Mary was paying that much attention. Instead, she'd cocked that dark head again, and was giving J.T. another of those long silent perusals.

"I suppose it is a bit like that," she agreed.

Then, as she heard her name called, she stood up. "Wish me luck."

"You don't need it. But . . ." He gave her a thumbs-up. And touched his fingers to the back of her hand in a way that had those expressive eyes widening. Revealing that she'd felt that spark, too.

She went up on the stage, sitting alone on the stool, answering questions from the audience, many of whom turned out to be theater students at the local community college.

"Do you have any regrets about this film going down in your filmology as your acting debut?" one young man with a goatee asked.

"Regrets?" She looked puzzled. "*Lady of the Lake* is a beautiful story, its script written with a deft and talented hand, and filmed with the most talented cast, all of whom were so helpful to a neophyte actress. Both the tale of the lady and the cinematography were also obvious love letters to my home country. Indeed, my own town — which would be a sister city to this one — where the lady is reputed to dwell."

Another earnest young woman dressed all in black popped out of her seat. "Surely you don't believe that? About the lady?"

"Surely I do," Mary said mildly. And turned back to the man who'd been interrupted. "Why would you believe I'd have any regrets?"

"Well, it's a horror movie." The scorn in his voice was obvious even to J.T., who knew nothing about the movie business.

"Millions of people are entertained by being frightened. Just as others prefer comedies or thrillers or stories about children growing up in a boarding school for witches. That's the lovely thing about films. There's something for everyone."

"Then you agree that *Lady of the Lake* is a horror film?"

"Some might see it that way," Mary allowed. "But they'd be wrong. It doesn't take a degree in cinema to understand that the story about the creature in a fanciful city beneath the water is an allegory about prejudice, the overreach of science, and the paranoia that can run rampant in small isolated villages, such as Castlelough, Ireland. Or, perhaps," she added with that warm smile he'd come to recognize as her professional one, "even Shelter Bay, Oregon."

"Yet," the professor, who apparently felt the need to have the spotlight turn back onto him, pointed out, "you can't deny that it's a very dark and negative ending."

"But I can. Is that how you see it?" she asked, with what sounded like genuine surprise.

"It's obvious that the scientists, who already killed the baby creature's mother, are not going to give up."

"Ah." She nodded, appearing to give the statement serious consideration. "That would be your view. And you're not alone in your belief. Especially since Quinn Gallagher, the screenwriter, purposefully left the ending ambiguous.

"But, as an optimist myself, after all the sadness and evil the scientists brought upon the creature and the town, because Shannon McGuire, who was quite a formidable person in her own right, teamed up with the wee creature, I view the ending as a message of hope." Her smile confirmed her words.

More hands shot up at that.

For the next hour, Mary answered questions and shared anecdotes, holding the audience in the palm of her hand. And if there'd been any people in the theater who hadn't been fans when the lights had first gone down, J.T. knew they'd been converted.

Had Bodhi not declared the time allotted for her question-and-answer period over, claiming that they needed to get ready for the showing of the first entry film in an hour, they probably would've kept her there forever.

As she left the theater, programs were thrust at her to autograph. J.T. was not surprised when she didn't refuse a single request.

It was only when they were in the SUV, driving back to the inn, where he'd intended to drop her off to chill out until it was time to leave for yet another party she was scheduled to be the guest of honor at this evening — this one for people who'd sprung for fifty bucks a ticket with funds going to local youth programs — that she leaned her head against the back of the seat and let out a long, deep, and weary-sounding breath.

"Would you do me a favor?" she asked.

"What kind of favor?"

She turned her head and opened her eyes. In her gaze he saw more amusement than frustration. "You're a cautious one, aren't you, J.T.?"

"You learn to be if you want to keep yourself, and your men, alive."

"That makes sense. But I'm not dangerous."

"Now, there's where you're wrong."

Her full lips curved. Just a little. "I could be offended. But I'm taking that as another compliment. Two in just a few hours." She nodded and seemed to regain a bit of the energy he'd watched drain away after they'd left the theater. "I'm making progress."

Which was exactly what he was afraid of.

"What favor?" he asked again.

"Could we go somewhere? Away from everyone, just for a while. And not to the inn," she said before he could point out that was where they were headed. "Somewhere outside. Where I can clear my head."

He thought a minute. "How do you feel about sailing?"

She sat up straighter. "You have a sailboat?"

"I don't. But Sax does." The only stoplight in town turned red. "We used to sail a lot growing up."

"You'd think sailing would be one of our most popular sports," she said. "Considering that Ireland is an island. But it's not. And I've never been."

It was ironic that just a few days ago he'd been thinking that he should take it up again, and now, because of her, he was.

"Well, then." Feeling more lighthearted than he had in a very long time, J.T. reached across the console between them and skimmed a finger down the slope of her nose. "That's something we'll have to rectify."

28

Boats of all sizes bobbed on the glassy waters of Shelter Bay. The fact that most of the slips were filled demonstrated the town's inseparable bond with the sea. While Mary might not have any personal experience with sailing, her eyes drank in the rows of gleaming white boats as they rested like pearls on blue satin.

J.T. had taken her hand, as if it were the most natural thing in the world to do, and surprisingly it felt that way as he led her down the bobbing wooden dock, stopping in front of a boat that, to her unschooled eye, appeared to be about twenty-eight feet long. It certainly wasn't the largest or fanciest boat in the marina. It was, however, beautiful, with sleek, graceful lines, and a dark blue hull seeming to reflect the water.

The deck gleamed with a varnished sheen, making her relieved she was wearing rubber-soled shoes instead of the high-heel boots she'd worn for the parade. It would be a crime to mar the perfection Sax Douchett had painstakingly achieved.

"I know little to nothing about boats," she admitted. "But it's beautiful."

"*She.* Boats are always feminine. This sloop especially."

Which explained the name KARA written in white block letters on the back.

"Don't you want to know why?" he asked.

From the wicked glint in his eyes, she knew she was being put on, but since it felt so good to escape from what had begun to feel like a never-ending day, she played along.

"A writer's always open to learning new things, since you never know when you'll need an obscure fact or bit of trivia. So why would boats, your brother's in particular, be named for females?" she asked.

"Because she's trim, responds well to a man's touch, and if the wind is favorable, she'll give a guy a helluva good ride."

"You really are terrible." The laughter in her voice ruined any attempt at a stern tone. "Now, do you intend to stand here for the rest of the day making more sexist jokes, or will you be taking me for that sail you promised?"

"Aye, aye, Captain Bligh." He stepped

onto the gleaming deck, then extended a hand to invite her aboard. The boat bobbed lightly on the soft swells of the bay.

Before casting off, he gave her a quick tour. Mary found the boat — sloop, she corrected herself — surprisingly roomy. The living area below the deck was tidy, utilitarian, but not nearly as cramped as she'd imagined it would be.

"This kitchen is larger than the one I had in my first flat in Dublin," she said.

"Same with me and my first place in California. And it's a galley."

"Thank you. I'd best learn that, since I believe my next selkie story is going to partially take place on a boat." She hadn't even dared bring that idea up to Aaron Pressler yet, knowing he wouldn't leap at the premise.

"You'll have to tell me about it," he said, as they went back up the short ladder to the outside.

"I don't usually talk about my work in the thinking stages. But since you're the only person I know who knows about boats, then perhaps I will pick your brain. If you don't mind."

"Sweetheart, the mood I'm in right now, you can have any part of me your heart desires."

The glint was back in his eyes, making him appear an entirely different man from the one who'd scowled at her just yesterday at the airport. Layers, she thought. This former Marine was turning out to be like a bloody onion. And as changeable as he was proving to be, didn't that make him even more interesting?

"Oh," he said, as he prepared to cast off, "another thing you'll need to know, while we're dealing with jargon, is sailors never go to the bathroom."

"Surely that must be very uncomfortable for them."

He rolled his eyes. "And you accuse me of bad jokes. On a boat, a bathroom is called a head."

"Why would it be called that? It seems a silly name."

"Not really. The word is a maritime term meaning toward the bow — front — of the ship. Which is also where the figurehead was. There'd be a special deck below sailors would climb down to. It had a grate over it, so they could, uh, relieve themselves into the sea, which kept the boat clean, and was more sanitary because the waves hitting the bow would also keep it washed clean."

"Well, isn't that one more reason to be glad I didn't live in olden times? And as interesting as it is, for the story I'm thinking of telling, I won't be needing it."

"Even so, you never know when you're going to be on a quiz show," he said. "That could well be the one bit of trivia that someday wins you a million dollars."

"And wouldn't that be lovely?" Though she imagined she'd win the lottery, which she'd never in her life entered, before she'd be appearing on a quiz show.

"Here." He handed her a padded life vest.

Although it wasn't the most flattering piece of clothing she'd ever worn, since she knew that the unique patterns on Aran sweaters were originally designed so people would be able to recognize drowned Irish fishermen, Mary didn't argue.

She loved watching him move around the deck with a lithe, masculine grace that couldn't be learned.

"Could I help?"

"Although being the youngest of three brothers put me pretty much on the bottom of the sailing totem pole, this is all about giving you a chance to relax before you have to jump back into public mode tonight," he reminded her. "So, why don't you just lean back, enjoy the ride, and tell me about the selkie and the sailor?"

"He wasn't a sailor," she said, tapping

down a twinge of anxiety as they sailed beneath the arched iron bridge, headed out toward sea. "But a fisherman."

Although she'd lived on the coast for most of her life, she'd always found it too wild and dangerous to want to do anything but walk along the beach or look down at the crashing waves from the top of the cliff at the edge of the Joyce family farm.

Yet now, watching the skill with which J.T. handled the fluttering white canvas sails, she found herself feeling safe enough that the nerves that had been sparking beneath her skin began to relax.

She leaned back against the sea blue seat cushions as the sloop picked up speed, skimming over the water in a way that made her feel as if they were flying.

"Since you've watched my movies, you'd know that seals have the ability to take on human form."

"Yeah, I got that. Though I doubt any of them look as good as you when they do."

She was used to men paying her compliments. They came easily and often, and, she'd found, it was difficult to value something so common.

Yet, to hear those words from this man, who'd originally seemed determined to dislike her on sight, caused a little rush of pleasure.

"Well, in this story, which I'm considering putting on film, although selkies need to live near the sea, if they actually go back into it, they revert to being seals and lose the ability to ever take on human form again."

"That's one hell of an internal conflict," he said. When she looked surprised, he said, "Hey, even history majors have to take a lit class or two. I know the basic elements of story structure."

Another surprise, and yet one more thing they had in common. She wondered if he was keeping track.

"Well, as it happens, there was a fisherman who'd lived many years all alone. One day he went out to sea, far beyond the breakers, and came back with a wife. Now, being a coastal village, every one knew of someone who'd either met a selkie or who probably was one, so although people recognized, at first sight, that she was one of the seal people, she was a good wife and a good neighbor, even though she was shy and didn't speak more than need be when she went to the market. Nor did she ever step foot in the church where most gathered on Sundays. Nor go to the pub to mingle with people.

"But those lapses are neither here nor there, because the people could tell that the fisherman was happier than he'd ever been, which led them to believe that the quiet, dark woman was a good wife. So, since they had kind feelings toward the fisherman, who always shared some of his catch with those in need before taking the fish to the monger, no one ever mentioned anything about her being a seal to the fisherman. And thus she came to be accepted by one and all."

"A generous village, seeming without prejudice."

"Aye, that it was. Yet as I said, she was not the first person in the village to have come from the sea. And undoubtedly would not be the last."

Comfortable in the telling of the story that had been asking to be told in her mind for some time, Mary didn't notice that she'd slipped into the lexicon of her homeland, as she often would do when tired, excited, or relaxed, which, since coming to America, was a rare thing.

"Well, as was his habit, the fisherman would often take his dory out to sea for several days, which saddened and worried his wife. Some who saw her walking alone on the cliff, looking out toward the sea, swore they could hear her calling to him in a strange, haunting language no human had ever heard.

"As is the way of nature, spring gave way to summer, which, in turn, became fall. The days grew shorter and nightfall would come sooner, and the seas and winds grew more wild, anticipating the long dark months of winter.

"The poor selkie was beside herself with fear. Those who'd pass their whitewashed cottage with the seashell trim on their way to the pub in the evening often heard her wailing as if Cromwell himself had driven a sword deep into her heart.

"But as much as he loved his wife, and did not wish to bring worry down upon her lovely shoulders, the fisherman assured her that he'd been fishing in these winter waters since he was a boy. Besides, he told her, as they lay in their bed, warmed by the glow of the peat fire, didn't he know the sky and the sea with the same familiarity he knew every curve of her body, every inch of her smooth, fragrant skin? He'd return, he promised as he kissed away the tears that glistened like sea foam on her cheeks."

"I don't see this ending well," J.T. said.

"Now, who'd be telling this tale?" she asked as they raced like the wind along the shoreline, past the lighthouse. "You're getting ahead of my story."

"And a fine one it is." He waved a hand. "Carry on."

"Tragically, perhaps because his mind was too much on his wife, or perhaps it was just the whims of fate, on that sad day, the fisherman misread the water and sky he'd come to know so well. The wind rose, turning the autumn waves rough and choppy.

"But still he was not concerned. Because he'd promised his wife he'd return home. And being an honorable man, he'd never, ever broken a vow to man nor woman. So he wasn't going to begin with his beloved bride.

"Even when the fog blew in, surrounding the dory, the fisherman wasn't afraid. A man could not fish off the Irish coast without knowing his way through fog. And though he might not be able to see six inches in front of his hand, didn't he still have his ears? All he had to do was listen and the gong on the buoy would lead him home.

"But the wind and the sea had other plans for the fisherman. The waves rose higher, until his dory was bobbing on the sea like a cork. The wind, blowing with a furious temper, ripped down his heavy sail, and broke the mast into splinters."

A thought suddenly occurred to Mary,

having her glance up at the *Kara*'s tall mast.

"Don't worry," J.T. assured her. "Unlike the fisherman in your story, I'm not one to tempt Mother Nature."

"I'm glad to hear that." Despite the breeze that was still blowing in over the water, J.T. was lowering the sail and switching to an engine. "I don't want to be distracted," he answered her question before she could ask. "So, I thought we'd drop anchor for a while. That way I can pay full attention."

He steered the gleaming white boat into a small cove carved into a cliff, cut the engine, then lowered the anchor over the side.

"Okay," he said, sitting down on a padded seat across from her and stretching out his legs. "You have my full attention."

It occurred to Mary that even in meetings with people who were considering whether to pay her a great deal of money, since she'd left Ireland, she hadn't had anyone as riveted to one of her stories as J.T. appeared to be.

"So," she continued, "for hours, as he drifted without his sail on the tides, the wind and the sea and the fisherman battled. Every time the elements seemed to be winning, the fisherman, who was as wily as he was stubborn, would outsmart his adversaries.

"Until finally, he was blown farther and farther out into the wild, windswept sea, and snow and ice began pelting him like stones, and his boat began to fill with icy water that chilled both his bones and his heart.

"Which was when the fisherman knew that his stubborn pride had finally gotten the best of him. He would not be returning home to his wife that night. Nor would he ever see her beautiful face again.

"So, with a heavy heart, he put his hands to his mouth and called out to her, shouting to be heard over the wail of the wind and the roar of the wicked sea, telling her that she was the only woman he'd ever loved. The only woman he *would* ever love. And he'd continue to love her to his death. And beyond.

"But even as his words left his mouth, they were whipped away by the cold, cruel wind, and the fisherman feared she'd never be able to hear them.

"His heart broken, he lay down on the bottom of the boat and prepared to die as snow fell from the midnight dark sky and began to cover him like a cold white blanket."

Mary bit her lip and blinked away the tears burning at the backs of her eyes.

Whenever she thought of this tale, it made her cry. Which was why she was certain that audiences would be as moved by the fate of the fisherman and his selkie wife as she was.

Unfortunately, the one thing she'd learned since moving to America was that the powers that ruled in Hollywood wanted more conflict than a mere man against the elements, which was, to her mind, the most basic of all. And while, because her films made money, they might be able to overlook a lack of car chases or explosions, when it came to romances, as she knew this love story would be marketed as, they wanted a hearts and flowers "happily ever after" ending tied up with a pretty pink satin bow.

She sighed and shook off her dilemma, deciding not to ruin a perfect afternoon borrowing trouble.

"What the fisherman had no way of knowing was that his words, given wings by the power of his emotions, and his love, did indeed carry across the sea, to the cliff where his wife was pacing, drenched to the skin in the icy rain that was slashing down like needles from the churning dark clouds overhead.

"Lifting her wet and heavy black skirts, she raced down the stone steps as fast as her feet would carry her. When she reached the rocky beach, she tore off her confining human clothing, dove headfirst into the waves, and swam out to sea to save her husband.

"She called as she swam, and in the same manner his words had reached her over the scream of the wind, the fisherman heard her and jumped up just as she reached the dory. He caught her as she leaped over the railing into his arms.

"Well, as you can imagine, they held each other tight, and there was much crying and kissing, and together they lay back down in the bottom of the boat and made the sweetest love they'd ever made together during all the days and nights of their marriage."

"So she saved him?" J.T. asked, clearly into the story by now.

"In her way," Mary said. "Without a sail, the boat continued to drift, and when the tide changed, as it always has, since the beginning of time, it drifted back onto the shoals. Where, the next morning, the villagers found the fisherman, sound asleep on the bottom of the boat, a seal covering him like a blanket, with her own blanket of white snow on her back."

"He was alive." J.T. moved next to her on the canvas seat. "But she had to return to the sea?"

"Aye. But at least, for that time they had had together, they shared a grand love. Which is, after all, more than many of us are granted in one lifetime."

"I guess I can't argue that. But you Irish do have a tendency for the dark and melodramatic."

Since she'd heard that more times than she cared to count, rather than take it as a criticism, she laughed.

"Aye, doesn't it seem that we do? But that comes from the ancient days going back two thousand years, when, in the Gaelic times, the ability to tell a rousing tale entitled a man to land and livestock, which, since cows were used as currency, could make him wealthy. He'd also be invited to sit at the high table with kings and noblemen, and even, in the most proficient cases, was given a voice on their councils.

"In those days, stories were always told, not written down as they might be now, and the master storyteller to the court must be ready to recite any tale which might be requested by his lord or lady to entertain the company at feasts and clan assemblies.

"My father, who was a seanachie, which would be an Irish storyteller, always said that the best tales included battles, forays, courtships, elopements, pursuits, banishment, tragedies, magic, wonders, and visions."

"From your films, it sounds as if you've followed in his footsteps."

"And won't I be taking that as another compliment, since he was known as one of the best, if not *the* best seanachie in all the country?

"But I do believe that it's why, rather than choose novels, as my brother-in-law has done, I prefer film. An oral storyteller can no longer earn a living by spinning tales for the court, or wandering from village to town, entertaining at market fairs. But film, while a visual medium, still, at least in my movies, depends on dialogue. So, in that way, I like to believe I'm doing my part to keep the oral tradition alive."

"You've definitely done that. In spades. You're also reaching a much wider audience than those old guys ever could have dreamed of."

The compliment, simply spoken, carried even more weight given that he hadn't shown any inclination to hand those out all that often.

As they exchanged smiles, Mary, who'd initially found him rude, edging toward unbearable, was unexpectedly, utterly charmed.

When his gaze moved down her face, sensually lingering at her lips before returning to her eyes, she had the impossible, inexplicable feeling that she'd known this man all her life.

As they sat there, side to side, thighs touching, heady anticipation sang in her veins.

Time froze. It could have been a moment.

An hour.

An eternity.

Mary's breath caught, then shuddered out as she watched. And waited.

Finally, as if he'd read her unruly mind, J.T. drew her into his arms.

29

He took her mouth with the easy confidence of a man who'd kissed more women than he could count. He didn't rush. His lips somehow managed to be both firm and soft at the same time. They plucked at hers, tasting at their leisure, lingering, wrapping her in gauzy layers of sensation.

Mary was no child. And, although she might not have grown up with the sexual freedom that girls in America possessed, neither was she innocent. She'd certainly been kissed before, beginning with the time, when she'd been fourteen, that Jack Kelly, who'd been delivering hay for his da, had caught her in the milking barn.

For the next two years, she'd had a wild schoolgirl crush on him, which had ended when he'd asked another girl to the May dance because she wasn't ready to have sex with him. But Shannon Fitzgerald, whom he'd taken instead, had been.

Given that he'd not only never been faithful, but left poor Shannon — whom he'd been forced to marry when she'd gotten pregnant that same spring — with four children for whom he'd provided no support, Mary knew she'd gotten the better of the bargain.

After that less than auspicious introduction to romance, other boys had followed Jack, and although Mary had welcomed their kisses with varying degrees of enthusiasm, none, not one in all those intervening years, had ever caused her mind to empty.

She should stop him, Mary told herself.

And she would.

Soon.

Which was difficult with the lovely golden light flowing through her veins and the mists clouding her mind.

His hands were wandering through her hair as if they had every right to be there. Fascinated, yet a tad frightened by the restrained passion in the depths of his steely eyes, Mary wanted to keep hers open. But when his teeth began nibbling on the exquisitely tender flesh at the inside of her bottom lip, her eyelids fluttered shut.

Seductive images floated behind her closed eyes, causing her blood to hum and her body to ache.

When that wickedly clever tongue traced a slow, lazy circle around her parched lips, she was hit by a rush of need so strong that had she not already been sitting down, she would have gone weak at the knees.

On the heels of that jolt came another thought crashing through her swimming senses — the unwelcome and totally unexpected realization that she was afraid.

Never had any man been able to bring her to the precipice with a single kiss.

He was drawing out every ounce of her will with his mouth alone. Without taking his hands from her hair, he was somehow creating havoc in every atom of her body.

Because she knew this was getting too dangerous, too fast, she managed, with effort, to force her eyes open.

Belatedly realizing that her hands were splayed across his chest — how had they gotten there? — she pushed against him.

And before she could utter a single word of protest, he released her mouth and his hands left her hair.

She was breathless when they drew apart. Breathless, needy, and, yes, frightened. Though not of J. T. Douchett. But of the desperate way he could make her feel.

Because she was still too giddy to think straight, she fell back on what she'd experienced in the past, ever since *Siren Song* had been released.

"I'm not that selkie on the screen."

"What?" She watched as ice flowed over the passion that had, only a moment before, been threatening to set her flesh on fire. "What the hell makes you believe I thought you were?"

Her head was beginning to clear, making her regret even having brought it up. But now, the only way to handle it, she decided, was to draw upon every ounce of dignity she possessed.

"You'd not be the first man to get them confused. Most I've known have."

"I'm not most men." The ice in his eyes was echoed in his cool, rigidly controlled tone. How could he remain so calm? "And while we're on the topic, there are a lot of women who mistake the uniform for the man."

Need and confusion were scorched away by the flash of temper that shot through her. "You flatter yourself." Though hadn't she herself imagined him in the dress blues of a U.S. Marine? "And while we're on the topic," she shot his words back at him through her teeth, "I'm not most women."

"Try telling me something I haven't figured out for myself."

They stared at each other for a long, silent moment. As she was wondering how something so wonderfully exhilarating could so quickly turn so wrong, the cell phone she'd turned on after leaving the theater rang.

This time, when her eyes closed, it was from frustration, rather than passion.

Muttering a curse, she snatched the phone from her purse. "I've got to take this," she said, proud that her voice was back to its calm, controlled tone.

"Go ahead." He waved a hand as if lacking interest in anything she did. "We'd better be getting back if you want to change for tonight's party."

"Fine."

She pushed the button with more force than necessary, listened to Aaron's assistant make her pitch, and perhaps it was partly because of lingering frustration from J.T.'s lack of response to that kiss that had tilted her world on its axis, or perhaps it was because telling the story to him had made her realize how much she loved the storytelling, but disliked the Hollywood model of making films as much as her grandmother Fionna had disliked the bishop back home, who'd kept trying to thwart her efforts to get a beloved nun canonized.

Or it could have been she was simply tired

of playing games and dodging what she knew would have to be her final answer in the end.

Whichever of those reasons, or perhaps all three, as the sloop began skimming over the water again, headed back to the Shelter Bay Marina, she told the caller, “No.”

There was a long moment of silence from California. Mary waited, feeling her frustration eased by the flap of the white canvas in the breeze, the wind in her hair, and the cooling sea spray on her face.

Although J.T. was busy guiding the boat, and not appearing to pay any attention to her, she could feel him focused on her. As she always seemed to be on him. Even when they’d been sitting in the dark. Or when she’d been up on that stage in the theater, answering questions, and her gaze had repeatedly returned to his.

“What do you mean, ‘No’?” Tammi asked finally.

“I mean that there’s no way I am going to take the soul from my story by injecting a vampire into the plot. And tell Aaron there’s no point in either of you coming up here to Oregon to try to convince me. If you want to make a vampire movie, find someone else to write you one. Because that person is not going to be me.”

That said, she pressed the end button.

"Good call," J.T. said as they sailed back beneath the iron bridge.

Then tension that had risen again between them after that shared kiss faded away like morning fog.

"It was the right decision."

"The only one," he agreed. "It was a stupid idea."

"Especially since movies take so long to actually get from screenplay to the screen," she said. "By the time we even got to editing, the entire vampire trend might have passed us by. And where would that leave us?"

"With that Aaron guy suggesting a selkie/scientist/zombie triangle?"

She laughed at that idea, even knowing that as outrageous as it might sound, it could actually happen.

Aaron Pressler wasn't going to be happy. Like most powerful men, he wasn't an individual to be crossed lightly, and Mary knew there'd undoubtedly be consequences. But right now, at this very special moment in time, not only did she not care what retribution he might try to think up; she felt exactly like Kate Winslet's Rose had in *Titanic,* when she'd stood on the bow of her massive ship, arms outstretched, and imagined herself flying.

30

The kiss had been a mistake. J.T. had known that even before he'd given in to temptation. Before his mouth had touched hers and sent explosions blasting through him.

He'd wanted her in a way that was familiar. Even reassuring, considering how long it had been since he'd felt such a hunger for any woman.

He'd spent the long, lonely hours of last night after leaving the inn attempting to assure himself that the attraction to Mary Joyce was nothing to worry about. She was, after all, a remarkably stunning woman. But more than her beauty, there was an almost magical luminosity that surrounded her.

Looking at her now, J.T. didn't see the celebrity movie star who'd dazzled everyone at the reception last night. Gone was the sleek and stylish parade grand marshal, and she'd left the polished interviewee back at the Orcas.

Even with her hair a wild dark tangle around her shoulders, her cheeks flushed, and her lipstick kissed off, not only was she the most dazzling creature he'd ever seen; she made it very easy to believe in mermaids.

Any male not attracted to Mary Joyce would have to be blind, dead, or gay. And J.T. was none of those.

Still, these unruly feelings she'd stirred up in him were one thing. Acting on them was an entirely different matter. Marines were known for their ability to handle any challenge. If he didn't allow himself to have sex with her, he wouldn't. It was as simple as that.

Or at least that was what he'd been trying to tell himself. And, for a short time yesterday and this morning, he'd almost managed to believe it.

Until he'd let his control slip. Now, as he watched her standing up to those studio hotshots, every instinct J.T. possessed told him that this particular siren was capable of luring him into dark, dangerous waters.

Over his head.

"This time it's me who owes you an apology," he said.

"If it's about that kiss, don't bother. It

was an impulsive, momentary thing. We were caught up in the story. Emotions got confused. Which is why, I suspect, so many actors believe they've fallen in love while making a movie. After all, if you're going to act as if you're in love, it's always helpful to *be* a bit in love."

"And what about you? Are you a bit in love with either of your costars?" Or both? Because he had not a single doubt they were in love with her.

"Of course. Well, to be perfectly honest, more so Sloan, who plays Cassidy." The scientist she spent a great deal of time getting naked with. And even if she *had* been wearing a bodysuit during those scenes, J.T. refused to believe that any man with blood still stirring in his veins could roll around in the surf or a beach or bed with this actress without getting aroused.

"And, before you believe all those stories about our alleged affair breaking up his marriage, which you undoubtedly ran across while researching me, those are merely tabloid lies. The truth is that his wife was the one who was unfaithful while we were filming on location."

He'd read that while researching her. He'd also read that the wife had claimed it was a get-even affair after Sloan Mercer had slept with his costar.

"Do I love Sloan? Of course. Which is why I felt so sorry for him when he was heartbroken about his shattered marriage. But my love for him was much like that I have for my own brother John. And, despite all this Tinseltown glamour" — she tossed her windswept hair and gave him a pose that brought to mind the glory days of Hollywood blockbuster stars — "in truth, I'm an old-fashioned Irish Catholic girl who'd never consider committing adultery."

"Point taken."

The point being that she was also not the type of woman a guy could have a quick, hot one-night stand with, then move on. He took her description of herself much the way any sailor would pay attention to the warning toll of those buoys leading out of the harbor into the sea. Or of the lighthouse they'd passed earlier.

"So," he asked, "what are you going to do now that you've burned that bridge and rejected the vampire story line?"

"I don't know."

One of the things that had made her a star was that every emotion she was experiencing showed on her face, and her openness proved even more compelling in person. What he was reading now was a bit of confusion, ultimately bolstered by resolve. If she had even an iota of regret about possibly endangering her career, she was hiding it well.

"However, since there's no point in borrowing trouble, and a great many people have expended a lot of effort to make the town's first film festival a success, I suppose I'll have to think about that tomorrow." The little tempest between them having blown over, she flashed him the smile Vivien Leigh had pulled out to charm the Tarleton Twins at the Twelve Oaks barbecue. "At Tara."

J.T. reminded himself that Hollywood was a town built on images and illusions, and although she was far more "real" than he'd expected, the illusion projected up on that silver screen could well be as false as the melted yellow grease most theaters poured over popcorn and insisted on calling butter.

He didn't believe she was a fake. But what was to prevent her, in the same way a selkie could change from seal to human, from adjusting to whatever environment she found herself in? It wasn't that large a stretch to think that the woman who could wow the red carpet on Oscar night, or charm the foreign press into giving her the Golden Globe, could also become a small-town girl that the fans who'd arrived for the festival and the residents of Shelter Bay could relate to.

Even knowing that didn't make the assault on J.T.'s senses any less devastating. And, he reminded himself firmly, it made her definitely out of his league.

31

As she showered and dressed for yet another command performance, Mary couldn't get that kiss out of her mind. It wasn't as if she hadn't been kissed before. Not just in real life, but in her movies she'd shared more than mere kisses with two actors so many women all over the world fantasized making love with.

So why had J.T.'s kiss tilted her world on its axis? Why did his lips, his touch, the way his eyes darkened when he looked at her, surpass anything she'd ever imagined?

She'd not been prepared for the turmoil, the aching need he'd created. She'd written about soul mates without truly believing souls could actually touch. Until that amazing moment when time had seemed suspended and she'd found herself caught between the erotic world of her dreams and reality.

"You're only an unpaid assignment to

him," she insisted as she put on a pair of earrings she'd bought in the boutique earlier. Created of blue and green sea glass set in silver, they hung to shoulders bared by a slender column of black silk.

He'd only taken on the job for the sheriff, who was about to become his sister-in-law. Not that any security was proving necessary. Which she'd tried to tell the committee from the beginning.

Now that Kara Conway and the committee had undoubtedly noticed that her fans were for the most part well behaved and certainly not dangerous, she could probably just request that he not follow her around like an overprotective guard dog.

One problem with that idea was that she didn't want him to go. Not until they'd explored whatever it was that was happening between them.

She still didn't believe Kate's declaration that her mother had sent J.T. to her. If Eleanor Joyce was somewhere in heaven, pulling romantic strings, surely she'd have arranged for an easier man. A more emotionally available one. A man who didn't keep giving her mixed messages.

Of course, although he didn't flaunt his masculinity, like many of the actors she'd met since moving to Los Angeles (not that any of them were the equal of J. T. Douchett), he was an extremely virile, intelligent man. In view of the fact that she normally dated only men who could charitably be described as "safe," it was inevitable that she'd be attracted to him.

That was all it was, Mary assured herself. Chemistry. A sexual fantasy for a man who'd lived through more than his share of danger. And wasn't danger always an aphrodisiac?

Despite his initial scowling behavior, she'd been drawn to him at first sight. And that attraction had only become stronger over the past couple days. Although she'd never been into sexual flings, she couldn't deny that the idea was seeming more and more inevitable.

Would that be so bad? They were both adults. And he certainly wasn't the type of man who'd call the tabloids the minute he left her bed. What would be wrong in allowing herself the pleasure J.T. could bring into her life?

Nothing. As long as she accepted that was as far as it could go. Although he'd only skimmed the surface of his military experience, she knew that the past years hadn't been easy. It would be surprising if he were ready to offer any woman any type of commitment.

Not that she was looking for happily ever afters with him. To expect a future where none existed was even more unrealistic than the movie scripts she wrote.

No ties. No commitments. Just two people, a man and a woman, enjoying each other for as long as their time together lasted. That was all this interlude with J.T. could be.

It was all she would allow it to be.

32

"Thanks for the use of the boat," J.T. said as he returned to Bon Temps. Although he would have been content to stay out on the water with Mary forever, they'd returned back to the harbor late, leaving her a little more than an hour to prepare for the party.

If he'd been asked only yesterday, J.T. would have guessed that the life of a movie star was pretty much sleeping until noon, drinking mimosas at brunch with other famous people at some trendy Sunset Boulevard restaurant, going shopping on Rodeo Drive, maybe spending some time at yoga or an upscale fitness club that never smelled of sweat, then getting dolled up to go out partying.

Yet sometime during that Hollywood life of leisure he'd imagined, she had also managed to write scripts, negotiate with studios, and act in her movies.

"Glad to help out. So, I take it the fact

that neither of you pitched each other overboard suggests you're getting along better?"

"Yeah." J.T. went behind the bar and, ignoring his brother's arched brow, took a Rogue Ale out of the cooler. "It's the first and only one of the day," he said.

"Did I say anything?"

"No, but you didn't have to. Christ, it's like living with Eliot Ness during Prohibition."

"Just watching out for you, bro. It's what big brothers do."

J.T. knew that. And he appreciated his brother's concern. But sometimes birth order sucked.

"So," he said nonchalantly as he sat down on the barstool, "back when you and Kara were in high school and you were hot for her —"

"That's a bit cruder than my actual feelings at the time." Sax put a dish of spiced nuts in front of him. "I loved her."

"Yeah. I know. I just wasn't sure you wanted to admit it."

Sax shrugged and began wiping the bar with a damp white towel. "Nothing to be ashamed of. It's not like I was going to do anything about it."

"Because of Jared."

"Yeah. But after a bunch of years and a lot of shit, things worked out. So, why are you asking now?"

"Kara might not have been rich, but she sure grew up differently than us. Her mother's a doctor."

"And her dad was a cop. Your point is?"

"She also was class valedictorian."

"So were you. And I'm still not getting where this conversation is headed."

J.T. dragged his hand through his hair. If he'd ever screwed up a notification conversation this badly, he'd have gotten himself a ticket back downrange. Which he would have preferred, but if there was one thing the past years had taught him, it was you didn't always get what you wanted.

"You weren't exactly a pillar of Shelter Bay society."

Sax threw back his head and roared at that, drawing appreciative looks from a pair of mermaids and a third woman who was inexplicably dressed in what appeared to be an *I Dream of Jeannie* harem costume, complete with a blond ponytail. They were sitting across the room, by the window, drinking pastel girlie drinks out of martini glasses.

"I was hell on wheels. And damn proud of it."

"Well, yeah. That's pretty much what I was getting to. So, all that time, speaking hypothetically, if Jared Conway hadn't been in the picture, would you have gone for it?"

"Told her how I felt? Sure."

"You wouldn't have worried that maybe you were all wrong for her?"

Another laugh. "Hell, there are probably some around town who think I'm wrong for her now. But all that matters is what she thinks. And Trey, because getting her to the altar would've been a lot harder if he'd kept those chips he'd had when we first met on his skinny seven-year-old shoulders."

He tossed the towel beneath the bar. "Are you worried about Kara and my marriage?"

"No." J.T. couldn't believe he'd screwed this up so badly. "I was just thinking how sometimes, even though people might be attracted to each other, when you're talking any real-life future, it's an improbable combination."

"That's one way of looking at it. Another is that sometimes the most improbable match turns out to be the perfect one. . . .

"Hell. This isn't about Kara and me at all, is it? It's about you and Mary Joyce."

"Maybe."

J.T. was a grown man. Like his older brothers, he'd been tested on the battlefield and survived. So why was he suddenly feeling as he had when he'd been twelve years old and asked Sax if you could really get a girl pregnant by dry humping her like some of the guys at school had sworn to be true?

"Are you saying you actually made a move on her?" Sax lowered his voice so their audience couldn't hear.

"It wasn't exactly like that."

"How was it?"

"When did my life become your business, anyway? First you rag me for drinking; then Kara tells me that people want me to stop running. Which, just in case you're interested, I intend to do tomorrow morning, so you might want to alert the town and have the governor call out the National Guard."

"That might be overkill. And — although if you tell Kara I told you this, I'll deny it and call you a damn liar — maybe a thing with Mary Joyce might be just what you need to shake you out of the doldrums."

For some reason, although he'd been expecting a big-brother lecture, Sax's suggestion irked. "She's not some easy Hollywood party girl who sleeps with any guy who happens to be handy."

Sax lifted a brow. "I didn't suggest she was. I merely pointed out that you're both adults. If she's willing, as long as you're both discreet enough to keep you out of the tabloids, it seems pretty much a no-harm, no-foul situation."

That was exactly what J.T. had been telling himself. So, what the hell was his problem?

33

Tonight's affair was a buffet dinner held in a banquet room of the Sea Mist restaurant. Along with the filmmakers who'd entered the competition, and those who'd bought tickets ahead of time, Mary recognized several faces. Including those of Kara and Sax, Cole and Kelli, Maureen and Lucien Douchett.

"Where's *Grand-mère?*" J.T. asked his parents after Mary had been introduced to a seemingly unending parade of bloggers, state politicians, and fans, most of whom had forgone their costumes tonight for dressier attire.

"They decided to stay home," his father answered.

"It's not easy to move in with your children," Maureen expanded on her husband's answer. "I suspect they just needed some personal time alone."

Remembering how confused Adèle

Douchett had appeared last night, Mary exchanged a quick glance with J.T. and knew he was wondering the same thing. Whether, perhaps, the older woman hadn't been up to yet another party.

As if sensing their concern, Kara looped her arm thorough Mary's. "There's someone I want you to meet," she said. She led them through the crowd to where a tall, dark-haired man in a dark blue suit and a woman dressed in a soft blue and green watercolor silk dress stood by one of the tall windows looking out onto the harbor. With them were Charity Tiernan and a man Charity introduced as her fiancé, Gabriel St. James.

"And this is Phoebe Tyler," Kara said. "She's going to be Maddy's sous-chef at the new Lavender Hill Farm restaurant and has agreed to help prepare my wedding supper."

"It's good to meet you," Mary said. "I love your dress."

"Thank you." The woman blushed a bit at that. "It's new."

Mary smiled. "So's mine." Leaving the beaded cocktail dress Leon had chosen hanging in the closet, she'd gone with a simple strapless black sheath and strappy turquoise sandals. "It's not often you find such a wonderful treasure of a shop in such a small town."

"We're so lucky to have Doris and Dottie," Kara said. "If it wasn't for them, I might be having to get married in my uniform."

They all laughed at that. Phoebe not quite as richly as the others. She appeared nervous, but Mary put that off to the fact that many people felt intimidated meeting a celebrity.

A little silence settled over them. Mary watched as the man who'd been introduced as Ethan Concannon, a local farmer, put his arm around Phoebe's waist, the gesture both comforting and proprietary.

"I love your movies," Phoebe offered. "They're so romantic."

"Thank you." From the way the hunky farmer was looking down at Phoebe, Mary understood why she'd be drawn to romantic films.

She was also wondering if there was anyone in this town who wasn't in love. Even Doris and Dottie, chatting about their husbands while ringing up her purchases, had still beamed after decades of marriage.

Thinking of the story she'd learned earlier, during the children's drama of the founding of the town, how that wealthy entrepreneur had bottled the springwater he'd sold as a cure-all, she couldn't help thinking that if she could only bottle whatever water the residents of Shelter Bay were drinking, she could probably sell it for enough money to fund any movies she might want to make for the rest of her life.

She was about to share that idea with J.T. when Reece Ryan, the *Shelter Bay Beacon*'s editor, came up to her.

"Ms. Joyce, I hate to interrupt you —"

"Don't worry; we weren't discussing anything important." Not only had she liked the newspaperman, but Mary was all too aware that this wasn't a private party. After introducing him to the others, she asked, "What can I do for you?"

"I was wondering if you had any comment about what *Variety* put on their Web site this evening."

"Since I haven't visited their Web site for a while, I have no idea what you're referring to." But his furrowed brow suggested that whatever was on the industry magazine's site wasn't good.

"About Aaron Pressler looking for a new writer for your fourth selkie film."

It was true, Mary thought. She'd written it before, but had never realized that you really did see little white dots floating in front of your eyes when the blood left your head.

"Oh, you know this business thrives on rumors," she said in what she prided herself to be a calm, reasonable voice. But she knew that J.T. sensed her discomfort when his hand moved to the back of her waist, offering silent support.

"So, you're still working on the script?"

"I am."

"But?" Oh, he was good. The investigative reporter he'd once been had caught her momentary hesitation.

"Let's just say that we're in discussions about the direction my character's taking," she said.

"Unnamed sources say you told the studio that you were off the project."

The floaty white moths turned to flames. Mary welcomed the flash of anger because it burned away her shock at being so blindsided. Even though now, hearing what Pressler had done, she realized she should have been expecting something like this. He didn't get to the top of the Hollywood elite without playing hardball. Which included crushing anyone who got in his way.

She'd always known that although he'd wanted to distribute her films because he saw them as guaranteed moneymakers worldwide, he'd also been behind the quiet movement to deny her an Oscar because she'd refused to just hand over her stories and let him dumb them down in an attempt to make even higher profits.

"I'm sorry." She gave him a faintly apologetic smile. "But I make a policy of never discussing contractual issues. Especially at such a lovely party as this."

"So, you're denying leaving the project?" he doggedly pressed on. "Or being removed from it?"

"I especially don't believe in responding to rumors. But I will say that I can't be removed from my own series. Because I own the rights to my characters. If any studio intends to produce a film using them, I'll be the one writing the script."

Which was true. Though as soon as she could get a minute alone, she was calling her agent.

As friendly as he'd been, Mary understood that Reece Ryan also had his own job to do, so she wasn't surprised when he wasn't quite done.

"Do you have any idea who would've leaked the story?"

"I've no idea if there even is a story to leak," she said honestly.

The studio head could be bluffing, hoping

she'd be scared enough to give in to his crazy vampire idea. She'd seen him do that before. She'd also watched some of the town's most talented writers cave in to him. Mary had no plans to be one of them.

"Why don't you ask Aaron Pressler?"

"I called as soon as the story broke on the site. To be perfectly honest, since he's obviously never heard of me, I was surprised he took my call. . . . He suggested I talk to you."

"Did he?" *Bastard.* She'd been an actress long enough that the smile she flashed, while forced, would appear genuine to anyone who didn't know how furious she was.

"Well, I'm sorry. But I'm afraid I really have nothing to say on the subject of my films, except that I hope viewers here at the festival enjoy their sneak preview of *Selkie Bride.*" She gave him another smile, even warmer than the first. "Now, if you'll excuse me, I really must get back to work and mingle."

After making a quick good-bye to the others, who appeared understandably confused by the discussion that had just taken place, she went back to working the room, thankful that apparently the paper's editor, hoping for an exclusive, was, for now, keeping the news of the story to himself.

34

She might not be a Marine, but Mary definitely had guts. J.T. knew that the bombshell that reporter had dropped on her must've shattered her evening, but not a person at the party would've had a clue by the way she charmed everyone like a politician picking pockets for campaign funds.

He watched the reporter studying her, appearing to be looking for something — anything — about her behavior he could write about, but she steadfastly refused to give him anything juicy.

He might have developed the ability to lock away his emotions in a steel box during his last assignment. But she was proving his equal.

During a momentary break, when they'd suddenly, finally found themselves alone, he bent down and asked next to her ear, "You okay?"

Her smile was bright. And yet he knew

her well enough to tell it was totally fake. "Absolutely."

"No." His hand went to her waist again. He'd found he liked touching her. So much so that although he knew it was playing with fire, he'd decided he was going to do a lot more of it before her time in Shelter Bay was over. "How are you *really* doing?"

"It's only moviemaking. Not life or death." When someone called her name, she glanced around, smiled brilliantly, and waved at a woman across the room. "I'll survive."

And survive she did. For another hour that, if it dragged interminably for him, must have seemed a lifetime for her.

Finally, they were able to escape.

"You didn't eat anything," he said as they left the restaurant.

"Of course I did."

"No. You carried a plate around for a while. Then put it down."

She shot him a look as they reached the SUV. "You don't miss much, do you?"

"Not a thing."

"Well, neither do I. You didn't eat, either."

"I had an oyster po'boy before picking you up. Want to stop somewhere?"

"I'm a little 'starred' out," she admitted. "Maybe I'll just raid the minibar."

"Or we can pick up something at the Crab Shack and go out to the beach," he said. One advantage of living this far north was that summer days were long. And today's weather was ending as well as it had begun.

"Granted, the beach isn't as crowded as in L.A., but we're still bound to run into people," she said. "And I'm really not up to that."

For the first time since she'd appeared in the door of that private jet, looking every bit everyone's idea of a movie star, she looked small. Sad. Vulnerable. And very, very human.

Looking down at her, J.T. felt the lock on the steel box inside him break open. Tenderness. It rushed over him like a sneaker wave. He skimmed the back of his hand up the side of her face. Then, because, for the first time in a very long while, he felt optimistic about something, he grinned.

"Not where we're going."

He dropped her off at the inn so she could change, then went back to Bon Temps and changed in the office, where he'd been sleeping on the sofa, and decided he really needed to find someplace else to live. And figure out what he was going to do with the rest of his life. His family was right. He'd been drifting rudderless for long enough. Too long.

Although Sax had told him that the Dungeness crab roasted in butter the Crab Shack specialized in was seduction on a plate, he decided that the two of them getting all greased up eating it might be sexy as hell, but since Mary was in the movie business, it'd probably remind her of that sex-drenched food-eating scene where Albert Finney's Tom Jones and Mrs. Waters give a new meaning to the word "appetite." And, although he wasn't lacking in self-confidence, he saw no reason to invite comparison.

So, he ended up with a bag of crab pesto sliders, rockfish tacos, coleslaw, and marionberry shortcake over biscuits topped with whipped cream. Along with a beer for him and a split of wine for her.

She was already waiting for him. J.T. thought it said a lot about her that she looked just as good in a sweatshirt, jeans, and sneakers as she did in that black dress and high heels she'd worn earlier.

"I really appreciate this," she said as they waited for a tall-masted schooner to sail beneath the opened iron bridge over the harbor. "Otherwise I would have ended up resorting to overpriced nuts and candy bars from the minibar."

"The Crab Shack's a Shelter Bay tradition," he said, leaving out what his brother had told him about the roast crab's alleged aphrodisiac powers. "It's not fancy, but it's good." The bridge lowered. "I also picked up some wine."

"After reading that blind item on *Variety*'s Web site, I need it," she muttered.

"That bad?" he asked as they continued toward the coast.

"Let's just say that Aaron Pressler believes in the scorched-earth policy of warfare. And I'm the earth he's currently trying to scorch."

"Want Sax, Cole, and me to go threaten to shoot him?"

"Of course not!" She'd been leaning her head against the passenger window, but at his comment, she turned toward him. "Tell me you're kidding."

"Yeah." He patted her thigh. And when she didn't complain, left his hand there. "I was. Though it's tempting."

"I have to admit it's tempting, too. But he's not worth you and your brothers going to prison for." She sighed.

"Can he do that?" J.T. asked. "Take your screenplay and give it to someone else?"

"Not my exact screenplay. Because, as I

said earlier, the characters and the worlds are mine. But since you can't copyright an idea, he can certainly change the name and locations and continue making movies about selkies."

She was sure that was the case. Unfortunately, her agent had turned out to be in Machu Picchu researching past lives. Since she was out of cell phone range, Mary had been unable to confirm that clause in her contract.

"Don't forget ménages with vampires and werewolves."

"Aaron doesn't like werewolves. He finds fur unsexy."

"Personally, I've always had a thing for zombies. That lurching walk, the empty eyes, the flesh dripping from them. Call me perverse, but that's really hot."

She laughed. "What I'll call you is a liar. You just said that to cheer me up."

"Yeah." He was definitely cheered up when she put her hand on top of his. "I did." He turned his palm, linking their fingers together. "Did it work?"

"Yes." She shook her head. "I've always considered myself too levelheaded to get drawn into Holly wood power games. But I guess I must have, because, for a few minutes there, I was more concerned what other people might think than how I felt about the situation."

"How do you feel?"

"Frustrated. Angry I didn't see it coming. But, I think, maybe a bit relieved."

"Because if they do decide to bail on your story, you've got your power back. Which sounds more like a win than a loss to me."

There was still enough light that he could see the surprise on her face. "That's very perceptive."

"Despite what my SEAL brother might tell you, not all Marines have muscles between the ears."

"I didn't think that," she protested. "You've already proven your credentials, J.T. It's just that Hollywood's a very strange and alien world."

"Yeah. I'm figuring that out for myself. The military might be its own universe, but at least you can usually trust your teammates."

"Imagine a jar filled with scorpions, and you've an idea of the way things work in the movie business. Though," she said, "there are some good people and I've made friends. But it's rare."

He turned onto a narrow, sandy road. "So what are you doing living there?"

"Believe me, I've been asking myself the

same question more and more," she admitted. Then looked around at the deserted ribbon of sand that hugged the cliff and stretched out in both directions. Sea stacks — bits of the continent that had broken away from the mainland — were still topped with fir trees.

"This is beautiful," she said as a pod of pelicans flew by in fighter wing formation.

"Our family used to hang out here a lot when we were growing up. In fact, my grandfather built that table when we were kids."

"It's perfect. It's so perfect." She leaned across the console and kissed him. A quick too-short kiss on the lips that still packed a helluva punch. "Thank you."

"And just think," he said, repeating the earlier words she'd tossed at him, "the night's still young."

35

It was better than perfect. Rather than sit at the table, J.T. had brought along a blanket and built a fire. The late-setting sun sank into the sea in a blaze of color that gilded the water. The sky turned indigo, then ebony, illuminated by the glow of the campfire and the full moon floating overhead.

After a meal that could stand up to any overpriced chichi restaurant in L.A., Mary sat on the red and black plaid blanket he'd spread out atop the cooling sand, leaned back on a driftwood log, and gazed up at the glittering stars that seemed just out of reach.

"This could get to be a habit," she murmured.

"The thought had crossed my mind." J.T. tossed another, smaller piece of driftwood on the fire, causing a brief flare of orange sparks. "As impractical as it would be. And if you did it all the time, it might lose its appeal."

"True." She took a sip of her wine. He was right, of course. The novelty was probably what made it so special. That and the man that she was with.

They could have been the only two people in the world. Moonlight streamed down, making the sand sparkle like diamonds. The only sound was the distant crashing of surf, and a bit beyond the blanket, wavelets lapped on the glistening sand. It was a night tailor-made for romance.

J.T. lay back on the blanket, folded his arms behind his head, and looked up at the vast expanse of sky. "Those stars look as if you could reach up and touch them," he said, unknowingly echoing her earlier thought.

"Mmm." Although she murmured an agreement, she wasn't looking at the sky. Instead her eyes were drinking in the way his brown T-shirt molded the hard lines of his body. Which, in turn, had her gaze traveling lower, lingering on his muscled thighs.

"When I was downrange, there were times when I'd look up at the sky and think how those stars were the same ones shining back here. I know it probably sounds dumb. But sometimes it helped, remembering that."

It was yet another rare glimpse he'd given her of that time in his life. "It's not dumb," she said quietly.

He turned his head toward her, just as Mary's gaze returned to his face. "Come here."

Her mouth was suddenly dry. She took a sip of her wine. Then another. It didn't help.

"I want to." More than she'd ever imagined.

"But . . . ?"

"I think I'm afraid."

"Of me?" When a gust of sea breeze ruffled her hair, J.T. sat up, leaned toward her, and brushed a few dark strands away from her face.

"No." She finished off the wine, which still didn't do anything to soothe her sudden tangling nerves. "I think I'm afraid of us."

"Us?"

"You." She pressed a hand against his chest. "Me." His heart was beating beneath her touch. Strong, but with a sped-up rhythm that equaled her own. "Us together."

"Believe me, sweetheart, I know the feeling." He did not sound all that thrilled about the prospect.

The air around them grew thick and heavy, and felt sparked with electricity, like heat lightning just before a storm.

Mary's mind, usually so logical and cautious, reeled with images, all of them erotic. All of them having to do with J. T. Douchett.

She imagined his mouth on her throat, her breast, his hot breath cooling her night-chilled flesh, trailing flames down her body until . . .

He lowered his head until his lips were a whisper away from hers.

Her eyes were drifting shut in anticipation of the kiss she'd been waiting for. Aching for.

Like their earlier shared kiss, this was more promise than pressure, a feathery brushing of lips, a slow stroke of his tongue, his teeth nipping at her bottom lip. Mary let out a shuddering breath as rich, liquefying pleasure flowed through her.

"This is crazy."

"Insane." He abandoned her lips to press kisses along the curve of her jaw. "But that doesn't stop me from wanting you."

"Nor me wanting you," she admitted.

His hands stroked her back with a confident, practiced touch, slipping beneath her sweatshirt. "You deserve better."

"You're underestimating yourself."

"I wasn't talking about me. Well, that, too, probably. But I was talking about location. You're a woman who deserves silk sheets, candlelight, and champagne."

"I slept quite well for years on muslin sheets before anyone thought to count threads. Champagne is overrated, and we don't need candlelight because we have the firelight. And the stars."

As she glanced up at the star-studded sky, thinking about him looking at the same stars while in Afghanistan, one went shooting across the black velvet sky, then twinkled out.

"I think," she murmured, "that if I ever build a house, I'm going to have a glass ceiling."

"Sounds great. Although a bit impractical."

"True." She sighed. Reconsidered. "My rental house in Malibu has five skylights. One in the foyer, another in the living room, a third in the dining room, yet another in the master bedroom, and a fifth in the master bath."

"Tinseltown decadence," he said teasingly.

"You scoff," she said, hitting him lightly on the shoulder. "But maybe when this festival is over, you can come visit."

It would certainly be no hardship. J.T. imagined making slow, smooth love to her in a wide feathertop bed with music playing from whatever hidden speakers the builder of the house had undoubtedly installed. Or better yet, in a Jacuzzi tub, with her up to her chin in bubbles, drinking the champagne he was now wishing he'd bought, her flesh gleaming like pearls in the starlight while he washed her back. Or her front.

Yeah. Like that was going to happen.

He paused, a desperate man caught on the edge of a jagged, treacherous cliff. One more step and he could send them both tumbling off.

Even knowing the impossibility of the fantasy, understanding that what was happening between them wouldn't — couldn't — last beyond the festival, he decided for now just to concentrate on the moment.

She drew in a quick breath as he began to caress her breasts. Sighed as his mouth captured hers in a slow, drugging kiss. She tasted like wine and sweet, forbidden fruit.

She shifted, lifting her arms as he drew the sweatshirt over her head. Then hummed deep in her throat as he drew her jeans down her long, slender legs.

He'd seen her body in her films. The bodysuit she'd told him about hadn't hidden all that much, and although the movies hadn't gotten anywhere near an X rating, there had been scenes when she'd obviously been bare breasted.

But as good as she'd looked on the screen, here, now, bathed in the glow of firelight, she was a thousand times more perfect in person and J.T. thanked whatever gods or fate had given him yet another gift by having her wear a front-fastening bra.

He flicked it open, filled his hands with her breasts, and felt her warm wherever his hands and mouth touched. He tasted the leap of her pulse at the base of her throat, then felt her heart hammer beneath a breast as fragrant as midnight gardens.

"I've dreamed of this," she murmured as he stripped off her lace panties, then nipped at the cord behind her knee.

"Have you, now?" His mouth trailed down to her ankle.

"I have." She sighed, and closed her eyes, as if reliving it. "Wicked, wonderful dreams."

J.T.'s senses filled with her until his own heart was racing, and although he'd already discovered that control seemed to disintegrate around this woman, even as the hunger clawed at him and his body screamed for release, he deliberately, ruthlessly slowed the pace. And experienced a rush of power as she willingly, eagerly surrendered, giving him her mouth, her body, in the same way her selkie character had surrendered to the human male.

"Well, then." Entranced by the true siren she'd proved to be, he lowered his still fully clothed body over her naked, lean one. "Let's see what we can do to make your wicked dreams come true."

Which he did his best to achieve as he drove her higher, again and again, to the edge of release.

When his roving tongue slid up the sensitive skin of her inner thighs, she quivered in response, her nails digging into his shoulders.

She was erotically hot. Wet. Ready.

But even as she moved under him, turning to quicksilver in his arms, still he retreated, rolling onto his side, leaning up on one elbow as his free hand stroked down that strong, slender leg, then back up again, stopping where her leg and hip came together.

"J.T." Her voice was rough with need as she arched toward him. "I want." She moaned low and deep in her throat as he cupped her. "I need. . . ."

"I know." All too well. If he didn't end this soon, he'd make an IED explosion look like one of those firecrackers he and his brothers used to set off on this beach on the Fourth of July.

All it took was a flick of his thumb, followed by a long stroke of his tongue, to send her over. She bucked. Shuddered on a gasp that gave way to a whimper.

Then went lax.

"Oh," she murmured dreamily. "That was lovely."

"And we've only just begun." He skimmed his fingers over her breasts, which tightened at the light touch.

"Well, then . . . please, sir," she asked, her eyes like blue fire in the starshine, "may I have some more?"

The look of her staggered him. And amazingly, for now, at least, she was his. "Much, much more," he promised.

He stood up and watched her watching him undress. He'd never had a woman look at him the way she was doing at this moment. She made him feel invincible, as if he could leap tall buildings in a single bound, as if bullets would bounce off him.

Like, he realized, he'd felt during battle, before he'd had his life sucked out of him.

But better, he decided, as his blood heated to near boiling when she unconsciously licked her lower lip.

After he'd rid himself of the boots Kara had complained about, pulled off his socks, then ripped off his shirt, tossing it uncaringly onto the sand, he desperately hoped, as her remarkable eyes followed his every movement, she wouldn't notice that his hands were less than steady as they struggled with the metal buttons on his jeans.

"Oh. Wow." She let out a long, lusty breath as he stood naked in front of her. "When you come to Malibu, I'm going to have to make sure to keep you all to myself. Because one look at that body and every female agent in town will be tearing each other's hair out to have you."

He noticed that the hypothetical trip to visit her after the festival had shifted from *possibly* to *when.*

But since this was so not the time to discuss their future, after sheathing himself with a condom from the stash he'd driven down to Newport to buy after leaving her at the inn last night, he lay back down on the blanket.

"Know this," he said as he braced over her. "The *only* woman I want, the only woman I want to have me, is you."

Finally free of the barrier of cloth between them, he covered her body with his, heat to heat, flesh to flesh, male to female. With a long sigh, and a dreamy murmur, she wrapped her legs around his hips.

"Now," she said achingly.

"Now." *Thank God.*

As he slid into her, she opened to him, taking him in, enfolding him. He moved slowly, in . . . out . . . in again as his rhythmic strokes went deeper, until he felt her contractions as she came again. With the sound of the surf roaring in his ears, swamped by what felt like a tsunami of sensation, J.T. gave in to his own release, which went on. And on. And on.

Finally, spent, he collapsed on Mary's warm, pliant body.

They lay there for a long silent time as the tide ebbed and flowed and stars whirled overhead. "Are you sure we're still on the beach?" she asked, sounding like a woman who'd polished off an entire bottle of that champagne he'd been wishing he'd bought.

He trailed a finger along her moist skin, between her breasts. "Last time I looked. Why?"

"Because I feel as if I just got swept away by a riptide." She laughed softly. "Or one of those sneaker waves all the beach signs warn about. Because you certainly sneaked up on me, J. T. Douchett." She lifted her hand and went to playfully bat his arm, but missed. When her hand fell limply to the blanket again, J.T. picked it up and pressed a wet kiss against the center of her palm.

"Although I hate to break this party up, we'd better leave."

"Do we have to?" She rolled over and pressed her lips on his chest, leaving a trail of sparks as she kissed her way down his torso.

"Unless you want to get washed out to sea," he said, fighting back the groan. "Tide's coming in."

"Oh." She lifted her head and looked at the water that was getting closer to the edge of the blanket. "Well, since I'm not Deborah Kerr and you're not Burt Lancaster, and this is real life, not the movies, I guess we'd better."

It was not her first choice. Then again, Mary thought with a little burst of sexual anticipation as they walked hand in hand toward the SUV, they did have the rest of the night.

36

Since it would be obvious to anyone who saw her what she'd been up to, she was grateful when J.T. called ahead and arranged for them to go in the back door and take the service elevator up to the suite.

Where, after a long steaming shower, which essentially turned out to be hot, wet foreplay, they took advantage of the oversized bed.

By the time a soft, silvery predawn light was filtering through the shades, Mary lay with her cheek against J.T.'s chest, drinking in the musky scent of his dark skin, listening to his steady breathing and the beat of his heart.

The night had passed in a sensual blur, a stolen, fantastic time apart from reality. Her dreams of him had been so hot, when she'd decided to make love to him, she'd feared the reality could never live up to those erotic images smoldering in her mind.

But she'd been wrong. Last night had been no dream, as the vague ache in her muscles attested to. The reality had proved amazingly better. And had her understanding, for the very first time, what her selkie queen had felt when she'd so totally given herself to that human scientist.

Mary had never known it was possible to feel so much; had never given herself so openly. So freely. Nor had she ever wanted to. Until meeting J. T. Douchett.

With a single look, a mere touch, the man could arouse her to desperation, inflaming passions she'd never realized were lurking deep inside her.

Displaying a stamina that was nearly superhuman, he'd shown her exactly how responsive her body could be, taking her places she'd never imagined possible. And in turn, he'd held nothing back, encouraging her exploring hands and lips to grow more and more intrepid until she'd learned to read his needs and desires as a blind woman would read Braille.

The upside was that she'd experienced a night of passion that few women could ever imagine.

The downside was that she was also realizing that she wasn't any good at casual sex. It struck her that if she was going to be able to distance herself from this man whose leg was over both of hers, effectively holding her hostage, she was going to have to do it now.

Years in a war zone had taught J.T. to sleep quick and light. Which was why he'd known the moment she'd woken up. Which was when, suspecting she might have regrets, he'd flung his leg over hers, to keep her in bed a little longer.

She was good, he allowed, as she carefully slid, inch by inch, out from under him. Although he'd never been one to believe in destiny, these past few days, especially the last hours, had J.T. wondering if, just perhaps, there was some unseen force working here. Some fate that had brought them together at this time, in this place.

Whatever the reason, this was the first morning in months he'd found himself looking forward to the day. To exploring whatever was happening between them.

The problem was, although last night she'd been the most uninhibited woman he'd ever been with, in the light of a new day, Mary didn't seem on the same page.

The bathroom door hinges squeaked, just a bit, when she opened it. He felt her tense, like a deer in the forest sensing a predator's approach.

He could stop her. He was, after all, larger. Stronger. Not that he'd have to use any force. Because it would take only a slow, deep kiss, a lingering touch, a hand to that slick, hot place between her legs, and he'd have her right back in this bed where she belonged.

He was still weighing his options when he heard the shower turn on.

While he'd been away, Shelter Bay had been designated a "green" town. Recycle bins were everywhere, plastic bags had been banned, and even Sax had gone out and bought energy-efficient appliances for Bon Temps.

The least he could do, J.T. thought, as he threw back the rumpled sheet, was do his part to save water.

The sun was shining, their morning love-making in the shower had been every bit as amazing as everything they'd shared the night before, and although he'd resisted the idea yesterday, J.T. hadn't balked when she'd changed into running shoes, shorts, a white T-shirt, and a baseball cap to run on the beach with him.

They returned to Moonshell Beach, which was nearly deserted, as he'd predicted it would be. They passed by Adèle and Bernard Douchett, who'd gotten there before them, beachcombing for shells and agates left by the receding tide.

Because it would have seemed rude to run by without a word, they stopped to exchange greetings.

Adèle's eyes swept over Mary. "As pretty as you were in that fancy dress the other night, I think I like this look better," she said. "Especially that *Whale of a Town* cap. I have one of my own, in blue, and while a lot of people might think it's touristy, it makes me happy to wear it."

"I feel the same way," Mary agreed. "It must be amazing to live where you can see whales all the time."

"That was the first thing that helped me get over my homesickness for the bayou," the older woman said. "I was down here gathering shells, just as we are today, feeling a bit blue, when a pod began riding the waves right in front of me, so close I was worried they'd beach themselves. I know it'll sound fanciful, but it seemed as if they were welcoming me. From that moment on, I felt as if I belonged here in Shelter Bay."

"I don't think it's fanciful at all," Mary said. "There have been so many stories about whales and dolphins interacting with people — maybe they somehow sensed your emotions and wanted to cheer you up."

Adèle's beaming smile lit up her face, giving Mary an idea of the beauty she must have been when the couple had first married. "Do you know," she confided, "I've often thought the same thing?" She shot a look at J.T. "This one's a keeper."

J.T. nodded as his grandfather did his best to smother a laugh. "I'll keep that in mind, ma'am."

Adèle's answering nod was sharp and satisfied. "You do that." Then she turned back to Mary. "My grandson's gone through a rough patch. But it's obvious even to an old woman whose eyesight isn't what it once was, and whose brain has turned into Swiss cheese, that you're good for him. And believe me, dear, you could do a whole lot worse."

"Believe me, I know," Mary said, speaking from personal experience.

"Well," J.T. said, beginning to jog in place, "I guess we'd better get going if we're going to keep to the schedule the committee has set up."

Mary knew her busy schedule was not the reason he suddenly felt the need to escape.

"She certainly seems fine this morning," Mary said as they continued running.

"She did, didn't she?" His relief was obvious. "Though now that Sax and Cole have settled down, it looks like she's got me in her marriage crosshairs."

"I think it's sweet. She cares about you and wants you happy. Which is the way families are supposed to be. You should've seen my father and grandmother trying to manipulate my sister and Quinn into a romance."

"I'm not sure people can be manipulated into a relationship if they don't want it themselves."

"You won't get any argument from me about that. And although Quinn didn't want to admit it for a long time, I think he was ready from the moment he and Nora met. It just took a while for the family to wear him down." The memory of that time had her smiling, even as it made her more homesick. "And it had to have been true love for me not to scare him off."

"How could you have scared anyone off?"

It was, Mary thought, another compliment. "I was a petulant Goth teen drama queen given to tantrums and door slamming. Looking back, I'm amazed anyone put up with me."

He glanced down at her. "I'm having trouble seeing you made up like a Goth girl."

She laughed merrily, feeling more light-hearted than she had for ages. "Let's just keep it that way."

As they rounded the cliff, J.T. waved to Lucas Chaffee, Maddy's new husband, who was throwing a stick into the surf for the dog Mary had been told he brought back from Afghanistan. Although the dog had lost a leg to an IED, it didn't seem to slow her down in the least.

The sight of the former Navy SEAL brought home the fact that while she'd mostly been thinking about J.T.'s last difficult duty, she hadn't given all that much thought to the years he'd spent in dangerous places where so many brave men and women had lost their lives.

If he'd been killed, which he well could have been, they'd have never met.

And whatever happened between them, wouldn't that have been a loss?

Although he was taller, her legs were long, and he was easily able to adjust his stride to hers, which had her thinking how well they fit together in so many ways.

Yet, as they ran along the packed sand, with the sea breeze clearing the last of the cobwebs from her sleep-deprived head, Mary wondered why, as they ran back past the place where just last night he'd shown her she could fly, she was feeling sorry for herself.

Because, she realized as they ran around the rock below the Shelter Bay lighthouse, she wanted more. As amazing as the sex had been, having shared her body with him, although she knew even just a week ago she'd have considered the notion foolish and overly romantic, Mary wanted to share her heart.

The problem was she didn't believe J.T. was ready to accept it.

37

"You really don't have to do this," Kara said as Sax flipped the CLOSED sign over in the window of Bon Temps. "I'm perfectly capable of driving to Portland to pick up my mother and John myself."

"I don't doubt that for a minute," he said. "But I want us to do this together because Faith's not only going to finally be my mother-in-law — she's Trey's grandmother and they're going to be grandparents to that baby you're carrying beneath what, may I point out, is a very sexy top."

The blouse in question was a simple cream silk, much like Kara knew her mother would've chosen. It was sleeveless, with a lace-edged scoop neck that, just a month ago, would have been considered conservative. Looking down at herself now, with her breasts seeming to have swollen to the size of cantaloupes, she could see that it was a great deal less so.

"You just like it because it shows off my boobs."

"*Mais* yeah." There were times, especially when he was frustrated or aroused, that Sax reverted back to the Cajun French that was still used in his family home. From the way his eyes were glittering with friendly lust, she knew this time it wasn't the former.

"We may be all adults, but she's still my mother," she reminded him. "A mother who didn't expect to have her daughter get pregnant twice outside of wedlock."

He drew her closer and nuzzled her neck. "Have I ever mentioned that I get really turned on when you talk like that straitlaced honor student the teenage me used to get a woody fantasizing about?"

She slapped his arm and pulled away to give him her sternest look. Which was impossible to hold when faced with that bad-boy grin.

"That's exactly what I'm talking about," she said. "Mom and John are only going to be here a couple days. Surely you can behave yourself for that long."

His expression was one of pure innocence. Kara didn't believe it for a minute. Fortunately, although there'd been a time when her mother hadn't hesitated to voice her disapproval of her friendship with Shelter

Bay's bad boy, this time around he'd won her over by proving that he was not only more responsible than most men; he loved both Kara and Trey.

Then, of course, there was that Douchett male charm, which seemed to appeal to every other woman in Shelter Bay.

But they could look and fantasize about him all they wanted. Because, Kara thought, as she lifted her lips to her soon-to-be husband's, Sax Douchett was all hers.

The flight from Japan was, surprisingly, on time. Since her mother and John had to go through first passport control, then customs, then take a shuttle to the terminal, Sax, Kara, and Trey went to the lower level to baggage claim, where they'd agreed to meet.

When her mother first appeared, the two women burst into laughter.

"We've changed places!" Faith said as she hugged her daughter in a way she had seldom done while Kara had been growing up.

It was true. Kara's blouse and dark slacks could have come from Dr. Faith Blanchard's old closet. While the T-shirt and jeans her mother was wearing had always been Kara's style.

"Doris and Dottie have been easing me

out of my rut," she admitted. "And you look beautiful."

That was also true. The brisk, professional neurosurgeon who'd left Shelter Bay had always looked as if she'd walked off the pages of *Vogue.* Her suits were always classically fashionable, her makeup impeccable, and even in rainy Oregon, Kara couldn't recall ever seeing a blond hair out of place on the short bob her mother had trimmed at Cut Loose every two weeks.

This woman's silver hair was pulled back in a loose braid, her smiling face was bare, and her clothes looked well-worn and chosen for comfort. And utility, since there obviously weren't dry cleaners to be found in medical-relief rescue centers.

"I feel good," Faith said. Then smiled up at John and put her arm through his. "Really, really good." It showed.

She turned toward Trey. "And look at you!" She swept him up into her arms and hugged him so hard she had him shooting a surprised look up at Kara. This was definitely not the grandmother who'd flinch whenever he'd play with his Hot Wheels on the wooden floors. "You've grown like a weed!"

When she finally released him so he could talk, he stuck out his chest with pride and said, “I’m gonna be a big brother.”

“I know. Isn’t it exciting! I know you’re going to be the best big brother ever.”

Her mother swept a look over Kara, pausing at her stomach. And immediately her smiling eyes misted. That was another thing. Kara couldn’t recall ever seeing her mother weep. Not even at Kara’s father’s funeral. Or afterward, when she’d returned immediately to work.

“May I touch?”

Since Faith Blanchard had *never* been a toucher, that heartfelt request had Kara’s own eyes misting up. “Of course.”

Faith touched a hand, almost reverently, against the front of the silk top. “Hello, little one,” she said softly, seeming totally unaware of the travelers bustling around them. “This is your grandma. Who already loves you so very, very much.”

She looked up at Sax. The mist had turned to actual tears. “Thank you,” she said. “For taking such good care of my daughter and grandson. And for . . .” She drew in a breath, obviously fighting for the calm she’d once worn like a second skin. “This glorious gift.”

“I didn’t do it alone,” Sax said. He waited until she’d done whatever bonding thing was going on, then gave her a hug. Which was something Kara knew he'd once never dared try to do.

"Well," John said in a gruff voice that revealed that he wasn't unmoved by the reunion, "let's get our bags and go home. We have a wedding to attend."

38

Unsurprisingly, given that Sax, Kara, Faith, and John were an important part of the Shelter Bay community, not a single person on the committee offered a word of complaint when Mary opted out of the film-character costume party to attend the wedding. She'd promised to award the trophies at the festival brunch before the sneak preview of *Selkie Bride* on tomorrow's final day of the festival.

The scene itself could have come from a movie. The scent from Sofia De Luca's gardens filled the late-afternoon air with perfume. On an emerald green lawn that smelled of fresh-cut grass, a string ensemble entertained the family and friends who'd gathered for the long-awaited double wedding.

J.T.'s parents and grandparents were in the front row, sitting next to Sofia. Next to them was Kelli, who kept sniffling into a tattered Kleenex. As if she'd been welcomed into the family, Mary had been given the seat beside her.

Gabriel St. James was seated on Mary's other side, and next to him was former Navy SEAL Lucas Chaffee: Sax's former teammate, and Maddy's new husband. On the other side of the aisle sat other former team members and close friends — Zach Tremayne, Quinn McKade, Shane Garrett, and Dallas O'Halloran — who had arrived with their wives from South Carolina and California to attend the ceremony.

The two grooms, Sax and John O'Roarke, stood side by side in the lacy white Victorian gazebo brightened by a fragrant profusion of scarlet climbing roses.

"Sax better unlock his knees," Gabe murmured. "Or he's going to fall flat on his face."

He'd no sooner spoken than John leaned over and said something to Sax. Who immediately shifted his weight.

"Looks like thanks to his future father-in-law, the Saxman just lost his chance for YouTube fame," Lucas said.

When the musicians segued into Handel's Air, the three groomsmen, J.T., Cole, and John's nephew Danny Sullivan, paired with bridesmaids Maddy, Charity, and Sedona, walked down the aisle, followed by Kara's son, Trey, who was carrying the rings on a satin pillow.

Watching the way Sax looked down at the seven-year-old boy he'd adopted caused a lump in Mary's throat. She knew all too well how painful it was to have a parent die.

When the quartet began playing Bach's Arioso, a light but beautiful piece of music that Mary had chosen herself for the place in *Siren Song* when her selkie first emerged out of the water onto the beach, the assembled guests all rose and turned to view the brides.

Both were beautiful, as brides always are on their wedding day. Looking at Kara, Mary could totally see her stepping off a movie screen. Unsurprisingly, given her police training, Shelter Bay's sheriff appeared cool and self-assured. The only sign of nerves was the splash of bright color on her cheekbones.

And her silver-haired mother, Faith, was so elegant in that dress and jacket Doris (who was seated behind the family, next to Dottie) had picked out, she could easily have been mistaken for Helen Mirren.

Watching the two grooms' stunned expressions as the women approached was an indication that although they may have known them for many years, they were suddenly seeing them in an entirely new light. Their absolute love and devotion had Mary tearing up.

"Do you have another of those?" she asked Kelli.

"Of course." She reached into a pink satin purse that matched her dress and handed Mary a handful of tissues. "I've always cried at weddings, so I make sure I come prepared."

"Good idea."

The wedding took Mary back thirteen years to a circle of stones overlooking the sea on the family farm in Castlelough, when Nora had married Quinn.

Mary had served as a bridesmaid, Kate as matron of honor.

Watching this ceremony took her back to that magical day, and caused a tug of homesickness in her heart.

As she reached Sax's side, Kara smiled up at this man she'd known so many years. The man with whom she'd shared so much.

Standing next to her, Faith Blanchard also offered a dazzling smile to the former sheriff's deputy J.T. had told her had apparently loved her for many years, but had kept his feelings secret because her husband, now deceased, had been his best friend.

Like mother, like daughter, Mary thought. Which again had her considering how alike J.T. and Quinn seemed to be. And how she and her sister had both found themselves attracted to men who were not easy to know. Nor would they be easy to love.

Not, Mary tried to assure herself, that she was in love with J.T.

There's no point in trying to lie to yourself, darling.

The voice was so clear, at first Mary thought one of the twins seated behind her must have said something. When she glanced back over her shoulder, although Doris and Dottie both flashed watery smiles, neither appeared to have said a thing.

Which didn't explain the silvery laughter Mary heard ringing in her head as she dragged her attention back to the ceremony.

The vows the couples exchanged were both simple and timeless.

To love. Honor. Cherish.

For richer or poorer.

In sickness and health.

Forsaking all others.

Till death do us part.

Mary heard more sniffles among the guests as, without taking his eyes from hers, Sax slipped the ring onto Kara's finger. Kara, in turn, put a gleaming symbol of promise on his.

Then it was Faith and John's turn.

A collective sigh of happiness could be heard rippling in the salt-tinged air as lips touched, in their first kisses as husbands and wives.

As the two couples walked back down the white runner while the musicians played Handel's perfectly named "Rejouissance," Mary doubted there was a single dry eye in the place.

39

The reception, held in the farmhouse's formal parlor, was as perfect as the wedding.

When the two couples danced their first dance to "At Last," sung by Maureen Douchett, who not only had turned down a Hollywood offer but could've given the late Etta James a run for her money, Mary felt herself tearing up all over again.

Watching Maddy, Charity, Sedona, and Phoebe Tyler, who had worked so hard to create such magic in three short days, had Mary envying their closeness.

Although she had several women friends, in truth, compared with the sisterhood these women seemed to share, hers were more business associates. And in her business, the unmentioned elephant in the room was very often colored the green of envy. Quinn had warned her that the more successful she became, the fewer close personal friends she'd have.

At the time, because she'd had so many friends at university, even after she'd first begun winning awards, she'd thought that his view was merely jaded. Unfortunately, she'd found that, like everything else he'd warned her about, it had turned out to be true.

"Something wrong?" J.T. asked.

"No." She shook off the slight depression. This was, after all, a time for celebration. "I was just thinking about work." Which was mostly true.

"Not tonight." He took the fluted champagne glass out of her hand and placed it on the tray of a passing waiter, whom Kara recognized as one of the film students from that first day's questioning. "We've never danced."

"We've only known each other four days," she pointed out.

"True," he said as he drew her into his arms. "So why does it feel like forever?"

"I hear they say that about swine flu, too," she said, trying to make light of his question.

"And here I thought I was the negative one." When his lips brushed her temple, the uncharacteristic public display caused hope to flutter in her heart.

"All I was saying was that this was a fling. A lovely one, but I'm leaving the day after tomorrow." She waited for him to tell her not to go.

"Yeah, you keep telling me that. But you know what you said about Tara?"

Because his breath fanning her hair was proving seductively distracting, it took her a moment. "That I was going to think about what I was going to do about my career tomorrow?"

"Exactly." He drew her even closer. "That's what I've decided to do about you going back to Tinseltown."

Although his tone was far lighter than that first day when it had been obvious that he hadn't wanted to be stuck with her, Mary felt something different about him tonight. Something edgy. Almost . . . dangerous.

As they swayed to his mother's husky rendition of Patsy Cline's "Crazy," which Mary thought probably suited hers and J.T.'s situation, his hands moved down her back, cupping her bottom, lifting her. . . .

"J.T.," she hissed as he held her against an erection he didn't attempt to conceal, "what do you think you're doing?"

"Dancing?"

He might call it that, but it was rapidly becoming the closest Mary had ever come to making love in a vertical position. When he nipped at the lobe of her ear with his teeth, she felt her knees weaken and dug her nails into his shoulders.

"How much have you had to drink?" she asked suspiciously.

"Only half a glass of champagne." He buried his face in her neck. And . . . licked? "But I gotta tell you, sweetheart, I don't need alcohol when you're around. Because you're intoxicating enough all by yourself."

Oh, God. Even as Mary told herself that she should back away from a potentially embarrassing situation, the swelling virility between his legs was making her ache in a way that had her own sexual senses suddenly, vividly alive.

"Do you have any idea how much I want you?" His voice was deep and dark with edgy passion that made even breathing an effort.

"I have a fairly good idea." She reached up and traced his lips with a fingernail, which caused memories of what the man was capable of doing with that sensual mouth to come crashing down on her.

"What would you say to getting out of here?"

Yes! her body shouted.

It wouldn't be polite, her more rational

head argued.

"We should wait until the brides and grooms leave."

"Look at them." He pulled her closer still. When he rubbed against her, she was amazed the friction hadn't created sparks hot enough to burn the farmhouse down. "They're lost in such a lovey-dovey world, they're not even aware that anyone else is here."

She followed his gaze to where Sax and Kara were swaying in much the same way she and J.T. were. The difference was that Kara had several levels of crinolines keeping the dance from becoming indecent. Nearby, Faith and John seemed equally enthralled with each other.

"You know," she said, "champagne always gives me a headache."

"Really?"

"It's true. I believe I feel a migraine coming on."

"Well, then." Despite their closeness, he deftly twirled her past the two twins from the boutique, who were dancing with their twin husbands. "Perhaps we'd better get you to bed." He was, Mary noticed, headed toward the door.

And she had absolutely no intention of stopping him.

40

J.T. pulled her to him, heat to heat, the moment they'd entered the suite, kicking the door closed behind them. Then took her mouth in a hard, claiming kiss, his tongue sweeping deep, mating with hers with a primal power that made her head swim. Clinging to him, Mary kissed him back, her avid mouth as hungry as his.

Outside the inn, the night rain, which had finally blown in from the sea, beat a hard percussion on the roof.

Inside, a storm swirled.

Unlike the other times they'd made love over the past two days, there were no words, no soft lovers' sighs. Only blurred movement, drugged sensations, blinding passion.

His hands, his mouth, were rough as they filled themselves with her and plundered. Mary heard the sound of silk ripping, and welcomed it.

Baring her to the waist, he tore away the

lacy bra and tossed it across the room, where it landed on a wingback chair. Then he took her breasts, his thumbs creating havoc on her nipples, which were straining to a point just this side of pain. When his teeth closed on one of those aching peaks, then tugged, desire shot through her like a whip: sharp, stinging, and oh, so very hot.

Desperate, needy, wanting to touch him as he was touching her, she reached for the zipper of his suit pants.

"Not yet."

His long fingers braceleted both her wrists, lifting her arms above her head as he used his superior strength to press her back against the door.

"Do you have any idea what I want from you?" he rasped as his free hand dove beneath the scrap of a dress that was now hanging low on her hips.

"What?" she managed to answer as he cupped her. Though she had a very good idea.

His eyes were hot, his smile carnal, as he whipped away the triangle of damp lace between her legs.

"Everything."

Freeing himself, he revealed admirable dexterity by managing to deal with the condom with one hand, then lifted her up.

"Wrap those long sexy legs around me, *chère,*" he growled against her mouth. "And hold on tight."

They made love without undressing, against the door, Mary's hands, finally freed, gripping his dark hair as they raced over that ragged edge together.

Somehow they made it to the bed, where this time the pace was slow, tender, and so beautiful that Mary ncarly wcpt. Colors, fading from the red of a bursting star of orgasm, to rose, to a cool, pinkish blue, were floating peacefully in her mind as she drifted off to sleep, her head on J.T.'s broad chest, her legs entwined with his.

The dream returned. But this time, instead of her warrior claiming her while a battle raged behind them, he was making glorious love to her in a meadow beside a lake she recognized all too well. Wasn't it the very same lake she'd grown up visiting? The one where Quinn had filmed *The Lady of the Lake?*

And then, as dreams have a tendency to do, it morphed, and she was walking on the cliff above a roiling, stormy sea, awaiting her sailor's return. Unsurprisingly, when the scene shifted out to the boat, it was J.T. fighting the sails being blown about by the wind.

Mary wasn't the only one who'd been dreaming. Waking up wanting her, J.T. rolled over, only to find her side of the bed empty. He waited a few minutes for her to return, then went looking for her.

She was curled up in a chair, wearing a silk robe, her feet tucked beneath her, madly scribbling on a notepad. When she didn't so much as look up when he entered the living room of the suite, he realized she was a million miles away.

He was about to leave her to go take a shower when she emerged from wherever she'd been.

"Good morning." Her smile warmed those lovely mermaid eyes that had cast such a spell over him in his hot dream.

"Morning." He crossed over to her, bent down, and kissed her. "I didn't mean to interrupt."

"You didn't." She put the pad down on the coffee table. "I just woke up with this scene in my head and I wanted to get it written down so I wouldn't forget it."

"The selkie and the fisherman?"

"The very one."

"So, you're going to write it."

"Yes. I've decided that it'll be my next project." She sighed. But it wasn't a sad sound, more resigned. And, he thought, perhaps somewhat relieved.

"I'll admit to being upset, and angry, at how Aaron handled things," she said. "But, in truth, we were never a good partnership. He'll find someone else to write his vampire selkie movie and if he doesn't miss the timing on the trend, it'll undoubtedly make the studio a lot of money. Which is, after all, the point. As he sees it."

"But you've never been about the money."

J.T. thought about his mother, turning down that Hollywood contract and never looking back, seemingly far more content performing with her family at Bon Temps. He wouldn't have expected a big-name movie star to have so much in common with his mother, but they were both strong, talented women who knew their own minds.

"No. As I told you when you took me on that lovely boat ride, it's always been about the storytelling. Going independent allows me to tell the stories I want. And if the audience is smaller, well, won't the pleasure of greater creative freedom make up for that?"

"Speaking of pleasure . . ."

He sat on the arm of the chair, and ran a hand down her hair, over her shoulder, then lower, to cup her breast beneath the ivory silk robe. "We still have time before you're due at the theater. What would you say to coming back to bed?"

She took his hand, lifted it to her lips even as her eyes warmed to sapphire, giving him her answer. "I can't think of anything else I'd rather do."

41

How could she want him again? Mary asked herself with a lingering sense of wonder. After last night? She'd lost track of the number of times they'd turned to each other, each time proving more satisfying than the last.

And this time was no different. But in one way it was, she considered as she sat across the room service table from him, eating the breakfast they'd ordered. A breakfast far more hearty than she usually ate, but as he'd pointed out, with a wicked wag of his dark brows, she needed to keep her strength up. Because he had plans for her.

Just those words, brimming with sensual promise, had her body warming all over again.

She took a long drink of ice water, willing it to cool the desire that had risen up like that sea storm in her story. Today was the last day of the festival and she needed to keep her mind on her duties. But after that . . .

"I have to fly to New York tomorrow," she said. "I'm booked on Letterman. To promote *Selkie Bride.*"

He lowered his fork, which was loaded with hash and on the way to his mouth, to the white plate edged with a lighthouse design border. "You're still going to do that? After what Pressler did to you?"

"The studio's releasing the movie. But this one, at least, is still my story, so I'm willing to do my part to fill seats because I believe people will enjoy it. Besides, I gave my word."

"And it'll also give you a chance to set the record straight about what happened."

Except for Quinn, there'd never been anyone in her life who truly understood the strange business she'd chosen. Nora, the rest of the family, and Kate had always been supportive. But they didn't entirely get it. J.T. did.

"There is that," she agreed. Then brought up the topic she'd been leading up to. "I thought that after I do the show, I might come back here."

"To Shelter Bay?" He did not seem as surprised as he might have been. Mary took that as a positive sign.

"It's a lovely town. I'd enjoy a chance to explore it. And" — she glanced over at the nearly filled pad on the table — "it definitely seems to appeal to my muse. It's been a while since I had such a burst of creativity."

"It's the sex," J.T. decided. "It loosens everything up."

"Do you think so?"

"It's a well-known scientific fact."

"Well, then." She gave him her best smile. The one the selkie queen had used to seduce her human scientist for the first time. "Perhaps I could hire you . . . as a creative consultant."

"A gigolo." J.T. nodded. "My brothers and Kara have been after me to find a new occupation. That sounds like something I could handle."

"You'd be getting no argument from me on that score. In fact, though I'd be having no actual experience in that matter, I'd say you set the standard."

Just as she hadn't had anyone to talk about her business with, Mary was unaccustomed to enjoying sexual bantering during breakfast. In fact — she gave it a bit more thought — even sharing a meal after a night of sex was a rare thing in the life she'd been living. Even before moving to the States.

Since she'd first appeared in Quinn's movie, all her attention had been directed toward becoming an actress. Then, even after her goals had shifted a bit toward writing, her main focus — her entire focus, if she was to be perfectly honest with herself — had been her career.

Men, and sex, had been merely something on the side. Until J.T. who, in these few short days, had landed directly in the center of her life.

"Then you wouldn't have a problem with that?" she asked.

"Having sex with you? Hell, no."

She laughed, although on one level her question had been entirely serious. "I was actually referring to my staying in town for a while."

He reached across the table, took her hand in his, and brushed his thumb over her knuckles. Although he'd touched her everywhere, both during their lovemaking on the beach and again last night, for some reason this simple gesture seemed even more intimate.

"You would," he said simply and, she knew, absolutely honestly, "make me a very happy man." Then winked. "Though I'm not going to deny that the gigolo gig definitely has its own appeal."

■ ■ ■ ■

The lovely morning peace was shattered as soon as Mary and J.T. walked out of the elevator into the lobby, where the press, seeming to have arrived en masse during the night, descended on them.

They shouted out her name, jockeying for position, microphones and cameras raised.

"I'm sorry," Mary said over and over again as microphones were shoved into her face and camera flashes blinded her. "But I have a schedule to keep to. I'll speak to you all after the awards and the screening."

It should have been enough. It was certainly more than she'd planned. But, unsurprisingly, with the scent of a juicy celebrity scandal in the air, her offer didn't satisfy.

Voices rose as J.T., his arm around her shoulders, guided her through the horde of entertainment reporters.

When a microphone boom hit her head, he stopped.

"That's enough." He didn't even have to raise his voice. Amazingly, the din immediately stopped, like water being turned off at the tap.

"Ms. Joyce has an event to attend. She'll speak to you all later. So long as you behave professionally and not like a shiver of feeding sharks."

"May I ask who you are?" a voice from somewhere in the middle of the pack asked.

"I'm Captain J. T. Douchett. U.S. Marine Corps. And I'm the guy tasked with getting Ms. Douchett to her venue on time."

Glancing up at him, Mary saw, for the first time, the warrior from her dream. His eyes were as hard as stone. As dangerous as a grenade. Not only did an absolute hush fall over the lobby; the crowd parted, reminding her of the iconic scene of Charlton Heston parting the Red Sea in *The Ten Commandments.*

"That was very good," she murmured as he drove the few blocks to the Orcas Theater. "I also just realized something. That first day, when so many fans showed up in Portland and Eugene, that was your doing, wasn't it?"

"Why would you think that?" he said, evading her question with one of his own.

"Because it makes sense. Your mission, as you pointed out, was to keep everyone away from me. So somehow you spread a rumor that sent people off on a wild-goose chase."

"People should know better than to believe everything they read on the Internet," he said mildly.

"Admit it. It was you."

Again he neither confirmed nor denied. "You've never heard that old saying 'The Marines have landed and the situation is well in hand'?"

"I may be Irish, but I am an expert on American cinema," she reminded him. "And the line has appeared in three movies that I can think of off the top of my head: *Doubting Thomas,* 1935; *What Price Glory,* 1952; and a shortened version in *Cocoon,* 1985."

He shot her a surprised look. "You weren't kidding about being an expert."

"I wasn't. Plus, I have an excellent memory and I clearly remember your claiming to be a *former* Marine."

"Yeah, well, I was wrong about that, because there's no such thing," he said as he pulled up in front of the parking space that had been set asidc for them. "Once a Marine, always a Marine."

And with those six little words, Mary realized that he was on his way back from that dark place he'd been, in the same way tending to his farm in Castlelough had proved her brother's salvation.

She'd turned her phone off during the awards presentation, which went well. Even the losers had presented excellent entries.

So much so, during the brief break between the awards and the screening of *Selkie Bride,* she'd approached the screenwriters, telling them that she thought they'd be good fits for her production company and would love to see more of their work. Needless to say, they jumped at the offer.

They'd just reached the part in the movie where the selkie was about to give up her kingdom for the man she loved, when the mayor suddenly appeared in the aisle next to Mary's seat.

"I'm so sorry to disturb you," she murmured, so as not to interrupt the film at such a vital moment. "But your sister's on the phone. From Ireland. She says it's an emergency."

Mary's blood, which had been so warmed by J.T.'s arm around her shoulder in the dark, turned to ice.

Memories flashed through her mind. A vague one of when her mother had died giving birth to her sister Celia. Another, more recent one, of her grandmother being nearly blown up in a shopping mall bombing in Ulster. And worst of all, her father dying of a heart attack on the way to the Rose, where he could always be found enjoying his Guinness and spinning his colorful, fanciful tales for the pub's patrons.

Emergencies were *never* good news.

She rose quickly, trying not to run up the aisle to the lobby, J.T. right beside her, as he'd been since she'd first arrived in Shelter Bay.

She took the phone the concerned-appearing mayor handed to her.

"Nora?"

"Oh, Mary." Nora's voice trembled. It sounded, Mary thought, as if she'd been crying. Please God, she prayed, don't let anything have happened to Quinn or the children.

"What's wrong?"

"It's Gran." There was a pause. She heard her sister draw in a deep breath. "She's in hospital. With pneumonia, and although John and Erin have been doing all they can, it doesn't look good." There was another pause. Her older brother John and Erin, Michael's wife, were both doctors, who'd set up a practice together in Castlelough. "You'd best be coming home, darling. As soon as you can."

"I'll leave right away."

Not wanting to waste time with particulars now, she hung up and turned to J.T. "It's my grandmother," she said, handing the cell phone back to the mayor. "She's gravely ill."

"We'll go back to the hotel and pack," he

said, going immediately into Marine mission mode. "I'll call the airlines and get us on the first flight out of Portland."

"Thank you. Here's my credit card." Her hands trembled as she reached into her bag and pulled out her platinum card.

He immediately squared his shoulders, and as she watched, something that looked a lot like anger glittered dangerously in his steel gray eyes. The same eyes that had managed to quiet an entire hotel lobby of shouting journalists.

"Because you've a very good reason to be upset, I'm going to forget you said that, *chère.*"

Again, those eyes didn't miss anything. Including her slight shudder at his tone.

He cursed.

"I'm sorry." He smoothed his hands over her shoulders. His voice and his eyes softened. "But this one's on me." When she opened her mouth to point out that it was her family, her problem, and she could certainly afford the tickets more easily than he could, he put a finger to her lips. "Arguing will only waste time," he said reasonably. Gently. "So let's get going."

Bemused, and still reeling from that phone call, Mary wondered if this was how he'd taken care of all the other women he'd known. With that beguiling combination of tenderness and strength.

Needing the tenderness, and knowing he was right about arguing being a time waster, Mary leaned on him, both physically and emotionally, as they walked out of the theater.

42

Although J.T. had been on several flights through Shannon Airport on the way to Iraq, he never got over the panoramic sight of fields and hedgerows and patchwork valleys set amid abrupt mountains.

"It looks like a postcard," he told Mary.

"Aye," she said. "Isn't that what everyone says?" She was already getting back into her native Irish lexicon, but her voice lacked the lilt he'd come to expect.

Her hands were clutched so tightly together he had to pry her fingers apart to take one in his own hand. Even as he rubbed his thumb against her palm, it remained stiff and cold.

"She'll be all right."

"No." She shook her head. "I have this horrible feeling she won't."

"It's natural to think the worst —"

"Not for me." She tugged her hand loose from his and pressed her fingers against her closed eyes. "What if Kate's right? What if I do have some bit of the sight? After all, didn't I dream of you before I'd even arrived in Oregon?"

"What? You never told me that."

"I did, too. I told you I'd dreamed of us making love."

"I thought you meant that first night. After we met."

"I did that night," she said. "But for longer. Even before I received the invitation to come to Shelter Bay." She met his gaze, her own eyes more tortured than argumentative. "How would you be explaining that, J.T.?"

"I don't know. Maybe I just looked like some guy —"

"No. It was definitely you."

"They say everyone has a double."

"Did you not hear me?" she asked on a flare of heat he found far more encouraging than that sad silence she'd sunk into during most of the flight. He hadn't been able to talk her into eating on either of the flights, or their layover in New York.

"I said I dreamed of you. Not some faceless man. Not some double. *You.* And then, suddenly, there you were. Which makes me wonder if Kate could be right about me having the sight."

He wasn't even going to attempt to address that here, now, while she was so upset and he honestly had no answer.

"Did you dream about your grandmother?"

"No," she admitted. "But I've been thinking about her a lot the past few days."

"Which couldn't have come from your meeting my grandmother?"

"I suppose so," she said as she turned back to look out the window again. The thatch-roofed cottages looked like small white boats on an emerald green sea. "I'm just so worried. I should have been here."

"You couldn't have known," he said, repeating what he'd told her time and time again.

Unfortunately, it hadn't helped.

Her brother-in-law, pulling strings from overseas, had arranged for the both of them to be taken from the arrival gate at JFK and whisked away to a private lounge where they could wait without her having to deal with adoring fans.

Fortunately, J.T. was nobody famous, and with her sunglasses, jeans, sweater, and flats, Mary could have passed for any attractive woman. Having been requested not to give away her identity, the flight attendants treated her the same as their other first-class passengers, giving no indication she was a celebrity.

Faith had given her a packet of sleeping pills to help her on the overseas trip. Although at first she'd refused them, J.T. had guilted her into taking one by reminding her that she had to be rested in order to be strong for the rest of her family.

So, although it had taken a while, sometime after they'd passed over Nova Scotia, she'd crashed and spent the last part of the flight snuggled up against him, her head on his chest, while he put his arm around her, holding her close.

If it hadn't been for the reason they were on the flight in the first place, J.T. would've found it a near perfect way to spend the night.

Since she was an Irish citizen, they were separated into different lines for the customs and immigration process. Afterward they went to the terminal coffee shop, where Mary's sister Nora Gallagher and her husband were waiting.

Nora was tall, curvier than her younger sister, with long flame-colored hair and kind eyes the hue of polished emeralds. Her husband, whom J.T. immediately recognized from his face on the dust jacket of his books, had the lean, rangy build of a long-distance runner. His face was harshly cut, his jaw square, his eyes dark. A scar marked his cheek, and the shots of silver at his temples added drama to the black jeans, boots, sweater, and leather jacket he was wearing.

"Oh, darling." Nora rushed forward and gathered her sister into her arms. "It's so good to have you home. I'm just so sorry it had to be under these circumstances."

Mary held on tight, then backed away slightly when the flash of a camera revealed she'd been recognized.

"Why didn't anyone call sooner?" she asked.

"There honestly wasn't time," Nora said. "It all happened so quickly."

"Why don't we discuss this in the car?" Quinn Gallagher suggested, nodding toward the crowd that was beginning to gather over by the take-out counter. He offered a hand to J.T. "Quinn Gallagher."

"J. T. Douchett." As he shook the older man's hand, they exchanged a look. Gallagher's was one of sharp appraisal. In turn, J.T. gave him that Marine stare Kara had wanted him for. In the brief, silent exchange, both men were measured. And found each other acceptable.

"The car's not far," Quinn said. He picked

up Mary's bag before J.T. could grab it. Deciding this was no time to get into a pissing match, J.T. shouldered his own duffel bag and followed them out to the black sedan waiting at the curb. It occurred to J.T. briefly that if Mary ever did decide to put vampires in any of her stories, she could certainly find inspiration in her own brother-in-law.

"I knew you'd want to get to the hospital as soon as possible," Nora said. "So I packed some tea and biscuits."

"The first morning I was here, Nora's father, Brady, told me that her tea was stout enough to trot a mouse across," Quinn said.

"Now, there's an idea," J.T. murmured.

Despite the seriousness of the reason for Mary's trip home, Quinn laughed at that. "That's exactly what I said when he told it to me. But it'll definitely give you one helluva caffeine jolt."

It turned out he wasn't kidding.

As they drove north along the River Shannon estuary, through rolling pasturelands that had once been inhabited by cattle barons and, in times long past, ancient Celtic kings, after welcoming him to Ireland, Nora explained, as best she could, what had happened to Fionna Joyce.

"She'd only had a wee bit of a cold," she

said. "When she refused to go to the doctor, Erin came to the house, examined her, diagnosed bronchitis, and gave her an antibiotic. Given her age, both Erin and John wanted to hospitalize her, but she insisted that since she'd had too many friends go into hospital only to die, she refused that, as well."

"She's so damn stubborn," Mary complained.

"Aye," Nora said. "But isn't that how she finally succeeded in getting Sister Bernadette canonized?"

"Your grandmother got a nun canonized?" J.T. asked.

"She did," Nora answered. "Tell him the story, Mary."

He could tell Mary was frustrated by the way her sister had sidetracked the conversation, but apparently not wanting to start an argument, she complied. "The entire time I was growing up, even before I was born, she pretty much dedicated herself to getting Sister Bernadette Mary — a Sisters of Mercy nun who'd worked to bring about peace during the Anglo-Irish War for independence — declared a saint. Sister Bernadette had been killed by the Black and Tans."

She'd been looking out the window during the drive, but now she turned toward him. "How much do you know about the sainthood process?"

"I must've missed catechism class the day that was taught, so pretty much next to nothing."

"Well, an important part of the judicial process is to document a candidate's life, holy works, and, most importantly, to provide proof of two miracles."

"While the first two parts were easy, it was the miracles that were difficult," Nora said. "Especially since the bishop at the time was no fan of women becoming saints and kept refusing to pass Gram's documents to the Vatican's Congregation for the Causes of Saints. She used to always complain that the only thing that would impress him would be a modern-day repeat of the wine-at-the-wedding miracle."

"She'd always said if Bernadette could only make whiskey flow out of the bishop's water tap, he'd recommend her before you could say Bushmills malt," Mary remembered.

And although her eyes were still heartbreakingly sad, that memory caused a faint curving of her lips. She reached over and for the first time since that phone call from Nora, it was she who took J.T.'s hand.

"But she finally got her second one after a person in Ulster, who'd claimed to have been cured of leukemia, went thirteen years without a relapse." Nora jumped back into the conversation. "Apparently ten years is required to even be considered for a cancer cure."

Although J.T. found that all a little bit off-the-wall, no way was he going to criticize what sounded like a good woman taking on a David-versus-Goliath cause, which had to take a lot of guts.

"To tell the truth, I think the real miracle was getting Gran's case past all those men in the Vatican," Mary said, showing that, once again, their thoughts were going in the same direction. "And getting back to her illness, how did bronchitis end her up on life support?"

"Apparently it turned into some sort of viral, fast-acting pneumonia that's resistant to antibiotics. But why don't we let John and Erin explain that?" Quinn suggested mildly. "Since they're her doctors."

Although he could tell Mary wasn't happy with that idea, neither did she argue. Instead, she just leaned back against the seat and looked out the window as silence settled like fog over the car.

As the road twisted through a maze of

hedgerow-separated fields, over narrow stone bridges, past whitewashed, slate-roofed houses, peat bogs, and cottages, which, even in these modern times, still possessed iconic thatched roofs, J.T. understood why Sax had always been so charmed by the country of their mother's roots.

They passed the sign welcoming them to Castlelough — home to the legendary Lady of the Lake. A second sign proclaimed the village to be the sister city of Shelter Bay, Oregon, America.

The tidy, medieval town of Castlelough, with its brightly painted shops reflecting optimism in this land of soft days and rainy nights, reminded J.T. of his hometown. If he and Mary had been here for any other occasion, he would have been charmed.

The hospital had, Nora told him as Quinn pulled into the car park, once been a workhouse. Before Quinn had settled in Ireland, townspeople had been required to drive to the district hospital in Enniscorthy. Apparently scaring the bejesus out of people with his horror novels paid very well, because the author had provided the seed funds for Castlelough to have its own medical facility. Taking in the gleaming white building with its tall Palladian windows, J.T. decided Mary's brother-in-law undoubtedly also contributed a bunch to its operation.

And not just Quinn, he noticed as they entered a lobby that had been painted in a buttery yellow he imagined would look like sunshine year-round. A small bronze plaque on the wall listed Mary as one of the hospital's patrons and a member of the board of directors.

Which was readily apparent by the warmth in how she was greeted by the nurses at the front desk. Not as some local girl who'd gone away and become rich and famous, but still one of them.

They were walking down a hallway lined with photographs of Irish scenery, which by now J.T. was guessing had been taken by Michael Joyce, when Nora paused and turned to her sister.

"Please," she said, "be gentle. Because as hard as this is on all of us, it's been ten times as difficult for John."

Mary's face was as pale as the whitewash on the cottages they'd passed. "I don't doubt that," she said, her voice tight. "Which is why he has to save her."

43

Back home in Shelter Bay, unaware of the drama taking place with Mary Joyce, Phoebe had taken the day off Maddy had given the kitchen staff and was spending it with Ethan.

"It was so wonderful," she was telling him, as they strolled on the wet sand between the surf and the cliff. Evening fog had come in, which, to her mind, only added to the romanticism.

"You were wonderful," he said.

Not wanting to let her out of his sight, he'd stayed in the new kitchen Chef Madeline had designed and Lucas had built. At first she'd been nervous, with him watching her, as if she'd been performing for an audience of one. But then, as she got into the rhythm she'd been taught, she'd almost forgotten he was there.

"I'll bet once the execs at the Cooking Network see that video, they'll want to spin you off onto your own show."

She laughed at his exaggeration, even as she felt so happy, she could float right up to the sky. "Hardly. But we did keep service running smoothly, just the way Chef Maddy taught us."

Not once had the staff of women from Haven House allowed any of the buffet servers to go empty. Phoebe knew that part of their diligence had been a lingering fear of imperfection, which many, if not most, might never completely overcome. But she also knew that the main reason for the successful reception had been the pride they'd all achieved. Pride that had once been cruelly stripped away.

"You know what?"

He smiled down at her, his heart in his eyes and on his sleeve. "What?"

"At first I was nervous with you in the kitchen." She'd learned that she could share her insecurities without having them be used against her. She'd also learned, by saying them out loud, they no longer possessed as much power. "But then I felt proud to have you see how far I've come since I was that terrified mess the day you first showed up at the house."

"Not a mess." Taking her hand, he helped her over a log that had fallen from the top of the eroded cliff. "You were so beautiful, you stopped my heart." He put the hand that wasn't holding hers over his chest, as if to make his point.

"I was too thin, I shook like a leaf in the wind, and my face was bruised."

"You weren't as strong as you are now," he allowed. "But you were special. So much so, you frightened me to death."

"Me?" She stopped and stared up at him. "How on earth could I have scared you?"

He might be a farmer now, but she'd immediately sensed the strength and power that lay beneath the surface. The steely core that had made him a good Marine. The same strength that had allowed him to overcome such personal tragedy.

"Because I knew I was going to fall in love with you. And I wasn't certain I could ever be so lucky to have a woman like you love me back."

"Oh, Ethan." Her eyes misted as her arms lifted up to twine around his neck. "Don't you know?" She went up on her toes. "I'm the lucky one."

Just as her lips touched his, there was a loud sound, like a firecracker going off on the beach. Or a car backfiring, Phoebe thought.

Until she saw the bright red stain blossoming on Ethan's chest.

He cursed. A rough, harsh curse she'd never heard from him. And then, as his legs began to fold, he said, "Call 911. Tell them you're on Moonshell Beach. And while you're calling, Phoebe, run. Run like hell."

"I won't leave you!" She was looking around, frantically trying to get her bearings and see where the shot had come from as she struggled to hold him up. But he was so heavy. And the blood was flowing all over her hands. "You need to come with me, Ethan. So we can get you to a hospital."

He yanked her hands from his arms. "Dammit, this isn't any fucking time to argue." Another word she'd never, ever heard escape his lips. Lips that had turned the color of the whitecaps. "Don't worry about me. Just run."

That said, he collapsed onto the wet sand at her feet, atop a pile of tangled green kelp.

44

As she'd feared when she'd seen that blood on Ethan's shirt, Peter came walking out of the swirling fog, an ugly black pistol in his hands. He was, inexplicably, dressed like Johnny Depp's Captain Sparrow.

"We have to stop meeting like this," he said.

"The police are looking for you, Peter," Phoebe said. "You'll never get away with this."

"Of course I will." He was calm. Seemingly reasonable. Insane. Or maybe, she thought as she glanced down at Ethan, unconscious at her feet, purely evil.

"I have two passports back at the inn." When her eyes widened at that, he smiled. "Yes, the Whale Song. Where I've been able to keep a close eye on you and your dirt farmer." He kicked Ethan with the toe of his black pirate boot. "You realize I have to kill him. For putting his hands on you."

"That would make you a murderer," Phoebe said. She stepped toward him, stopping when she heard the quick, deadly click of the pistol. "He's nothing to me. I'll go with you, Peter. Right now. Tell me what you want, and I'll do it."

"And where have I heard that before?" He cocked his head. "I remember. Right before you had me arrested."

"You shot an elderly lady," she reminded him.

"Because she got in my damn way!" The gun was steady, but wild hatred raged in his eyes. "I'd come to take you home, Stephanie."

"I'll go now," she tried yet again to get him away from here. Then she'd figure out how to help Ethan.

"Too late. Do you realize what you did to my reputation? To my family's good name? You made the Fletcher name a laughingstock all over the Internet."

"Nobody believes anything they read online."

"So you say. Then why did you testify in court that I was some sort of monster?"

Because you are.

When she didn't, couldn't, respond, he kicked Ethan again. This time hard in the ribs. When that drew no reaction, Phoebe's heart sank.

"The tide will be coming in soon," he said. "It'll wash your farmer's body away. And crabs and sharks will eat him."

If a snake could smile, it would look exactly like Peter Fletcher did at that moment.

He bent over, pressed the barrel of the gun against Ethan's head, and just when he looked as if he was about to pull the trigger, this time for real, Phoebe leaped on him at the same instant Ethan's fingers curled around his booted ankle and pulled him off his feet, which sent the gun flying into the surf.

Which was the good news.

The bad news was that Peter had no sooner tumbled to the ground than a sneaker wave, which Ethan had taught her was like a mini-tsunami, engulfed them all.

It was dark. And icy cold. Phoebe was tumbling in the water, totally out of control, sand scraping across her skin like shards of glass as she felt herself being pulled out to sea. Although she was a good swimmer, the power of the wave was too strong, and even as she fought against it, she couldn't get up to the surface to breathe.

Just as she was certain that she and her

baby were going to die, she felt a strong arm wrap around her waist.

Her first instinct was to fight; then, as she was pulled to the surface, breaking the water, she realized it was Ethan. Somehow holding her up with his single good arm.

"We've got to stay away from those rocks," he shouted against the roar of the surf. "But don't worry, Phoebe. I have you."

And he did. As he held her and as he kicked his way down the beach, away from the outcropping of rocks and back to the shore, she kicked along with him.

Twice, they were sucked back under. Twice, he pulled them to the surface. Like when she'd been unable to tell which way was up as she'd been tossed wildly in the surf, time ceased to have meaning. Even when they were above water, it was difficult to know where they were because of the thickening fog.

Until they hit the beach and he pulled her to her feet with his good arm, and, staggering, began dragging her away from the water.

Out of nowhere, another man suddenly appeared. With his face indistinguishable from a distance in the fog, at first Phoebe feared Peter had somehow managed to survive.

"Dillon Slater," the deep voice said as the man quickly took in the situation, braced Ethan beneath his wounded shoulder, and added heft to the rescue. "I was on the cliff when I saw the wave hit you guys and called 911."

Just as they reached the grassy dunes, the sound of a siren cut through the fog.

"Thanks," Ethan said. "Appreciate the help."

The man shrugged. "You would've made it on your own. I just provided backup."

"You called for help," Phoebe said. "Which neither one of us could have done." Then she turned on Ethan.

"How did you do that?" she gasped. "With a bullet in you?"

"No way was I going to lose you." Breathing heavily, one arm hanging limp at his side, he lowered his head and finished the tender kiss that had been so cruelly interrupted.

The man who'd introduced himself as a basketball coach at the high school gave his report to a Shelter Bay deputy, and Ethan and Phoebe were put into the back of the ambulance. As they lay on the gurneys, the EMTs taking their vital signs and tending to Ethan's wound, he reached over and took her hand.

And in that moment, as she held on tight, Phoebe truly knew that she and her baby would be all right.

Just as she and Ethan would.

45

John Joyce was standing beside their grandmother's hospital bed, when the others entered. As upset as Mary was, one look at the pain on her brother's face, and the anguish in his gentle brown eyes, had her anger dissolving like sea foam.

They exchanged a silent message in the way of siblings. His offering apology, hers telling him that none was needed, before she turned to her grandmother.

Fionna had always been the most vital woman Mary had ever known. Her passion for her Bernadette campaign had blazed like an eternal flame. And even as she was grateful that the quest had been fulfilled, a part of her wondered if only Fionna Joyce still had that mission left to fight for, if she might fight harder for her own life in order to achieve it.

"Gran." She pasted an indulgent, slightly scolding smile on her face as she walked over to the bed. "What are you doing, scaring us all to death like this? If you were that eager to have me come for a visit, you'd have only needed ring me up."

"Well, you're here now, which is all that matters. I've said my good-byes to Nora and the other children. I just was waiting for my famous movie-star granddaughter to arrive before I joined my dear Declan and your father and mother in heaven. And, of course, St. Bernadette."

"As happy as I am about Bernadette becoming a saint, I suspect, after all the work you've done on her behalf, she'd be wanting you to have some time to enjoy yourself and your great-grandchildren."

After Quinn adopted Nora's son, Rory, they'd gone on to have twin girls. While Michael and Erin had three sons. Celia, who was finishing art school, had yet to have a serious boyfriend, from what Mary had been told. And John had been so busy, first with his medical studies, then establishing a practice, he'd not married, either. Mary suddenly realized, with a little stab to her heart, that if she was ever to have children, they'd never know this very special woman.

She picked up her grandmother's hand from where it limply lay on the white sheet. She'd grown up seeing those hands in rapid-fire motion, wielding steel knitting needles like heroes in her father's fanciful stories had wielded their magic swords. Now that same hand, which was an unhealthy blue hue, felt as dry and frail as a bird's claw.

"Although it's glad I am to be back home, the only place you're going at the moment is to the farm. Where you belong."

"Oh, Mary, darling." Her grandmother sighed. Then began to cough, struggling dangerously for breath. John moved forward and helped her sit up and readjusted her oxygen tube. It was obvious that talking took a major effort.

"You don't have to talk, Gran," Mary said, feeling a familiar knee-jerk guilt at causing her grandmother additional discomfort as the elderly woman's eyes fluttered closed.

"Aye, I do," Fionna corrected with a bit of her familiar spirit. "And I will." She glanced past Mary to J.T., who was standing just inside the door. "Come here, young man, so I don't have to shout."

He immediately joined Mary next to the bed. "You'd be the man my daughter-in-law sent to our Mary," she said.

John shot a quick, questioning look at Mary, who felt color, the bane of the Irish, flood into her cheeks. "He's just a friend from America, Gran."

"Don't be wasting the short time I have left with foolish arguments," she said. "What's your name?" she asked J.T.

"J. T. Douchett, ma'am."

"Douchett?" A brow lifted. "Eleanor sent Mary a Frenchman?"

"Cajun, ma'am."

"Ah, well." She nodded at that. "And didn't your Acadian ancestors suffer the same diaspora as we Irish? Which gives you both something in common."

"I suppose that would be right," J.T. said.

"Well, of course it is." She coughed again. "You'll take good care of our Mary," she instructed him. "She might be rich and famous now, but money can't keep you warm at night, and fame is often fleeting. She needs a man who'll stick. In good times and bad."

Even as Mary desperately wished her grandmother would find someone else in the family to focus on, Fionna seemed bound and determined to say what was on her mind. So what else was new? In a way, as embarrassing as it was, Mary found her grandmother's behavior reassuring. Perhaps everyone was exaggerating her condition. And even if they weren't, wasn't Sister Bernadette's canonization proof that miracles did happen? Why couldn't the saint pull off one now?

"Something tells me you're that type of man," she said. "Though, like Quinn" — she shot a look at her eldest granddaughter's husband — "you look as if you'll prove a challenge. Which will be good for the girl. No Joyce woman would ever want a man who'd let her run over him. We're strong-willed females, J. T. Douchett. It's best you know that going in."

"Yes, ma'am," he said. "And I promise you that I'll take good care of your granddaughter."

"Aye, of course you will. Eleanor hasn't made a mistake yet."

Seeming satisfied, now that she'd settled that, Fionna lay back onto the pillows. As her eyes drifted closed yet again for the very last time, a single tear trailed down Mary's cheek.

46

Even out in the west, the preburial Irish wake, which they'd held when Mary's father had died, had mostly gone out of fashion. Quinn, whom the family had come to count on to take care of things, had made arrangements with Dudley's Funeral Home. The father and son had come from Dublin some years ago, looking for the slower and friendlier pace of Castlelough life.

After the funeral mass and burial held the next day, the family went home to the Joyce farmhouse, which Quinn had expanded to allow for his writing office and more living space for Nora; their three children; Celia, when she was home from school; himself; and Fionna, who'd spent all but her last forty-eight hours in the house she'd been born in.

Urged by Nora to rest, Mary had gone upstairs to the room her sister had readied for her and J.T., and, still jet-lagged and emotionally spent, immediately fell like a stone into sleep.

It was evening when she awoke to find J.T. sitting in a chair by the window, watching her.

"How long have you been awake?" she asked.

"Long enough to decide that you're the most beautiful woman God put on this green earth." He stood up and crossed over to her. The mattress sighed as he sat down on it and brushed a tender hand over her hair.

"How are you doing?"

"As well as can be expected." She felt the dreaded tears rising again behind her lids and momentarily squeezed her eyes shut as she dragged a trembling hand through her hair.

"I know she had a good and full life, and she accomplished her life's goal, but even when I was in America, it was comforting to know that she'd always be here, with her knitting and her tea, and her sharp and clever tongue, whenever I'd come home."

"She'll still be with you," J.T. said. "Just here." He touched her temple. "And here." Her breast over her partially broken heart.

Which was when, after doing her best to hold her pain in, Mary finally lost it. She pressed her cheek against his chest, clung to him, and let the flood of tears, more than the single one that had escaped at the hospital, flow.

He stroked her hair as she wept, murmuring tender words, encouraging her to let it all out.

And when she'd finally wept herself dry, he cupped her face between his large and gentle hands and kissed away the salty tears from her cheeks.

"Poor you." She lifted his hand to her lips.

"Why poor me?"

"Because you no sooner escaped having to comfort grieving women than here you are again, stuck in that same situation."

"Not the same at all," he corrected. "Because being with you is no hardship."

"And isn't that a lovely thing to say?" She sat up and glanced over at the clock. "I've nearly slept the day away."

"You needed it. Even without what you've gone through the past forty-eight hours, I didn't let you get any sleep the night before we got the call from Nora."

"That night was certainly no hardship," she tossed his words back at him. "Where's the family?"

"They've gone into town to arrange for Fionna's stone."

"Ah. Da bought his own before he died." She sighed. "Although Nora was upset that he'd spent the money, I always thought the real reason she got angry at him was she didn't want to think about him dying."

"Perfectly understandable."

"True. I wonder if he had a premonition."

"Oh, perhaps your mother gave him advance warning."

She couldn't tell from his expression whether he was teasing or serious. But his words did bring back what her grandmother had told him.

"About Mam sending you to me," she said.

"Yeah. I was thinking about that while you were sleeping."

Terrific. Now he'd think they were all crazy. "And?"

"And I was trying to figure out how to thank her."

Even if he didn't mean totally mean it, it was the perfect thing to say.

"Are you up for a ride?" she asked. "Because there's something I'd like to show you."

"I'm willing to go anywhere you take me."

Since she assured him she was rested, and the only experience he'd ever had driving on the left side of the road was a few days in London, he didn't argue when she got behind the wheel. As they drove through the countryside, J.T. drank in the scenery — the stone fences, the fields, the meadows splashed with purple, white, and yellow wildflowers. Nearly every crossroads — and there seemed to be hundreds for such a small area — boasted a statue of the Virgin Mary in a small stone grotto, often adorned with seashells.

After parking the car on the side of the road, they began walking up a narrow trail, where they passed a cemetery, high Celtic crosses standing like sentinels over rounded stones covered with green moss. After continuing up the twisting mountain trail, they came upon a mound of earth blanketed with yellow poppies and decorated with more shells and stones.

"It's a cairn," Mary said. "Built about five thousand years ago. We have quite a few in this part of the country. They're like a tomb, but since the ancients believed in an active afterlife, they were often buried with tools, weapons, and household goods."

"Which saved them from having to go shopping to get stuff for their new life," he said.

She smiled for the first time since she'd received the phone call. "Aye. The ancients didn't have the benefits of Target or the Internet."

J.T. had grown up hearing stories about the Grand Dérangement, the forced expulsion of the Acadians from Nova Scotia by the British in 1755, which had resulted in his family settling in Louisiana. You couldn't live in Shelter Bay without hearing the story of that town's founding. Yet both events were like yesterday when compared with this land that had, in many ways, remained unchanged for millennia.

They left the trail, and were climbing over ancient, rounded mountains that were on the way to crumbling back to dust. Next they came to a towering hedge covered with shocking pink flowers. The thick greenery extended in both directions as far as the eye could see.

"There's a secret passageway that leads to the lough," she told him.

J.T. followed her through the bright, fragrant passageway, stopping in his tracks to look down into a valley that appeared to belong in an illustrated book of fairy tales.

A lake, surrounded by feather-crowned reeds, was a bold splash of brilliant sapphire on a mottled green carpet. Two swans — one white, the other black — that looked as if they'd just flown in from Sleeping Beauty's castle glided serenely on the water. On the far bank of the lake a stone castle, slowly crumbling, was painted gold and crimson by the setting sun.

"It's stunning. And very peaceful."

"It is now," she agreed. "We Irish have a saying: *ciunas gan uagineas.* It means 'quietness without loneliness,' which I've always thought suits the scene."

J.T. agreed.

"This is also the lake where the Lady is supposed to live."

The one Quinn Gallagher had written about. The movie she'd first appeared in. "I recognize it from the film." He hadn't seen it at first, because, he supposed, he hadn't really expected anything so stunning to exist in real life.

"But I didn't bring you here to tell you the story, which you mostly know from having watched the film, although Quinn does admit to taking liberties."

"As it seems most storytellers do."

"True. Myself included . . . This place wasn't always so peaceful," she said. "The truth is that this land my family has lived on for centuries was the scene of many battles."

Perhaps because he'd spent so many years in war zones himself, J.T. could picture them. And hear them. The clash of swords, the shouting, the confusion, the battle horses.

And suddenly, inexplicably, this place, which he'd never before seen, became very familiar.

"This is where we are together when I dream of you," she said. "There's a battle raging behind you and you come striding out of the smoke, with your armor and your sword, and take me." She glanced down at the flower-strewn meadow. "Right here."

Hell. It was probably his own imagination, but . . .

He shook his head. "It's impossible."

"Aye, it is."

But he knew she believed it. And the crazy thing was, thinking back on those spirits at Little Bighorn, J.T. did, too.

He took her in his arms. Not to arouse, nor soothe, but to be close. "I want to give you what you deserve," he said against her hair. "What you want." Because this might be one of the most important conversations he'd ever had in his life, he had to be honest with her. "But I can't."

When she would have pulled away, he tightened his arms around her. "Not now," he said.

She looked up at him, hope warring with

pain in those remarkable eyes that were exactly the hue of the lake.

"When?"

And wasn't that the question he'd been asking himself for the past twenty-four hours?

"Give me two weeks. Then I promise, we'll meet back here."

Although there was a sheen of tears in her eyes, the lips he could taste in his sleep turned up, ever so slightly, at that.

"At least you're not making me wait until New Year's Eve," she said.

"I'd never make it that long," he admitted. "But as you undoubtedly figured out, I've been drifting since I came back home. There are some things I need to settle before we talk about the future."

She sighed. Heavily. With resignation. "Fortunately for you, Fionna was right when she told you we Joyce women would never be happy with a man we could push around."

"Two weeks," he repeated. "Then you can push me around all you want."

"That may be the first lie you've told to me, J. T. Douchett," she complained. "But two weeks it is. And not a day longer."

"I promise." He touched his mouth to hers as the sun set behind the castle ruins.

"A chuisle mo chroi," he murmured against her lips.

Mary's head came up so fast, it hit beneath his chin, causing his teeth to bang together. "What did you say?"

He had been as surprised as she looked to hear those words coming out of his mouth. "I don't know."

"You don't speak Irish?"

"Not a word."

"Yet you called me the pulse of your heart."

"Well . . . it definitely fits. Because you are."

"But how did you know that?"

He smiled, a slow, satisfied smile, as he gave himself up to this place. To her. "Easy." He took her lips again, this time taking the kiss deeper. Longer. "Magic."

47

Coastal Community College was set up on a bluff high on a hill overlooking the harbor. While certainly not the largest college in the state, it was one of the most charming, set in a grove of fir trees, its buildings painted lighthouse white and topped with a red cedar shake roof.

Inside, colorful Native American art lined walls painted the same buttery yellow as the hospital in Castlelough, the color designed to bring in sunshine during the darkest of rainy Pacific Northwest days.

J.T.'s meeting his first morning back in Shelter Bay was with the president of the college, the vice president of instruction, the human resources director, the dean of college relations, and the director of the college foundation.

"Well," the president, a dark-haired woman who appeared to be in her late forties, said, after going through the file he'd brought with him, "your credentials are definitely impressive."

"Thank you, ma'am."

"Which makes me wonder," the human resources guy broke in, "why, after teaching at the War College, you wouldn't consider a community college a step down."

"That's not the case at all," J.T. said. He'd had plenty of time to think about it on the long flight home from Ireland. "As your brochure states, community colleges are the way forward into the future. Especially these days with so many people out of work, they offer the opportunity for a quality education close to home. In the community, thus their name."

"Yet what's to prevent you from getting bored and moving on to greener pastures?"

"I like the pastures just fine, here," J.T. said easily. "This is, after all, my hometown. I have family here. Three generations of connections."

"We have a great many ROTC students." The vice president of instruction pointed out what J.T. had already unearthed for himself online. "I have no doubt that you'd be a great help preparing them for any deployments they may experience."

"I like to believe my wartime experience would prove helpful," J.T. said. "But there's more to fighting wars than what happens on the battlefield. I believe a strong grounding in war history also helps in decision making. Both at the command level and on the ground."

"Well put," the director of the foundation said. "I was with III MAF at Khe Sanh."

Although the Marine Amphibious Force had landed in the tactical victory column of the Vietnam War, what became known as the hill battles, J.T. knew it had been a hairy time.

"Then you'd know that Marines don't quit."

Although he was responding to the director, he shot a look at the HR guy.

"I also believe that military history serves everyone," J.T. added. "Not just those fighting our wars."

"Well put," the fellow Marine, who was obviously on his side, said. *Semper Fi.*

The rest of the interview went well, and thirty minutes later, J.T. left the administrative building an employed civilian.

His next stop was at Take the Cake bakery. Not because he was in any need for a cupcake, although he had to admit the German chocolate was the bomb, but Sax had said that, having been a CPA before turning to sweets, the baker was the best person in town for financial advice. Which turned out to be true.

"So, what do you think?" he asked his brothers, as they stood on the piece of property overlooking Moonshell Beach.

"I think you're going to be teaching a lot of classes to pay for this," Cole, always the pragmatist, warned.

"You guys know there's not a lot to spend your money on when you're deployed," J.T. said. "I could cover the land. And the cottage." He pointed toward a small cottage he'd decided he and Mary could live in while building their own home. Then they could turn it into a guesthouse for when her family visited from Castlelough.

"Have you even asked her if she wants to live here?" Sax asked.

"Not yet. But Sedona — and thanks for telling me about her, because she's brilliant — said that since this is a buyer's market, the seller would give me time to change my mind if she doesn't go along with the deal. It's been on the market over a year and I'm the first bite the seller's gotten."

"The cottage is, to put it mildly, a wreck," Cole pointed out.

"It just needs a little TLC," J.T. argued. "I figured we could do the painting and repairs, while our women took care of the inside. Getting furniture and all that decorating stuff."

"Which will probably cost more than a new roof." Cole glanced up at the moss-covered roof in question.

"I can handle it," J.T. said yet again. Sometimes it sucked being the youngest brother. Especially when Cole got into elder mode.

"Well, then," Sax said, giving his brother a one-armed man hug, "I'd say, since you promised Mary you'd be back in two weeks, we'd better get our asses in gear."

48

While setting a romantic meeting place and time might work very fine in the movies, Mary was finding, yet again, that the movies were far different from real life.

After her agent returned home from Peru with the revelation that she'd once been an Inca queen who'd lived in a mountain city above the clouds — which had immediately had Mary thinking of the Neil Young song — she'd gone on to confirm that although Pressler could hire writers to create a mermaid/vampire story, he could not use either her world or her characters.

Which was a relief on more than one level, since Mary had only ever seen the story as a trilogy, from the first. To her mind, once her selkie queen gave up her kingdom to live on land with the human she'd chosen to mate with for life, the story had its happy ending.

So, trying not to go crazy while she was

waiting for J.T. to return to Castlelough, and her, she began work on the story of the fisherman and the selkie that had been stirring in her mind for so many months. And while writing somewhat took her mind off the stubborn Marine she'd fallen in love with, the problem was that since she'd told the story to him that day on the boat when he'd first kissed her, it did nothing to ease the need that was growing exponentially with every passing day.

Then finally, it was time.

After tiring of her pacing a path in the floor, Nora had finally shooed Mary out of the house, causing her to arrive at the lake early.

Where she waited.

Then finally(!) he was coming over the hill, his hair as dark as a moonless night over the Burren, eyes the color of rain. But much, much warmer.

He was striding toward her on long, determined legs that ate up the ground.

His jaw was wide and square, his rawboned face as chiseled as the stone cliffs into which the lake had been carved by glaciers eons ago.

Although clad in jeans and an Aran Islands sweater, he was still every inch a warrior.

Having grown up in a country that had

suffered centuries of hostilities from battling factions, Mary still hated war.

But she loved him.

He stopped in front of her, eyes so warm as they looked down into hers, she felt her body melting, like a candle left out too long in the summer's sun.

"Do you have any idea how much I've missed you?" he asked.

"And wasn't that your own doing?" she countered, placing her hands on her hips when she wanted to fling them around his neck.

He laughed. "Your grandmother was right. You Joyce are strong-willed females." He skimmed the back of his hand down the side of her face. "And ooh-rah for that."

"We're also known for getting straight to the point," she reminded him. "So, what have you decided?"

"What I'd already decided before I left. That I want you."

"Leaving was an odd way of showing that."

"I needed to get a life back. A life I could ask you to share."

This was still not the romance she'd been hoping for. But he was getting closer.

"First I need to know something. . . . Are you going back to Malibu?"

"No." She'd already decided to return to making the films she loved. The films that had first garnered her an audience. Which might be smaller, but her work would be her own.

"What would you say to spending part of the year in Shelter Bay?"

"I'd say, if you're asking me to be spending it with you, yes."

"Okay." He let out a long breath, and suddenly she realized that she wasn't the only one who'd come here today with nerves all in a tangle.

"I have a job. Teaching history at the community college. Most of the students will probably be ROTC, on their way to the military, who I think I can help. As for the others, who'll be going into civilian life, I still believe it's important for them to know more about their country's past, too."

"Coming from a country with a great deal of past, you'll be getting no argument from me there," she said.

"And I bought a house. Well, not exactly a house. But some land with this cottage I thought we could live in while we built one large enough for our family. And then we could use the cottage for a guesthouse for your family. It's on the coast. Overlooking Moonshell Beach."

"Our beach?"

"Yeah. Our beach. Because I knew, after making love to you there, I'll never be able to think of it any other way."

"That's so lovely. And romantic. And where would we be spending the rest of the time?"

"I was thinking here. Well, not exactly *here,*" he amended as he looked around at the lake and castle. "But in Castlelough. So you'll have your family around you. After all, it'll be good for our children to know their cousins."

He tightened his arms, drawing her closer. "I know this all happened fast, but if there's one thing I've learned during my time in the corps, it's that since life doesn't come with a time guarantee, we shouldn't waste a moment. I love you, Mary Joyce. With every fiber of my being. And I want to spend the rest of this life, and any others we might be gifted with, together. So . . . will you marry me?"

"Well, since my entire family would undoubtedly disown me if I didn't . . . I believe I have no choice but to let you talk me into it."

And wasn't this the romance she'd been waiting for? "*Failte abhaile,* Captain

Douchett." She lifted her smiling lips to his kiss. "Welcome home."

ABOUT THE AUTHOR

New York Times bestselling author **JoAnn Ross** lives with her husband and three rescued dogs in the Pacific Northwest.

The employees of Thorndike Press hope you have enjoyed this Large Print book. All our Thorndike, Wheeler, and Kennebec Large Print titles are designed for easy reading, and all our books are made to last. Other Thorndike Press Large Print books are available at your library, through selected bookstores, or directly from us.

For information about titles, please call:
(800) 223-1244

or visit our Web site at:
http://gale.cengage.com/thorndike

To share your comments, please write:

Publisher
Thorndike Press
10 Water St., Suite 310
Waterville, ME 04901